SMART MOUTH

SMART MOUTH

ERIN McCARTHY

BRAVA

KENSINGTON PUBLISHING CORP.
http://www.kensingtonbooks.com

BRAVA BOOKS are published by

Kensington Publishing Corp.
850 Third Avenue
New York, NY 10022

ISBN 0-7582-0595-3

First Kensington Trade Paperback Printing: April 2004
10 9 8 7 6 5 4 3 2 1

Printed in the United States of America

Many thanks to Lori Foster for her generosity and advice, and to Kate Duffy, for making this all possible. And for my husband, Heath, for always believing in me.

Chapter One

"Where is it? You said it was going to be here." Derek Knight looked around the front and back seats of the rental car again in impatience as he spoke into his cell phone.

Nothing. No envelope.

Which meant his informant was an imbecile and he was dead meat.

He was so close to busting this case wide open. All he needed was a little more evidence, which was supposed to have been dropped in this car by the speaker on the other end of the phone.

"Well, I put it there," came the anxious whisper.

Derek rubbed his eyes. Jesus. Dealing with this guy was giving him heartburn like he hadn't experienced since the first messy days after his divorce. He fumbled in his pocket for antacids and popped two in his mouth, chewing the chalky tablets rapidly.

Movement to the left caught his attention. He looked up and saw nothing but legs. Female legs. That stretched firm and smooth from the ground right to eye level as he sat in the driver's seat. At one point those legs were covered by a short skirt the color of an olive, but it didn't matter.

They still beckoned him, toying with him, distracting him from the task at hand. He sent the window down with a soft

purr and listened to the sound of her heels hitting the concrete, echoing around the dark garage as her hips rolled and
swayed and those legs bent seductively at the knee with each
step.

He looked past the legs to the narrow waist, the luscious
chest, and to the straight auburn hair flowing across her
shoulders. She turned, met his gaze. Her eyes went wide with
awareness, her plump lips opened as she clutched her rolling
suitcase tighter.

Do something, he thought through an unexpected haze of
lust, painfully aware that it had been months and months
since he'd been on a date.

Talk to her.

Then the voice coming over the phone line repeated insis-
tently, "I'm telling you I put it there myself thirty minutes
ago. In the red Ford Taurus."

Derek heard the last words and snapped to attention.
"Hold it. You said the green Ford Taurus."

"No, I didn't. I said the red one. It's parked in the far corner under the second floor sign."

Derek swore. He had to be the only agent in the history of
the bureau to have a color blind whistle-blower. "Okay, I'll
call you back."

He could see the car in question. It was across from him.
And damn if it wasn't Legs unlocking it and popping the
trunk.

"Excuse me," he called over to her as he threw open the
car door and stood up.

She flung her suitcase in the trunk and ignored him, heading to the driver's side door of the car with her cute little
backside to him.

"Excuse me, miss, I think you have the wrong car." Derek
started to jog over to her, images of his butt hung in an FBI
sling by Nordstrom, his less-than-happy boss, flashing through
his mind.

She opened the door and turned to enter the car. She frowned as she hastened to get in the car. "Don't come near me," she yelled. "I have Mace."

He stopped and stared in astonishment as her hand popped out holding a spray can in a threatening manner.

Christ, she thought he was attacking her. "No, you don't understand. There's been a mix-up with the cars and . . ."

The door slammed shut, the lock clicked, the engine roared, and Derek had to leap back to prevent a broken foot as she backed up with the speed of a NASCAR driver.

"What the hell?" he muttered, then realized that months worth of planning and negotiating were fleeing in that car with her. Not to mention those awe-inspiring legs.

With his own burst of speed that made his bad knee scream, he went back to the green Taurus and followed her, on her tail in sixty seconds as she swung around the first floor curve of the garage.

After his last case, when he had skirted procedure a time or two, Nordstrom would be more than happy to see him in the basement pushing papers for the rest of his life.

He was not giving up those documents without a fight.

Reese Hampton tossed her purse and the Mace on the passenger seat, her eyes trained on the exit sign in front of her. She was exhausted. A hot shower and room service were the next order of business, and the only things that could redeem a flat-out lousy day.

The flight from New York to Chicago had first been delayed. Then they had encountered a storm front over Pennsylvania, sending half the passengers scrambling for their airsick bags. The man in the seat next to her had snored, and his hand had fallen in her lap three times. Given that she didn't even want to be on this lame *you're a girl so you do it* assignment, she was not in a good mood.

Then walking across the garage, struggling to keep her flipping suitcase rolling without toppling over sideways, she had looked up and met the gaze of the most gorgeous guy she had ever seen. Caramel brown hair. Chocolate eyes. A deep summer tan and shoulders as wide and rock solid as the Grand Canyon.

The smelly damp garage had receded, replaced by images of rolling in a floral meadow with him, naked in a world of sensual pleasure where STD's don't exist.

But then the whole fantasy had been shot to hell when he had started towards her, an intense and somehow *dangerous* look in his eye.

Dangerous was sexy in theory. The reality was less than titillating.

A man running towards her in a dark secluded parking garage was a little nerve-racking, no matter how cute. Ted Bundy had been cute, and look how he had turned out.

It was a sad testimonial to her pathetic life that the only man to show interest in her in ages was probably a psychiatric ward escapee.

Exiting the garage, she put double chocolate fudge eyes out of her mind and tried to figure out where she was.

"Shoot!" Reese saw immediately she had turned the wrong way down a one-way street.

Doing a quick U-turn, she hit the control on the car panel that would call Map-Star, the live service that tracked down the car you were in and offered directions. It was why Reese always used this particular rental car company.

For being an investigative reporter, she had an appalling sense of direction. She had estimated that she had called Map-Star at least forty-seven times in the last two years. She was starting to get to know the employees by name.

They had even sent her a Christmas card the year before, which was thoughtful.

"Thank you for using Map-Star. This is Paula. How may I help you?"

"I need to get to the Crowne Plaza Hotel on North Wabash, please."

"One moment."

Reese flipped the rearview mirror down as she idled at a red light, checking her lipstick. Just as she had suspected. Gone. Good thing the society wedding she was covering for the paper wasn't until tomorrow. They would slap an apron on her and send her to the kitchen with hair like this.

She flipped the mirror back up, then frowned. What was that flash of green behind her? Why did that car look familiar?

"Okay, you need to head towards the airport exit on I-190 East for two point seven miles."

"I can do that." She checked the mirror again. The green car was still behind her. And there was something about the driver . . . She was terrible at placing faces.

"I'm on I-190 now."

The green car stayed right behind her.

"Now continue on I-90 East for five point eight miles."

Darting her eyes back and forth from the road and the mirror, Reese felt a flicker of annoyance. She knew who that was. It was the guy from the garage. He was following her.

Of all the nerve.

Her hands tightened on the steering wheel as she tried to tell herself it was a coincidence. It was possible that he needed to go in the same direction she did. People did that. Go in the same direction.

It was also possible he was following her on purpose.

Without thought, she jerked the wheel hard to the right and squeezed onto the exit ramp, just missing the guardrail.

"You've gone the wrong way."

The car was still behind her.

She went left at the light at the exit, her tires squealing as she took the corner at forty-five miles an hour, her high heel slipping on the gas as she floored it.

"Miss, you're not supposed to be turning."

There was no question now that he was following her. He was right on her tail, the psycho, and Reese checked the doors to make sure they were all locked.

If this were New York, she would know where she was going and could head to the police station to file a stalker report. Or call a friend to meet her. But here, in Chicago, she had no idea where she was and no one she could call.

But Reese had no fear of speed.

She weaved in and out of traffic, a certain thrill racing through her. "Heh, heh, think you can catch me?" she gloated to the rearview mirror.

"Ma'am?"

A beer truck cut her off, causing her to slam on her brakes. The green car was back on her tail.

"Shoot! Okay, maybe you can catch me." Along with alarm, she felt grudging admiration. Clearly this guy was a professional weirdo, as opposed to your run-of-the-mill weirdo.

"Ma'am?"

"What do I do now?" she wondered out loud, gliding through a stop sign.

"I don't know, because you're not following my directions," came the exasperated voice of the Map-Star employee.

She jumped and threw her hand over her heart as her pulse leapt in fear. Yeesh. She had forgotten all about the Map-Star call she was still connected to.

Reese took another left turn and said, "Someone's following me! I need you to call the police."

There was a long silence. "Are you sure?"

"Yes!" What, like she was making it up? Call her what you want, she'd never been paranoid. She knew a lunatic when she saw one.

It was eight o'clock and any minute now Reese knew that daylight would be disappearing and night would cover the city in a shroud of creepy darkness. She would be utterly vulnerable, and annoyance was about to turn to fear if this guy persisted.

"Call the police."

"I can't call the police if you don't stop and park some-where. They'll never find you spinning in circles."

Okay, the attitude from Miss Map-Star wasn't helping. She would call the police herself from her cell phone.

Reese slammed on her brakes at a red light and said, "Fine." She clicked the button to disconnect the call, making a mental note to complain to Map-Star. Shouldn't they call first and ask questions later? She could have been being car-jacked or having a heart attack, for crying out loud.

Knuckles rapped on her window.

"Aahh!" She let out an involuntary scream. It was him, the gorgeous guy, who apparently was certifiably insane as well as movie star good-looking.

"Go away!" Some people had a really hard time taking a hint.

"No, you're in the car I was supposed to get. There's something . . ."

Reese didn't wait to hear the rest. She turned right, ignor-ing the no turn on red sign. She was really starting to freak out. She'd seen a lot of strange things as a journalist, and come to think of it, even stranger things as a single woman trying to date, and every one of them was running through her mind right now.

She cut her thoughts out right there. That wasn't going to help her get out of this situation alive and intact. This was no trickier than fending off her boss Ralph's groping hands. The idea was to dodge and weave.

Glancing in the mirror, she saw that the green car was no longer behind her. Her foot eased on the gas, and her shoul-ders relaxed. Well, see. He had given up.

Much better. She reached for the Map-Star button to get step-by-step directions to her hotel. She hoped like hell the paper hadn't gone cheap on her and gotten her a crummy hotel room. She deserved a freaking feather pillow after this, at the very least.

Without warning, the green car came from nowhere and pulled out in front of her, cutting her off and forcing her to slam on the brakes. Her car skidded as she screamed, and rode up onto the sidewalk a little. She was reaching for her cell phone to call the police, someone, anyone, when the man appeared at her window again.

"Listen, I'm sorry to bother you like this. Can we just switch cars, please? I left something in the car you have."

He sounded normal. He looked normal. But there was nothing normal about nearly running her off the road in pursuit of his forgotten wallet or whatever it was he'd left in the car.

Thoughts tumbled in Reese's head. If she opened the door, he could push her in and abduct her. But if she didn't open the door, he would stand here all night, she was sure. She could throw the car in reverse, except a produce truck had slipped into the spot behind her. She couldn't go forward. She could call the police, but she didn't know where she was, and there were no street signs visible.

Telling the police you were somewhere near O'Hare outside a bookstore and a deli wasn't going to cut it.

She could handle this. No problemo. Even if her knees were vibrating.

Trying to sound authoritative, she said, "Get back in your car and I'll get out, okay?"

She would dash into the deli and abandon the stupid rental car. Let him have it. Of course, her suitcase was in her trunk, along with her laptop computer, but she could live without her PJ bottoms and her purple toothbrush. The paper probably had insurance for her laptop. If they didn't, tough toenails, this was her safety in question here.

Estimating distance, she figured it was only fifteen feet to the front door of the deli, and people were entering and exiting on a regular basis. He couldn't murder her in a deli, she didn't think.

"Listen, lady, it's not what you think. I'm with the FBI."
He started to put his hand in his pocket.

With hours of cop TV under her belt, Reese said, "Freeze!
Get your hand out of your pocket."

He stopped, startled. "I'm trying to show you my badge."

"Yeah, right, you're an FBI agent, and I can bake a cake
from scratch." Like she'd fallen off the turnip truck yesterday.

His lip twitched.

The loony was laughing at her. "Get back in your car!"
she ordered him, fury overcoming fear.

"Okay, that's fine." He held up his hands as if to reassure
her and went back to his car.

The minute he closed the door, she grabbed her purse, her
briefcase, and her Mace, and flung open the car door.
Stumbling a little as her heels hit the sidewalk, her briefcase
slipped out of her hand.

Instinctively, she bent to get it and the white Tyvek envelope that had slid to the ground with it.

"Hey, that's my envelope!"

Oh, no. His voice sounded like it was coming from outside
the car. She should have known not to trust a lunatic. Reese
grabbed everything and ran for the door, still half hunched
over. With her free hand, she pushed open the door and tumbled in just as she sensed his presence behind her.

His voice was smooth, low. It sent shivers dancing up her
spine.

"I just want the envelope in your hand. If you hand it to
me, I swear I'll walk away and you'll never see me again. Or
at least let me show you my badge."

When she bit her lip and paused, he added, "You realize
you're interfering with official FBI business."

She wondered if she should believe him. He looked sexy
enough to be a federal agent. Way better than that wimpy
paranoid Mulder.

Besides, he didn't really look like a lunatic. But who really knew what a lunatic looked like?

Taking stock, Reese realized she had not recovered the Mace after dropping it outside. Clutching her purse and briefcase, she looked around the room at a total loss as to how to act.

His hand touched her elbow just as she caught the eye of the twenty-year-old clerk behind the counter. She shot the clerk a pleading look, then took a deep breath.

Her dad had taught her always to speak up for herself.

"Don't touch me!" she yelled, her elbow slamming into her pursuer's stomach. "Someone call the police! Help me, he's attacking me."

She heard a grunt, stomped on his foot for good measure with the spiky heel of her shoe, and started running towards the kitchen, wishing she hadn't quit aerobics back in ninety-nine after the ripped leotard incident. Crap, she was out of shape.

A middle-aged woman behind the deli counter beckoned her forward. "Come in the back while we call the police."

Reese fought the urge to look back to see if she was still being pursued. The fear must have been obvious on her face.

"Don't worry, there're about three guys wrestling him to the ground right now," the woman said, slipping a maternal arm around her.

Reese's teeth were making a clattering sound like a baby's rattle. She squeezed her lips shut and sank onto the hard wooden chair the woman pointed out to her in the stockroom.

"You poor thing. It's not even safe to walk the streets anymore, for crying out loud." The woman wiped her hands on her apron. "You just sit there and try to relax. I'll get you some coffee, and the police should be here soon."

Reese crossed and uncrossed her legs, waiting impatiently. It was a solid five minutes before the woman came back and the look of sympathy on her face had evaporated. There was no coffee in her hand, either.

"Did you know that man is an FBI agent?"

Reese snorted. "Don't tell me you fell for that. Just saying you're an FBI agent doesn't make you one."

The woman threw her a chastising look as she headed back towards the door. "The badge, the gun, and the police patting him on the back were enough for me."

Reese sat up straighter. Okay, this could be bad. "You mean . . . he really is an FBI agent?"

"Umm-hmm." With that and a toss of her head, she left. "I'm going to get an autograph for my grandson. He's into law enforcement."

Darn it. Reese jumped out of the chair and started pacing. FBI agents should know better than to pursue an innocent civilian before identifying themselves. She wasn't a mind reader.

She conveniently ignored that he had tried to tell her and had tried to show her his badge.

If he had been less *weird* she wouldn't have elbowed him in the gut.

Which technically speaking, meant she had assaulted him.

There was only one thing to do. Grabbing her briefcase and purse she headed for the back door. She was going to hail a cab and put as much distance as she could between her and the crazy man with the chocolate eyes before she found herself in the slammer instead of the Crowne Plaza.

Chapter Two

Derek stared at the floor and tried not to groan out loud. Man, he hadn't handled a case this badly since he was a rookie. It had never occurred to him that Legs would think he was stalking her.

Nor had he anticipated she would put up such a fight.

Thanks to her quick thinking and tenacity, he was face-down on a dirty deli floor with four guys behind him, holding his arms and threatening to sit on him if he made one move.

"Listen, this is all a mistake," he said to the floor, trying to twist his head. Of all the humiliating things to have happened. He hoped this little escapade wouldn't get around the office.

They never would have gotten him on the ground if there hadn't been four of them, and he hadn't been preoccupied with watching to see where Legs was going. Not to mention the agonizing pain in his foot where her heel had penetrated.

He still might have been able to take them, but at the last second, his bad knee had buckled and he'd gone down when one of these idiots had jumped on his back. Now here he was on the damn floor, and his evidence, the compilation of months of planning, was in the back room with a woman who thought he was a serial killer.

"The only mistake you made was pulling your scumbag

act here in front of us," a voice from behind him said, squeezing Derek's arm for emphasis.

It figured he would encounter an overzealous bunch of Good Samaritans.

"If you get out my wallet, you can see for yourself. I'm a federal agent, and you're interfering with an investigation."

"Yeah, right," the voice scoffed.

He attempted a shrug, but his shoulders were pinned to the floor. "Look for yourself."

"I'm not digging in your pocket." Horror was clear in the young deli clerk's voice.

Derek pulled hard on his hand, freed it a little and pulled out his wallet. He tossed it next to him. "Have a look."

A moment later, hands eased up. "Is this real?"

Derek took the opportunity to move out from under his captors' hands and sit up. He brushed dirt off his sweatshirt. "Yes."

He spotted the men in blue coming through the front door as the four guys in their early twenties gaped at him. Derek said, "Ask the cops."

The kids nudged each other and looked sheepish. Derek found he couldn't be that angry with them. Hey, at least they were sticking up for what they thought was a defenseless woman.

The deli clerk said, "No way. Did we like totally screw up? Was that woman like a major criminal?"

The one with fluffy poodle hair nodded. "I bet she's one of those madams running a call girl ring for senators and stuff."

His friend scoffed. "There are no senators in Chicago."

Derek sighed. He was strongly starting to suspect this day wasn't going to turn out the way he had hoped. Which pretty much summed up every day for the last two years.

The two patrolmen sauntered over. The older of the two glared at them each in turn and said, "What the hell's going on here?"

"Dude, we didn't know he was FBI, man. We just saw him

grabbing the chick and we were trying to help her. Totally innocent, that's what we are." The deli clerk started to scoot back away from Derek, his hands in the air.

His three friends nodded vigorously. One said, "Seriously, man. We were just trying to protect the hot babe, and then it turns out he's FBI. No way we could have known that."

The cop turned to Derek, who had managed to get himself and his stiff leg off the floor. Jesus, he was like an old man as things popped and creaked when he righted himself. His knee throbbed, giving him just one more reminder of his past poor judgment.

"What's your story?" the cop asked, tucking his hands into his belt and looking resigned to his life.

"I'm a federal agent. I was in the process of apprehending a female who has pivotal evidence in her possession when I was ambushed by the Mob Squad here." Derek glanced over to the door where Legs had retreated. "I need to see if she's still on the premises."

The cop, who had taken his badge from the clerk and was studying it, said to his partner, "Go check it out. Bring her out here for Agent Knight."

Then he handed Derek his badge and clapped him on the shoulder with a grin. "Caught you off guard, did they?"

Derek stuffed his badge back in his pocket and tried not to grimace. "It happens."

"Where are you going?" The cop stopped the boys, who were inching away steadily, with a frown.

They all froze and Derek saw a smirk cross the cop's face before he glared at them again. Derek didn't bother to listen to the ensuing stammering explanations, and headed towards the door to the kitchen.

The other cop came back out right as he reached the door. "Nobody back there."

Derek swore. Not that he was surprised. Legs didn't look like the kind to hang around when there was a handy back door available.

He felt a jump of desire again, that was totally out of line given the situation.

But those boys had been right about one thing. That was one hot chick.

As an older woman came up and asked him for his autograph, which made him want to laugh, he pictured that glossy auburn hair falling across his pillow, and those long creamy legs stretching, wrapping around him as she gave up little moans of pleasure.

Damn. He needed to get out of the house more.

It took another ten minutes to clear up the whole mess with the police and track down from the rental agency the name and address of the woman in the red Taurus.

After a lot of hemming and hawing on their part, and threats on his part, they released her name to him.

Reese Hampton. She was staying at the Crowne Plaza.

Derek got into his green car and wondered how exactly he was going to go about cajoling Reese Hampton into surrendering the evidence without her macing him in the eyes.

Charm. He would just have to be charming. Which he was sadly out of practice doing. So he would try calm. Matter-of-fact.

You're-interfering-with-FBI-business, ma'am, kind of attitude.

And if that didn't work, he would just have to grab the envelope and run.

Reese toweled dry her wet hair and wondered why she'd given up smoking. Now would be the perfect time to flop in the chaise artfully arranged in front of the window and light up.

Except she had quit three years earlier and even the basest of urges couldn't force her to put on clothing and leave this room right now after the day she'd had. She'd order room service instead to satisfy her oral needs. If she had other oral needs that had been ignored for the last decade or so, well, that was her lot in life.

Undersexed and underpaid. Story at eleven.

Lucky for Ralph, and his sorry behind, the room was satisfactory. It was tucked away at the end of the hall far from the elevator, with a king-size bed and a view that didn't include the parking garage.

Plus there had been a fluffy white robe in the bathroom, which she was now wearing.

After calling room service, she lay on the bed and tried to put herself in the right frame of mind for the wedding tomorrow. Think of it as a stepping-stone. Maybe she would run across someone important attending the wedding. A businessman with connections. A senator she could charm over the spinach puffs.

Or more likely it was a complete and total waste of her time and the only pressing news would be whether the bride wore a John Galliano dress or a Vera Wang.

Disgusted with her boss, her job, and her life, Reese reached for her briefcase to check her notes. She couldn't even remember the name of the damn bride, which could make things awkward.

Who are you here for? The bride or the groom?

Oh, I'm just here because my boss won't take me seriously due to my breasts.

She had an attitude problem and was well aware of it. Stuck in a rut at twenty-six.

A white envelope fell in her lap as she wrenched the briefcase to her side. Curious, she picked it up. Understanding dawned on her.

The envelope. That's what the pushy yet mouth-watering FBI guy had wanted.

Her breath hitched. Her heart raced like she'd taken a hit off that cigarette she'd been craving. Oh, no, this was bad.

Or good, however you wanted to look at it.

Something was in this envelope. Something that the FBI wanted.

Something that could take her career from the depths of the entertainment section to the heights of the front page.

Reese debated the ethics of opening the envelope. For about a microsecond. Then she tore with gusto.

A note fell out. Tight, spidery handwriting stared up at her. *Is this enough to prosecute?*

Yeesh. Reese clutched it with growing excitement. The thrill, the anticipation, the surety that there was something wonderful and great and monumental ahead coursed through her like a sugar rush.

If only sex were this good.

Flipping through the pages, she began to bounce up and down on the bed, muttering over and over, "Whoa, whoa, *whoa.*"

Pharmaceutical company price-fixing. An intentional withholding of patents for generic drugs to force the price of the name brand product high.

This was so illegal. This was so awesome.

Grabbing her digital camera out of her briefcase, Reese took a picture of each and every document, then checked to make sure they were clear and visible.

Setting the camera aside, she was about to start reading the documents again, more slowly this time, when there was a knock on her door. She'd forgotten about the room service.

Tugging her robe closed, she quickly shoved all the papers back in the envelope, put it back in her briefcase, and went to the door.

Pasting a generic smile on her face, she opened it. And found herself face to face with double chocolate fudge eyes.

Shit. She tried to slam the door shut.

Which was stupid. He was an FBI agent. Keeping doors open was probably like day one in agent training camp.

His foot and his hand landed in front of the door, stopping it from closing as he took a step forward. Reese backed up and tried not to swallow her tongue.

"Reese Hampton?"

Not good. He knew who she was. "Maybe," she said, clearing her throat.

He smiled. A slow, wide *women adore me* kind of smile. Reese was suddenly way too aware of the fact that she wasn't wearing underwear.

"You're not sure?" he asked.

"Can I help you?" Striving for professional, she came off sounding more like a sullen McDonald's clerk.

He took another step forward, forcing her back instinctively. With the added space, he moved clear of the door and closed it behind him.

That wasn't good.

"Hey, I didn't ask you in."

"I don't care." He smiled, reminding her that he was crazy. No matter that he was as cute as a kitten and built like every woman's fantasy. He was still wacky and in her hotel room.

"Do I have to call security?" She yanked tighter on her robe as if tugging would suddenly cause undergarments to materialize on her body.

He laughed and reached into his pocket. "Not this again." He opened his wallet and stuck his badge in front of her. "They can't touch me. But I'll leave as soon as you give me what I want."

In another time and another place, that might have had a nice ring to it. But now it just annoyed her. This guy was starting to tick her off with his creepy smile and hot body.

Ripping the wallet out of his hands, she studied the badge. She still wasn't convinced it wasn't fake. She knew a guy in the Bronx who could make one of these for thirty bucks.

"So, Agent Knight, what is it that you want?" Besides the Tyvek envelope, because she wasn't giving that up. Not when her first and probably last chance to do a real, newsworthy story resided in that envelope.

"Call me Derek."

Oh, ho, ho. Mr. Smooth. She narrowed her eyes at him

and wondered just how he could manage to make jeans and a navy sweatshirt look so sexy. He was moving into her room, glancing around with no attempt at discretion.

Reese stayed by the door, hoping he'd get the hint. Of course, the guy had chased her into a deli, so it was likely he wasn't going to be satisfied with a brush-off. Now she knew why he was so tenacious about his envelope. Given only the quick glimpse she'd had, that evidence looked very incriminating.

Several pharmaceutical companies in collusion to price-fix, fleecing little old ladies who needed their beta-blockers out of their Social Security checks was big time. Probably earn Agent Knight here a gold star, or whatever the hell the FBI gave out. Maybe a class at Quantico named after him.

Scaring the Pee Out of Unsuspecting Reporters 101.

"What do you want, *Derek*?" She emphasized his name to show him she was annoyed, if he couldn't tell by her violent scowl. She'd known a Derek in grade school and he had been fond of tripping her on the playground and snapping her bra strap. The bias against the name was deep seated and this Derek's current behavior wasn't working to counter it.

"That is, besides shaving ten years off my life from fright by chasing me half across Chicago."

"Sorry about that," he said, running his hand along the dresser in her room as he turned and walked towards the window.

Reese barely heard him. My God, she'd gotten the first glimpse at his backside. His butt was amazing. She felt inspired to write poetry. To sculpt. To overlook his professional insanity . . . uh, intensity, and do a little investigating of her own.

Exhibit A. The finest ass in the lower forty-eight states.

"Where's the envelope, Reese?"

He turned around abruptly and she was left staring at his front side. That wasn't so bad either. Her body agreed. She realized with utter mortification that she was aroused, as in no-need-for-lubricants-here wet. Since she was naked but for the robe, it was disturbing and uncomfortable.

Like being wrapped in a damp towel.

"What envelope?" she said, sticking her chin out at him. Jerk. Clearly he was used to getting his way, even if he had to run innocent investigative reporters off the road.

And make them horny.

He stopped scanning the room and looked at her. "Come on, you know what I'm talking about. The white envelope you had in your hands when you ran into the deli. It's mine and I need it back."

Reese wondered where he kept his gun. Everything looked so hard, solid, like she could run her hands across his chest and find nothing but rippling muscle and toned flesh. Was it tucked in his pants? On his leg?

"Sorry. Can't help you."

He stepped towards her. "We can do this the easy way. Or the hard way. The easy way is you give the envelope to me. The hard way is I get a search warrant and *then* you give the envelope to me."

There was no doubt in her mind he would, either. The thought of forcing him to leave and come back had a certain appeal, but she wanted to get cracking on studying those documents. If she gave him the envelope, he'd be none the wiser and she could print out the pictures she'd taken and start picking through the evidence.

She wasn't sure if there was enough to go to press on in the envelope and she would have to do some research on the parties involved. All on her own time, before and after the stupid wedding that all of Chicago's movers and shakers would be at tomorrow.

"Don't get all threatening and cop-ish, Knight. Maybe I have it and I don't know it. Let me look around."

Putting her hand on his arm to brush past him, she squeezed a little. Ooh, very nice. A cheap thrill ran through her. Too bad she had better things to do than engage in a rip-roaring affair with a Fed.

Like try to pretend she had a career and a life.

Derek watched Reese saunter over to the bed like she had all the time in the world, plus a day to spare. This was unreal. If he had been thinking with his brain he would have gotten the warrant first or called for backup. She wouldn't have the nerve to play this game with him if he wasn't alone.

Of course, that would have meant admitting to someone else in the bureau that he had screwed up. Again. He had thought intimidation would work, after all, withholding the envelope from him was illegal. And there wasn't any good reason Reese would want it.

Unless . . .

Her rental car slip had listed her employer as the *Newark News*. Unless she was a reporter who had smelled a story.

She turned and handed him the envelope with wide innocent eyes that were as fake as his mother's fur. "Is this it?"

It was, and it had been ripped open. Dammit. Not only had he lost the stupid thing in the first place, he'd lost it to a freaking reporter. Who was hotter than hell and half naked.

"It's been opened." He yanked it from her hands.

"It fell open when I dropped it."

Yeah, Tyvek was known for flying open. Usually he just about needed a knife to pry the stuff apart.

He stared at her with a scowl, trying to scare her into the truth. Instead, her lip twitched like she was going to laugh and right then he was more concerned with the way she kept tugging at her robe than this case.

She was minutes out of a shower, and her auburn hair was still damp, clinging to her head and neck, little wisps of hair trailing down her cheeks. A heady smell of peaches and mint clogged his nostrils and made the room seem smaller than it was.

When was the last time he'd been with a half naked woman? Long enough to make him sweat now.

He had a good head start on a boner, too.

"Why do you keep tugging on your robe? What have you got on under there?"

The semi-smirk fell off her face. "My bra, my panties, and thick flannel pajamas."

He bent over and picked up a satin bra that was lying on the bed. Sliding his thumb across it, he said, "Then what's this?"

"I have more than one." She let her hands drop from the robe and land on her hips. "Now if you're done fondling my bra, can you please leave? You've got your envelope."

He also had a major problem. "Look, Reese, I know you're a reporter. I know you looked in the envelope. Now I need you to promise me you're not going to print any of that information. You could jeopardize the whole case if you do."

"Who says I looked?"

Spinning her bra on his finger, he said, "Yeah, right. And you've got those flannel pajamas on right now. You're a good liar, but I'm not stupid."

He wasn't leaving this room until he got some cooperation. He hadn't gone this far to have the whole case shot to hell by a brassy reporter with bad timing.

"I can't promise you anything." Green eyes flashed, met his in defiance, and locked into a battle of wills.

Derek looked away first, pissed as hell. And he wasn't sure if it was because she could ruin this investigation for him, or because he was almost overwhelmed by the urge to toss her back on the bed and screw her brains out.

Odds were two to one on the second.

Reese jumped as Derek said, "Shit!"

He continued to maul her bra as he added, "Jesus, I don't need this crap. Like I don't have enough problems, I've got to deal with you now."

Someone needed Prozac.

Intent on saving her expensive bra from destruction, she inched towards him. "Hey, relax, I'm not out to ruin your life."

"I'm not reassured." Tossing her bra on the bed, he dropped the envelope next to it and raked his hands through his hair.

Giving her bra a glance to check for torn seams or busted underwire, she sighed in relief. All intact. "I didn't ask for this to happen either."

But she was so glad that it had. Not only did she have a chance at a real investigation and byline, but she got to do it alongside the sexy and hot-tempered Agent Knight. It was an orgasm just waiting to happen.

She decided to re-categorize his looniness as tenacious and determined. Career driven. If he had to drive her off the road to get his envelope, he would. She could live with that. After all, she was willing to stand here with hard nipples in front of a gorgeous man for a story.

Talk about a hardship.

He shook the envelope in front of her. "What did you see?"

"Look, Knight, don't get all worked up. Maybe we can help each other out."

"How the hell can you help me?"

The man had no people skills. Too much time spent on bulking up those muscles and not enough on social graces and communication.

"Calm down and I'll explain."

The knock on the door didn't help his glare. In fact, it made it more pronounced. "Who's at the door?"

"Well, gee, I don't know. Let me adjust my x-ray eyes and tell you." She rolled her eyes. "What do I look like? A Powerpuff Girl?"

The sarcasm went unheeded. Knight was slipping his hand under his sweatshirt in what Reese determined was an instinctive check to make sure his gun was there. She about came on the spot.

Since when had she developed a weapons fetish?

Since double chocolate fudge eyes had arrested her.

A laugh ripped out of her. God, she cracked herself up.

Giving her a wary look, Knight called, "Who is it?"

"Room service."

Reese's stomach growled. "Oh, that's right. My chicken wings are here."

Knight said, "You ordered wings at nine o'clock at night?"

He opened the door and nodded to the room service attendant. Reese salivated as the tray was brought in and deposited down on her tiny table in the corner.

"There's no time limit on wings. Besides, I just got in from New York and there was no food service on the plane. I haven't eaten since noon."

"You're all set. Is there anything else I can get for you?" The middle-aged attendant smiled at her, eyes dropping to her robe for a split second.

"That's all. Thank you." She headed for her food, her stomach in danger of digesting its own walls if she didn't eat soon. "Knight, give the man a tip, would you?"

She gave him a sweet smile as she took her seat in front of the tray.

He frowned at her, but was already reaching for his wallet. "Let me guess, your money is with your flannel pajamas."

"No. My money is in my purse on the bed. I just don't feel like getting it."

The attendant chuckled as he accepted the tip from Knight. They exchanged one of those guy looks, the kind where they lament the vagaries of womankind with a single lift of the eyebrow.

"Have a good night," he said as he backed out of the room.

Reese patted the seat next to her at the cozy little table. "Sit down. Share some wings with me."

He came towards her, dripping with suspicion, flipping his hair back out of his eyes. Given the unruly nature of his hair and the fact that his sweatshirt was probably older than she was, she decided he had been a while without a female influence.

Perfect.

Because she intended to influence him. To give her first dibs on the price-fixing story, and to convince him that it would be a brilliant idea to sleep with each other in the near future.

"Let's discuss how we can help each other."

"You can help me by staying out of this, Reese. Forget anything you saw and go back to doing whatever it was you were doing before."

Interviewing B grade actresses and local mayoral candidates? No thank you. The truth was, she didn't even work for a real newspaper. No *New York Times* for her. She was stuck with the *Newark News,* which was one third obituaries, one third sports, and another thirty percent delegated to entertainment. Her beat, lucky her. The remaining three and a half percent was for the news and current events.

With this story, she could blow off the *Newark News,* give her boss Ralph the finger, and wave the scoop in front of the highest bidder. Meaning any halfway decent paper that offered her a job. Anywhere in the Continental U.S. She might even be willing to consider Alaska if the pay was right.

"Okay, just give up on that idea right now. I can't forget what I saw. And if you hadn't chased me here, there, and everywhere for it, I probably never would have looked. But you made me curious." So really he had no one to blame but himself.

A heartfelt sigh issued forth as he dropped into the chair. "I'm too old for this crap. I need to retire."

It made her laugh as she reached for a chicken wing, setting it on her paper plate. Room service didn't extend to anything breakable she guessed.

"I think you've got like thirty years ahead of you before you can do that."

"Try twenty. I'm thirty-six," he said, reaching out and grabbing her stalk of celery. He gave a vicious bite and sat there chewing in a major sulk.

Since Reese had put him in the somewhere between twenty-nine and forty category, she wasn't surprised at all. But confirmation of his age made her take a peek at his ring finger to see if there was a Mrs. Crabby FBI Agent.

The finger was bare and there were no telltale tan lines to indicate he slipped it on and off at will.

"You're just going to eat celery?" Reese said around a mouthful of chicken. "There's plenty for you, too."

"Ulcer," he said, eyeing the wings covetously.

Reese saw the signs of someone feeling seriously sorry for himself. A little balloon of empathy for him rose in her chest, which was dumb since she had every intention of using him to suit her purposes.

Yet she said lightly, "Is that standard issue with your gun and badge? I swear, every cop has one."

He just grunted and tossed the celery down, rattling the plastic fork and knife on the table. "Along with the bum knee?"

"Were you shot or something?" He was growing more and more appealing by the second, if a little on the moody side. She pictured him dodging bullets and wrestling bad guys to the ground. Chasing a crook with the same single-mindedness with which he had chased her.

Shiver. Why had she never dated in law enforcement before? This was so sexy.

"Tire iron. Took it in the knee."

"Owww." Her own knee throbbed in sympathy.

His lip twitched. "That about sums it up."

Then he sank back into his chair and said, "Sorry. You don't want to hear all this, I'm sure. But I haven't been having the best few months. Year. Two years."

Sex could fix all that. Or at least make him forget. It was

perfect. She could sleep with him and have no guilt that she was using him to get this story. In fact, it would be like a public service. Sending a federal agent back into the field relaxed and ready to defend innocent Americans.

And there were no moral snafus because she wanted him. She really, really wanted him.

"Well, if you're going to have a pity party, I want to join." Wiping errant blue cheese dressing from the corner of her mouth, she said, "You think your life sucks? Try mine. I'm twenty-six." She stopped to take a sip of iced tea.

"And how is that supposed to make me feel bad for you?"

"Hold on, I haven't gotten to the bad part. I'm not old but I'm too old to still be working the crappy job I do. I'm not a real reporter, Knight."

"You're a fake one?" he said, the corners of his eyes wrinkling as he smiled.

"No, I'm not a fake." She allowed a pitiful and drawn out sigh to emerge. "I'm a reporter, but I work for a rag paper. Only it's not even a good rag. We haven't even been sued for slander. Our circulation is so small we could print that the president is lovers with Tom Cruise and no one would care."

He laughed, a full rich laugh that reminded her she had never bothered to dress, and the only thing separating his hand from her thigh was a layer of terry cloth. Oh, and a table. But it was such a small table.

He shook his head. "I kind of wondered what exactly the *Newark News* was."

"A pit of despair for young aspiring journalists, whose idealism is ground under the boots of Ralph Greco, managing editor. Ralph is also fond of onion laden sandwiches, which, given the small confines of our office, makes life almost unbearable."

He said, "My boss would be happy to see me shuffling papers for the rest of my life. He's demoted me twice and lies in wait for me to screw up so he can gleefully slap me with an infraction."

So Knight understood a hostile work environment. This was great. She grinned at him. "What did you do? Sleep with his wife?"

Laughter disappeared as he blanched. "Damn, that's a scary image. Lord. Let's just say Mrs. Nordstrom has an excess of facial hair."

Reese snorted.

"No, I just tripped him by accident on a take down. He was supposed to be first man in, and when he moved past me, he tripped." Grinning, he reached over and picked up a chicken wing. "He was first man in alright. First in on his face."

Oh, that was good. "So both our jobs suck. I bet I can beat you for crap factor with my personal life."

His eyebrows raised. "I doubt it." He took a bite of chicken and leaned forward, a definite gleam in his eye.

Reese bent towards him, sucking the excess sauce off her finger with slow deliberate movements. "Give it your best shot, Knight. You've got nothing on me."

"You want to bet?" His voice was low, hoarse, teasing.

"I do."

If she were a betting woman, she'd bet that this night was going to get a whole lot more interesting fast.

All she had to lose was the robe on her back. And shedding that was exactly according to plan.

Chapter Three

Derek was going to regret eating the wings.

He wasn't going to regret being with Reese. His mood had been darkening like an incoming storm, until she had teased him right out of it. She was right. He'd been feeling sorry for himself, which was pathetic.

Hey, he still had his job and he could walk. What the hell else did he want?

Right now he wanted Reese Hampton so bad he was salivating. It wasn't helping that he knew damn well she wasn't wearing any flannel pajamas under that robe. He'd caught a glimpse of pale flesh more than once.

"How about this? If I win, you have to tell me exactly what you saw in that envelope and what you plan to do with that information."

She smirked, pulling a hair out of her mouth. "Okay. And if I win, you have to let me print the story when it's time. First rights to insider info."

"In the *Newark News*? I don't think so."

Her cute little button nose wrinkled. "No! In the paper that I give the story to. The paper that will then hire me and change my life from sewage to meaningful."

Derek weighed his options. He didn't think he could trust Reese any more than he could a politician, but she'd already seen the documents. He didn't want to send her running off to print the story with half the information.

If he strung her along throughout the investigation, it would keep her out of his way. She could have the story once several executives were in the back of a car on their way to prison.

Besides, she wasn't going to win.

He had the record on lame and boring lifestyles.

"It's a bet."

She grinned. "I'll go first."

Wiping her hands on a napkin, she tossed her hair back. "Okay, it all started approximately twenty-four years ago when my mother had the bad taste to die on me, leaving me at the mercy of my father and three older brothers."

"Hey, I'm sorry about your mom." Derek pictured his mom baking cookies for him and cheering him on at Little League. When was the last time he'd called her?

"No, no, don't feel sorry for me. Yet. It's not like she did it on purpose, or like my dad was unfeeling. The total opposite. He loved me so much he was terrified he'd screw up raising a daughter. So instead, he just raised me like a boy. Sports, jeans, spitting, the whole bit."

That explained a lot. It didn't explain the way she could move around the room with a total sensual femininity, but it explained the stare-him-straight-in-the-face brass balls attitude she had.

"I bought my first bra by myself at Sears when I was twelve, with money from my allowance because my dad was in denial. The saleswoman took one look at my clinging baseball T-shirt showing everything and then some, and rushed me off to the fitting room. I emerged with a B cup and a whole new world of information."

So far, she had him beat.

"I'll spare you the rest of the horror of my entrance into puberty, but let's just say I had to fight tooth and nail for my dad and brothers to acknowledge that I had different plumbing than them. And when I expressed an interest in boys, all hell broke loose."

Looking at her, he could only imagine. He could see her, too, defiant, yelling back at her family, sneaking out of the house to meet a guy.

"I had to lie that prom was a different day, say I was sleeping at my friend Jeannie's house, then pull my dress out of a duffel bag and put it on in the rest room at the party center."

"What was their objection to prom? Every kid goes to prom." A flash of taffeta and a bad tux rose in his memory. Christ, he couldn't even remember his date's name. Damn near twenty years ago.

She folded her hands across the table and raised an eyebrow. "Three older brothers had all been to prom. I'm guessing their experience was somewhere along the lines of a drunken orgy. They weren't about to let me have that much fun."

That was pretty damn sad. Though he didn't imagine she'd taken it lying down. "Did you have that much fun? Have a drunken orgy of your own?"

"No. My boyfriend threw up on my dress and passed out by eleven o'clock."

Derek laughed.

"Hey!"

He shrugged. "It's funny."

She stuck her tongue out at him. "So, that's the story of my childhood. I don't even remember losing my virginity because I was so sure one of my brothers was going to walk in and murder the guy. I spent the whole five minutes watching the door over his shoulder."

"Five minutes? Christ. You probably weren't missing much anyway, then." If he ever had Reese beneath him, he'd need a hell of a lot more time than that. He was thinking hours. A whole night. A month, maybe.

"Oh, please, like you were any better when you were eighteen."

"I was better than five minutes, that's for sure." None of his girlfriends had ever complained.

She snorted. "So do I win the bet?"

She wished. Derek settled back in his chair, stretching out his bad knee. "Not so fast. You've got me beat with life before twenty-one, but I've got you after that."

Stacking the dirty plates one on top of each other, she said, "How?"

"You ever been married?"

"No."

"I have." Five years of indentured servitude and it still hadn't been enough to keep Dawn around. "So I win, right there."

"Why?" She narrowed her eyes. "Just because you were married? What's so bad about that?"

"Says you who haven't been married." He crossed his arms.

"Lots of people are married and seem happy."

"Including my ex-wife." He didn't have bitter feelings towards Dawn. In fact, he didn't have a whole lot of feelings for her at all, which seemed wrong given they'd lived together for close to six years. But sometimes he wondered if he'd have made different choices if he hadn't been with Dawn.

If he hadn't been so worried that he wasn't measuring up in her eyes.

Back when he'd been at the academy, he'd always pictured himself working in violent crimes, out on the street, right in the action. But he'd gone into the financial crimes division because that had seemed the fastest route to a directorship, which was what Dawn had wanted, and he had wanted to make her happy. It hadn't worked.

Water under the bridge now.

"Dawn wanted two things I couldn't give her. Money and sperm."

Reese's eyes went wide. She dropped a paper napkin. "You don't have sperm?"

That made him laugh. "No, I've got as much as the next guy, but Dawn wanted a kid and I didn't. I think I knew the marriage was going south and a kid was only going to make that worse."

"Oh." She closed her mouth. "So what happened?"

"She left me and married Chicago's prosecuting attorney and moved into a fancy house. She is currently six months pregnant with their first progeny."

"Damn, that's cold."

He shrugged. "She has a right to have what she wants."

But Reese stood up, yanking her robe belt tighter as she moved away from the table. "So where does love fit in all that? It's just 'sorry, you're not giving me what I want, so see ya?' That's wrong."

He didn't say anything. He didn't want to talk about Dawn anymore, was sorry he'd started the subject. No thoughts of Dawn belonged in this room where a gorgeous woman was only a few feet in front of him. Touching distance.

If he reached out and tugged on the belt . . .

"So I think you win post twenty-one. So we're tied." She nibbled the tip of her finger in a gesture that had him shifting in the chair.

"Okay, I know a deciding factor to see which of us has a crappier life. When was the last time you had sex?"

He shouldn't have been surprised by anything Reese said, but he still felt his mouth flapping in the breeze. Then answering. "Uh, five months."

Which right now felt like five hundred years. The stupid teasing robe was gaping at the chest again, and he saw the rise of her left breast. Flannel pajamas, his ass.

Reese felt a surge of triumph. Listening to his marriage woes, she'd been afraid she was actually going to have to admit defeat. "Hah! I've definitely got you beat. It's been *fourteen* months since I've had sex!"

It came to her a split second later that maybe that wasn't something she should be bragging about.

But she'd suck it up for the sake of winning.

Only he didn't look impressed. "Yeah, but you forgot about my ulcer and the bad knee, plus I'm ten years older than you. I think that makes us even."

She was about to argue, just on principle, when he spoke again in a voice that made her wish she was still sitting with her legs crossed. Tightly.

He sat there, legs straight out in front of him, arms across his chest as he flicked his gaze over her. "Besides, I'm sure you've had plenty of opportunities."

Yeah, they were just dropping at her feet left and right, begging for it. Please. The only men interested in getting their hands on her were her boss and the short little guy who worked the register at her grocery store.

"Not a one."

"I have a hard time believing that."

"You want to bet?" Her social life was nonexistent. Women in nursing homes got more action than she did.

"We haven't settled our first bet, I'm not entering another one."

Reese paced back and forth, slowly, next to the table. She lifted her hair off her shoulders and tossed it back. It was still damp and heavy, and she knew it was probably doing a Chia Pet imitation.

Knight was right. They were running about head to head in the Whose Life Bites Royally competition. There was only one thing to do.

"Let's arm wrestle."

His relaxed slouch disappeared. He gaped at her. "What?"

"Yeah. It's a great idea. That's the way my brothers and I always decided a tie."

"Reese." He shook his head. "It would be pointless because there's no way you can beat me."

Typical male arrogance. "You think so?"

Yes, obviously. Gag. He was flexing his muscles and she suspected he wasn't even aware he was doing it. He just squeezed his wrists and popped out his elbows as he studied her, certain of his strength superiority.

"You can't beat me."

"You're ten years older than me," she taunted, enjoying the sudden irritated flare to his nostrils. "And that chicken wing ought to be kicking your ulcer in gear right about now."

With an expression of disgust, he shoved their dirty dishes to the very edge of the table and slapped his elbow down. "Alright. Give it your best shot, tough girl."

Reese sauntered over to the table, planning her strategy. It was true there was no way she could beat him on strength alone. Especially since she hadn't seen the inside of a gym . . . ever. But it wasn't hopeless or she wouldn't have suggested it.

As a kid, she had always provoked her brothers during the match by making faces at them. Ryan had laughed and lost his grip on her hand every single time, allowing her to take advantage and win. Riley had run about fifty-fifty, and with Rick, her oldest brother, she had soon learned not to challenge him at all. He had never even blinked.

Sticking her tongue up into her nostril was probably out of the question in front of Knight, but the theory still applied. She just needed a different tactic.

One that didn't require her to taste snot.

Rolling up the sleeve of her robe, she eyed him.

He looked amused. "Oh, are we that serious then? Maybe I should take my sweatshirt off."

Now there was an unexpected perk. Trying not to pant, she said, "Suit yourself."

"Not that I think I need it." Knight leaned back and

crossed his arms, grabbed his sweatshirt, and ripped it over his head in one motion.

Dammit, he had a T-shirt on under there. Reese sucked her breath in and swallowed hard. It was still a mighty nice view, full of tight cotton, rippling muscles, and a holster strapped across his shoulder with his gun tucked into it.

Fourteen months was too long to go without an orgasm. She was turned on by a flipping white T-shirt. If he showed her any skin, there was no telling what she might do. Whimpering was coming to mind.

As he casually tossed his sweatshirt onto her bed—her bed, for hell's sake—she took the seat across from him. His elbow was back on the table, he was leaning forward, his fingers stretched up and fidgeting.

"Ready when you are."

She put her own right elbow on the table and lined it up with his. He didn't wait. Strong fingers enveloped hers, clasping her tightly with a warm naked squeeze. The gasp she'd been planning to fake wasn't fake at all, but painfully real. Deep, gut-wrenching, tingling, mushy real.

Knight was doing an extended version of the previous nostril flare.

"On the count of three," she managed to say, her voice coming out like a sixty-year-old smoker's.

His thumb wrapped tight, but his fingers drummed across her knuckles. Reese leaned closer, shifting in her chair. The smell of the chicken rose up between them, spicy and pungent. He had a little bit of chin stubble, not noticeable until she was this close because it was lighter than his hair. The rough fawn colored beard made her want to reach out and scratch it, digging her soft fingertips into that masculine hardness.

"One." As she shifted her shoulder forward, her robe split open, offering a hint of cleavage.

"Two." She slid her tongue out and moistened her lips, with deliberation and agonizing slowness.

Knight's hand relaxed as he watched her, his jaw clenched. Reese sighed a little, drawing her breath quickly back in, causing her chest to rise and fall. She gave a deep lean. A sharp hiss came from Knight, his eyes plastered to her chest.

She tossed her hair back and caught a flash of the top of her breast through the corner of her eye. He had to see it, too, since his gaze hadn't moved a quarter of an inch.

"Three." Reese squeezed hard, pushed with everything she had in her, and dropped his arm to the table before he could even react.

She pulled her hand out of his slack grip and indulged in a little gloating as he sat there stunned. "Ha, ha! Told you I could beat you."

"Hey, I wasn't ready."

"Oh, don't give me that. It's not just about strength, it's about reflexes. I was obviously quicker." She grinned at him, enjoying the sour look on his face.

"You cheated," he accused.

"How?" she asked innocently.

"By flashing me."

"What? What are you talking about?" She sat back and crossed her leg over her knee, swinging it up and down.

"Your robe gaped and it distracted me."

"I'm not responsible for your being distracted. If you can't keep your mind on the game, it's not my fault, you pervert." Reese stood up and pulled the belt on her robe tighter, trying not to grin in triumph and probably not succeeding.

"So I win the bet and I get the scoop on the drug story."

"I want a rematch."

"Yeah, because you lost. I'm not falling for that."

Knight ran his fingers through his caramel colored hair and shook his head. "You're nothing but a con artist."

She leaned over him, propping herself up on the table. "That's the risk you take. That's why they call it gambling, Knight."

It was meant to be fun, additional rubbing of his face in

the loss. She expected him to persist in a rematch. Or to laugh. But more likely to protest, argue, and further amuse her with his annoyance.

Instead, he said, "I knew you weren't wearing a bra. And there isn't a stitch of flannel on you anywhere."

Then his finger reached out and hooked around the trim of her robe. One little tug and he had pulled it back until the swell of her breast was showing, his eyes dark and edgy.

She blushed. From surprise, a hint of embarrassment, and most of all from hot jolting desire that reached deeper inside that robe than his finger was. All the way inside, snaking everywhere until her body pulsed and throbbed and burned with it.

"What the hell are you doing?" she said, with forced indignation.

"Confirming that I can't trust you as far as I can throw you."

"Given that wimpy display of arm wrestling, I guess that wouldn't be too far." She held on to her control with a great deal of effort. It was tempting to just tumble herself into his lap, which was so inviting, hard, and denim.

With a bulge that wasn't a gun.

Oh, damn, she wanted that.

"You're a real comedienne. You want to see how strong I am?" He stood up fast, surprising her, his thighs coming awe-inspiringly close to her mouth.

His chest brushed her arm as he stretched to his full height, which was a good eight inches more than her five foot six. He filled the space around her, smothering her with his largeness, his broad chest eye level.

She stayed bent over, refusing to admit how flustered she was. And hot. Was terry cloth flammable? If it was, she was dead because any second now a fire was about to ignite between them.

"I'm not interested, Knight. All I want to know is how much information you're going to give me about Delco Pharmaceutical." It just about cost her her soul to spit out those words that were nothing more than total bullshit.

His mouth was next to her ear, his fingers brushing her hair back off her cheek as he drew her to a standing position. She shivered as he said, "Uh-uh-uh. You're doing it again. Lying to me."

"You can't prove it."

Lips grazed along her jaw, forcing her to gasp against her will, her eyes fluttering shut like some newly awakened virgin. Reese completely, one hundred percent appreciated the fact that she was female, despite what her father wanted to think.

"Want to bet?"

Then he shifted and kissed her.

Chapter Four

Derek knew he was screwed. He might as well kiss the last of his career good-bye and apply for a security position at the mall.

The minute his mouth touched Reese's he forgot about the case, Nordstrom, and his ulcer, feeling nothing but a hot pit of desire, intense aching want that was owned by this woman.

He thought to be cautious, to taste and savor before going deep. But Reese didn't wait for him to do more than brush her lips, and took him instead. She grabbed on, held, sucked on his bottom lip and moaned an honest pleasure into his ear, making him feel about as manly as he was capable of being.

Reese kissed the way she talked, with vibrant movements and a single-minded determination to get what she wanted. She wanted the upper hand and having caught him off-guard by her response, she had it.

Until Derek broke off and trailed his lips down her long smooth neck, touching the tip of his tongue along her clavicle bone. Reese's grasping, taut fingers slackened a little and a funny little sound like a hiccup came out of her.

He loved the way she tasted, soft and sweet, like sucking on a juicy apple, golden delicious. Settling all of her body against his, he moved up to her ear, tickling it with his tongue and dusting kisses across her cheekbone until he was back to her mouth.

This kiss was his, slow and soft, wide open lips and gentle pressure. Nudging tongues and quiet sighs. Reese's fingers slid down off his shoulders to the edge of his shirtsleeves, then clung there.

He moved his knee between hers, wanting closer, everything touching, and he felt the crush of the neck of her robe between them. Taking her mouth again and again he wondered through a fog of lust if this was a good idea, before his fingers ignored the question and headed for her belt.

But Reese stepped back, knocking his hand away, the complacent passion receding a little from her eyes. She panted as he clenched his lips together, disappointment pulsing through him, paralyzing him for a minute while he regained control.

"While this is a nice distraction, we haven't settled our bet. You haven't actually agreed to information-share with me."

Derek should applaud her for bringing them back around to the subject. But all he wanted was to toss that robe out the window and spend about a million years tasting every inch of her.

His hard-on ached in agreement.

Reaching out, he played with the belt of her robe, debating just tugging her back into his arms. "I'll information-share. Now let's get back to what we were doing."

Her shove at his hand wasn't convincing. But she still persisted, "I'm serious. You have to tell me everything."

Everything was a very broad and all-inclusive word that he had no intention of committing to. He smiled at her, slow and deliberate. Her eyes went wide.

"There are things I can show you, too, you know."

Starting with his chest. He wanted out of this T-shirt, so when he got her naked she would slide across his bare skin with her nipples.

She eyed him, her arms snaking across her chest. "I just bet you could. But I'm not interested."

"You don't want to see it? I've been told it's big, hard, and fast. Stop you in your tracks and rip the breath right out of you." He bit back a grin.

"Knight!"

"What?" He laughed, undoing the shoulder holster as a prelude to taking his shirt off. "I'm talking about my gun."

"You're a sick man." The shock on her face gave way to annoyance.

That auburn hair that he was fast starting to develop an obsession for pooled around her face, and she tucked it behind her ears.

"See?" He held his gun up for her to see before tossing it on the table.

Reese shrugged. "I've seen bigger."

That pulled a surprised laugh from him. Damn, she was unlike any other woman he'd ever met. And a fascinating complication he really didn't need in his life right now.

"Ouch. Talk about cutting a man down to size."

"Well, I didn't say it's small, I just said I've seen bigger. Don't feel bad; not every guy can be issued the big guns." She didn't even bother to hide her smirk.

Derek took a step towards her. "It's all about how you use it, isn't it?"

Dammit, how did he do that? Make her think she had the upper hand, then yank the control rug right out from under her. But she had to admit, she wasn't ready to complain just yet. Not when she was enjoying herself so much she was in danger of giggling.

Giggling was a girly habit she'd abandoned at about age four, when her brothers had wrestled and shoved every last giggle right out of her. She'd learned to express herself through grunts, snorts, and eye rolls, yet here she was feeling every inch a female and liking it.

"So you're good with it, is that what you're saying?" Reese stuck her foot out to increase her area of personal space, hoping he'd stay back and yet simultaneously praying he'd walk right up to her and kiss her senseless again.

"Very good with it. Do you want me to show you?"

"How? By shooting me?" They weren't talking about firearms, but she wasn't about to admit that. Let him say it first.

Two more steps and he was flush against her. She had to pull her foot back to avoid stumbling. Knight's hands gripped her arms and he looked down into her eyes, his gaze dropping to her lips then back up again.

"Reese."

"What?"

"Be quiet."

If he had given her a second, she would have told him to go to hell. As it was, his lips were on hers before she could even form a word, and then she didn't care how bossy he was being, or how stupid this was, and that it was still possible he was stringing her along about giving her the drug co-exclusive.

All she cared about was that for the first time in a long time her body was in tune with a man's, and that nothing else was going to matter or get addressed until she had sweated through some hot sex with Knight.

So when his hand slipped inside her robe and stroked along her breast, she was all for it. She gave an encouraging moan, pulling back a micro-millimeter from his mouth with hers, until he pushed forward and claimed her again, nudging back her lips with his tongue.

While his tongue dipped and tasted and did amazing things to her mouth, his hand went back and forth on her breast, caressing and plucking, pinching and playing until she arched her back and let her head roll to the side in delirious pleasure.

She made a mental note to thank Ralph for sending her on this trip, though she never would have predicted anything more exciting than drinking free champagne at the wedding when she'd boarded the plane. This beat a couple of glasses of Don Perignon any day.

His wet mouth left hers and closed over her nipple. Yep. A vat of champagne served by dancing baboons on the top of the Eiffel Tower couldn't be more exciting than this.

"Yes. I like that." Just in case he got any ideas about stopping.

"Mmm," he said, and sucked harder, the slickness of his lips raising goose bumps on her chilled flesh.

"Oh," she said, wishing there was a way she could say *if you stop I'll murder you* without sounding like a lunatic.

But he did stop, the lousy tease, and murmured into her neck. "Reese, what exactly are we doing here?"

"Right now we're doing nothing. A second ago you were kissing me and if you don't mind, I'd like to get back to that." Frustrated and heading towards irrational, she put her hand on his chest, ready to haul him back.

He nipped her ear. "I want you. Can I make love to you?"

Yes, five minutes ago. Reese raked her hand across his chest. All muscle. She rubbed her thighs together to stop the swollen need, but it only made her more aroused.

"Is this what you always do with women you've chased into delis?"

"I've never chased a woman into a deli before. And I've never slept with a reporter before, either, but you have a strange effect on me."

She could sympathize with that. "So what happened in that deli, by the way? Did those clerks get you on the ground, or what?" Somehow she doubted it, but she liked teasing him.

"Reese," he said, his voice a low warning, his thumb circling her nipple again before giving it a light squeeze.

Enough talking then. "Oh, fine. Yes, I want you too. Yes, you can have me and do X-rated things to me. Right now. And if you screw me over and withhold evidence from me at least I'll always have the Crowne Plaza."

His shoulders vibrated as he laughed soundlessly, his breath tickling her ear. "Don't do that."

"What?"

"Make me laugh."

"Why not?"

"Because it distracts me from doing this."

Before Reese even knew what he was planning, he had un-knotted her robe belt. While she swallowed a softball-size lump of desire in her throat, he pushed the sleeves down her arms and let the robe drop to the burgundy carpet.

The chilled air of the temperature-controlled room danced over her naked body and her nipples puckered. Knight shook his head a little as he studied her, then whistled.

"Damn, those are some pj's you've got on."

She leaned back against the table, propping herself up with her straightened arms, enjoying the frank appreciation on his face. She bent one knee as she said, "Smart-ass."

"I was smart enough to come to your room, wasn't I?" His words were muffled as he dragged his T-shirt off over his head.

Then he dropped it to the floor on top of her crumpled robe and Reese's mouth went bone dry. His muscular chest looked even better without the shirt, and his jeans had sunk a little low on his hips, revealing a faint tan line left over from summer.

"Turn around," she told him, intent on torturing herself a little further.

He had popped the button on his jeans and stopped with his hand on the zipper. "What? Why? Don't tell me you've gotten shy."

"No, not shy." That wasn't the word that came to mind. She had never been shy, but she'd never been reckless before, either. She felt that now, a stimulating, flowing, powerful abandon that defied common sense and felt heady and erotic.

"Did I tell you you have a gorgeous body?" Those choco-late eyes roamed over her again, dark and greedy.

"No, but thanks. Now turn around."

"Why?"

"Because I want to look at your ass." He wasn't great at taking orders. They'd have to work on that.

Then again, neither was she.

"Excuse me?"

"What part don't you understand? I want to check out your ass. I caught a glimpse of it when you came into the room, but I want another one."

The poor man looked aghast. She didn't care. "Come on, I'm standing here naked, you can show me your fine be-hind."

A little bit of color raced up his neck, turning his cheeks into two bright spots of copper-red. Which only thrilled her further. "You're blushing! Hasn't some woman ever checked out your butt before?"

He scowled. "Well, sure, but we never discussed it, for Christ's sake."

"We wouldn't be discussing it if you'd just do what I told you."

They stared each other down, both willing the other to cave. Reese licked her lips and tumbled her hair out of her eyes. Knight broke eye contact and swore under his breath.

A second later he made a big production of turning around. "For the record, I'm doing this under duress."

"Duly noted." And disregarded. Because she was looking at perfection.

The seat of his jeans had just the right amount of droop and snug, and bronze skin rose above the waistband, making her dry mouth suddenly flood with saliva. Her inner thighs experienced a similar sensation.

His legs were long and built, but not bulky or brawny. He just looked healthy, strong and all man. Reese closed the two feet between them and slid her hands across his back pockets until she was cupping those firm cheeks in her eager fingers.

Knight started. "You said you'd be looking, not touching."

"Do you really mind?" She moved her hands around past

the seam of his soft, worn jeans and found his erection. Closing her hand around it, she squeezed, her nipples pressing against the hot flesh of his back.

A hiss came from him. "No, I don't mind." His normally mid-pitched voice had dropped to bass.

"Oh, good." Closing her eyes, Reese leaned against him and concentrated on stroking up and down on the length of him through his pants.

She could feel all of him, even his testicles on the underside of his zipper, and her fingers starting moving faster, wanting more, loving the reaction as he throbbed beneath her. Spreading her thighs a little on either side of his leg, she pressed her mound against him, the soft denim of his jeans wiggling through the hair and rubbing her clitoris as she moved. They groaned in unison.

"Reese."

Why did he insist on talking? "What?"

With her teeth, she nipped his back. He was salty-tasting, with a lingering smell of musky soap. She was practically crawling up on top of him, rocking against his leg and continuing to stroke him.

"Do you have a condom?"

Oh, God, there was a mood killer. Reality didn't belong here where she about to have a one-night stand with an FBI agent who had clearly been issued one big gun.

She stopped trying to insert her hand into his pocket to cop a better feel and said, "No. But you have one, right?"

Silence.

Every overexcited nerve in her body stood up and yelled *Shit.* "You have one, right?"

He groaned. "No."

"Oh, Knight!" This was the story of her life, temptation followed by fate laughing cruelly at her. Fate usually took the form of one of her brothers in her mental imaginings.

He hadn't moved, but was still breathing hard as she lay

draped across his back like a wet Kleenex. Pulling her hand off him, she was startled when his own hand closed over hers, drawing it back to his erection.

"We can either stop and I'll go to the store, or we can find . . . other ways to satisfy each other," he said.

Now the man was talking. Reese groped along him and said, "I don't want to wait for the store."

"Me either." He took her hand, turned around, and covered her mouth in a deep, rough, wet kiss, his fingers laced through hers.

"Of course, maybe this is fate telling me I shouldn't sleep with a man who ran me off the road and wanted me for my envelope."

"Fuck fate."

Okay. She wasn't going to argue with that. It had been a futile attempt at rational anyhow. It would take more willpower than she had to walk away from him, stark naked, and go their separate ways.

Tomorrow she had to go be the dippy reporter for the *Newark News,* firmly entrenched in her crappy life. Tonight she was a woman, a successful, sensual woman who had a hot fed at her mercy, ready and willing to satisfy all her desires.

A fed who was bending over again, closing his mouth over her nipple, scratching her with his beard on her soft skin as he flicked his tongue over her.

He said, "You could argue that fate put you in my rental car. That fate wanted you to sleep with me."

Reese squeezed his shoulders as his mouth moved to her other breast, his finger rolling across the nipple he had left painfully hard and slick.

"That's true." As he moved his leg in between hers, she felt his erection pressing into her. Her eyes snapped open. "Wait. We can't. No condoms."

Remember that, she commanded herself. *Be smart, be safe, be mature.* Arguably all things she struggled with. But not when it came to sex. She'd never been stupid about sex and no matter how many times Knight touched her below the belt, she wasn't going to give in on this one.

"I know." He did that ear thing again, where he whispered into her, making her shiver and cling to him like sticky tape.

"I'm just going to suck you and finger you until you come. Is that alright?"

He wouldn't have far to go.

"It will make you feel better. Just a little something to take the edge off," he coaxed, all the while his hands sliding down her sides, big hands. Man hands. Hands that held a gun and went without gloves in the winter.

Rough hands, with bumps and calluses and hard skin, that scraped her waist and made her feel about as strong as dandelion fluff. Whereas a minute ago naked had felt powerful, controlling, now she was vulnerable, exposed before him and his fast-moving fingers.

She curled against him, closing her eyes, not wanting to see, just to feel what he was doing as he cupped his hand over her mound, his mouth hovering an inch in front of hers. His breath tickled her lips, she could taste him and his closeness, feel the hardness of his chest and the soft hair there brushing against her nipples.

He hovered, holding, breathing, still, until her vaginal muscles quivered with anticipation, waiting for the moment when he would touch.

She pushed forward, impatient, needy, and said, "Knight. Come on."

Keeping her eyes closed, she heard him exhale, a pleased soft laugh before his tongue startled her by touching the center of her bottom lip. Reese looked at his angled masculine face, so close she almost went cross-eyed. She dropped her head back as his tongue entered her mouth, hard and demanding at the same time he kicked her thighs apart with his foot.

Then before she could groan, his finger was inside her, sliding in and out to match the rhythm of his tongue, a double assault that had her mindlessly clawing at his back and struggling to stay standing.

He didn't mess around. He went straight for the kill, something she'd have to remember when she wasn't praying for salvation like she was at the present.

In and out, he stroked her over and over until she had to stop him, had to regain some level of control. Otherwise she was going to beg him to never stop, to keep her and take her at his will.

To hell with that.

She jerked back her mouth from his, panting. "You don't play around, do you? You get right down to business."

His finger paused for a second. "You strike me as the kind of woman who wants action, not words."

Her answer was cut off when he added a second finger to the first. "Oh, God," she said, deciding that control was overrated.

Derek watched Reese, arching and bumping up against his fingers, forcing him deeper. She was like whipped cream, pale and soft and sweet, not the least bit healthy for him but too damn good to pass up. His throat was tight, his cock hard, as she pressed forward in impatience, gray-green eyes glazed with desire.

He was burning in his jeans, a sheen of sweat covering him as he fought with himself to stay sane and not plunge himself into her. Maybe it was a good thing he didn't have a condom. A tiny fear niggled at him that once he was in her, he wasn't going to be able to leave.

So much for the matter-of-fact approach to getting his envelope back.

An hour after arriving at her hotel, and here he found himself with her naked in his arms, bucking on his fingers like a rodeo rider. He stopped moving and let her take over, raising up and down, a woman who knew what she wanted and wasn't one bit shy about getting it.

That turned him on, set him panting, but it was a dangerous thing, too, a woman who is ambitious. He'd been there,
done that, had the fucking T-shirt. He'd promised himself
this time around if he ever got seriously involved with another woman he was going to find a sweet librarian type,
content with her life, full of maternal instincts, and adept at
baking.

Reese didn't exactly fit that description.

"Jesus, Reese, you don't even need me, do you?" It didn't
bother him, quite the opposite.

She had established her own rhythm, her breathing ragged
and quick, her hips rocking her onto his two fingers, the air
sweet and heavy with the earthy smell of her body.

The fit of her around him was snug, moist, and when he
pulled his fingers apart into a V, she shuddered, head rolling
back, auburn hair tumbling over plump lips.

"I do need you," she said.

That pleased him so much he added a third finger, a tight
pulsing stretching of her that had them both moaning into
each other's mouths. He held the back of her head, hand slipping in her soft hair, keeping her lips against his while he
stilled his fingers, feeling her muscles clenching.

"You're going to come."

"No," she shook her head in denial.

"Yes, you are."

Another shudder sent her shoulders twitching. "No, I can
handle it."

"It's not too much for you?" He pulled one finger back.

She sagged against him. "No, it's not too much."

"No bigger than my cock, is it?"

Reese started moving again, her curvy bare chest leaning
against his while she got herself off on his fingers. "I don't
know. I've never seen your cock."

He laughed softly. She constantly surprised him. "You
want the other finger back?"

Licking her lips back and forth, leaning over to suck on

her neck gently, he still held her head, twirling that hair around his hand, wanting to hold her there for a very long time.

"I don't care, it's up to you."

Reese was a very good liar, but Derek wasn't buying it. "Then I want it back in."

When he pushed inside her, she came on a low moan, her eyes opening to lock with his as she rode out her pleasure. He kept his fingers in place, let her feel him filling her as she jerked in his arms with rigid shudders.

It was long, tight, her nails raking down his chest as she enjoyed the orgasm with little pants of pleasure. Derek enjoyed it nearly as much, the way she held onto him, the way her thighs clenched, and the way her moist inner muscles vibrated on his fingers.

"Told you you were going to come."

Her forehead landed on his shoulder as she murmured, "For once I don't mind being wrong."

When he slid out of her, she sighed, and Derek wrapped his arms around her, holding her against him, breathing in her sweet womanly scent. Then he kissed the top of her head, in a move that startled them both.

It was too intimate, too caring for what they were doing here, a little casual sex. Yet he didn't feel casual, he was having too much fun to call it that. Reese interested him way more than just about any woman who had come into his life in the past two years.

Which scared the shit out of him.

Had the chicken wings been laced with Ecstasy? Christ, he was acting like an idiot.

He did not know this woman. He had no reason to trust her. For all he knew, she was planning to kick him in his bad knee, steal the Delco evidence along with every dollar in his wallet, take his gun, and hit the highway.

The smart thing to do would be to distance himself from

her, not get closer. Not kiss her on the head like a boyfriend would.

Get out while he could, take his evidence and his pride and forget he'd ever had the misfortune to glimpse her long luscious legs.

Then she unzipped his jeans and slipped a delicate soft hand inside his briefs, giving him a long stroke with cool fingers. He forgot that leaving would be the best thing to do in this situation.

He forgot that he shouldn't trust her.

Hell, he forgot his own damn name.

Chapter Five

Reese had known Knight was packing, but this was ridiculous.

As she took him into both her hands, she said, "How many fingers did you say you were using?"

"Three." His voice was tight and edgy.

Studying the smooth expanse of his erection, she shook her head in wonder. "Damn, this has that beat."

He looked at her like he thought she was joking.

This was no laughing matter. And her body, still tingling from that orgasm, was enthralled by the sight of him, big and pulsing in her hands. What would it feel like to be filled by him? To have him pound into her, holding her flush against the bed, stroking her into ecstasy.

Or standing up, having his man hands on her ass, lifting her cheeks while he thrust up inside her.

Reese swallowed the excess saliva in her mouth and hoped Knight was planning a very fast trip to the store soon, or she was going to be forced to drop into Drug Mart in nothing but this robe and ransack the condom aisle.

"Your hands are so smooth, so feminine," he murmured, his dark gaze shuttered.

Moving around the length of him she said lightly, "Still strong enough to throw a fastball at forty miles an hour and break my brother's nose."

"Or beat me at arm wrestling?" he said in a dry voice. She chuckled. "Exactly."

Giving in to impulse, she leaned forward and ran her tongue across his chest, giving his nipple a little tug. Knight drew his breath in sharply, his hands reaching out and holding onto her elbows, squeezing hard.

"Take my pants off," he demanded.

Without thinking, she did, shoving on denim and his cotton briefs until they were down around his knees, caught between her legs and his. Glancing down to follow through on her task, she had an eye-popping view of his erection. Free of the briefs, it was even more majestic as it rose up, ready for release.

This was dangerous. This was her brains being scrambled and her body being tortured. But she wanted to touch him, feel him, stroke him into the mindless desire that he had given her, and a quick hard release.

If she had to squirm along the way, then that was okay. All the more reason to work fast and send him to the store in search of latex.

Yet when her hand closed back over him, she forgot about herself as he gave a low soft moan. Instead, all she could think was how wonderful he felt, how it pleased her to please him, how relaxed she was with a virtual stranger.

Not so strange anymore. He had touched her, kissed her, sent her rushing into a frantic orgasm and now she could do the same for him. To him.

Moving faster, she built a rhythm, rushing over the length of his shaft, then up and over the head, her thumb moving separately in little circular strokes over the smooth skin. With her free hand, she snaked around and planted a firm grip on that rock solid ass of his that she had admired earlier.

He gripped her head, urged her forward for a long languid kiss that surprised her in its fervor, yet thorough intimacy. It wasn't just slapping and mating, it was deep, intertwining, knowledgeable. A stake-a-claim kiss.

It sent her heart racing in her chest, her fingers rushing faster over him, surprise mingling with passion laced with fear. This was different, wrong . . . right. Reese had indulged in a one-night stand a time or two in her life, probably out of what some therapists would claim was defiance of her father.

She had always lived her life like she had something to prove. That she was tough, strong, and smart, and that she was all of that plus a highly sensual, bra-wearing woman.

This was different from those other times where she had matched wits and blended bodies with men. It had never been personal.

When Knight muttered, "Pull back, Reese," it was personal.

She followed him with her hand as he tried to maneuver out of her reach. He swore and yanked on her elbows trying to jerk her hand off him.

"I'm going to come. Pull back."

The hell with that. She had come all over him, creamy wet and clawing nails. It was only fair he do the same, driven wild and desperate.

"I know. I want you to come on me."

His jaw clenched, his arms tensed, his shoulders hunched up. "Don't tempt me."

Her thumb moved across the top of his penis, sliding slickly when it was met with the clear fluid signaling how close he was to an orgasm.

"I'm tempting," she breathed, pressing her breasts against his arm, her nipples firming as they touched his flushed skin.

She used his own desire to wet all around in a circle, then she stroked down in a quick tight motion. Knight grabbed the back of her head, crushed her lips to his in a rough kiss, and moaned as he gave up the fight. His forehead rested against hers and hot breath spilled into her mouth as he panted in heavy silent gasps.

Warm heat spilled over her fingers, rolled across her fingernails, and touched her belly as she continued to hold him through his pulsing orgasm. He drew in a huge shuddering breath and shook his head.

"Christ. I can't believe I just did that."

Reese kissed his jaw, finally releasing his ass, which she'd been holding like a prisoner. "Believe it."

She couldn't resist another taste of his mouth.

He accepted her kiss, sucking gently on her bottom lip before he said in a voice she hadn't yet heard from him, "Let me get you a towel."

Tender. That's what it was. He sounded tender.

It made her damned uncomfortable. Pushing back, she pulled her hand off him and grabbed the robe off the floor. She wiped the worst of the moisture off on it and said, "I'll just go wash up, it's fine."

Appalled at the tiny quiver she heard in her voice, she thrust her head up and gave him a wicked smile. Tossing her hair back she ignored her suitcase full of clothes and strode to the bathroom naked, glancing back at him over her shoulder.

He was standing there, looking bemused and confused, his pants still half down and his arms at his sides. Those chocolate eyes were trained on her rear, and the nostril flare was back.

When she returned to the room, having applied a fresh layer of deodorant and brushed her teeth after washing her hands, she found him lounging on her bed, jeans back up.

And snapped.

Damn.

Etiquette would deem it appropriate for her to put something on over her naked body, but she had never been one for rules. Instead, she crawled up next to him and positioned herself so that her breast draped across his chest.

For a second he tensed. Then his arm shot out and wrapped around her back, pulling her in for a soft kiss.

"Mmm. Minty fresh."

"Hey, Knight?"

"Yeah?"

"This was supposed to make it better, right? Take the edge off." She nibbled on his bottom lip.

"It didn't work for me," he said.

Good thing. She would probably turn his own gun on him if he rolled over and fell asleep, or left her right now. "Me either."

"There's a drugstore around the corner. I could be back in ten minutes."

"Six if you jog."

"Patience isn't one of your strong points, is it?" He gave her a gentle nudge away from him and slipped off the bed.

Reese rolled onto her side and propped her head up with her hand, enjoying the sensitive feeling of the bedspread on her bare skin. "No."

Knight glanced over at her as he swiped his sweatshirt off the edge of the bed. Then he nearly ripped the shirt in two. "Oh, Christ, Reese, I'll never leave if you do that."

"Do what? Lie on the bed in a naked seductive pose designed to drive you wild and torture myself?" It was definitely working for her. She clamped her thighs together and licked her lips.

He growled. The shirt fell.

He took one step toward her when his jeans beeped.

"Shit." She said that, not him, as she saw his interest shift immediately from her crotch to the crotch of his pants.

It was his pager, and he was digging it out of his pocket, fingers wiggling around right where she wanted hers to be. One glance at the message, and his face lost the last of its desire.

He switched back to an FBI agent, and pulled his T-shirt on over his head. Reaching for his gun, he said, "I've got to go."

Only an appalling and immature woman would whine and argue. Reese wasn't either of those. But she was sexually frustrated, which compromised her rationality and dignity.

"No!" She punched the pillow and collapsed back, willing her body to forget she'd ever set eyes on Knight. She and her vagina had been humming along unused just fine until she'd spotted his double fudge eyes and poetic buns.

Derek watched Reese pummeling the bedsheets and saw flickers of his ex-wife. Dawn had never liked his hours either, and he had left the house a lot of times feeling guilty about his career. Which was ironic, considering he had taken the job paper pushing white-collar crime instead of pursuing violent crimes like he had wanted.

Shoving his gun into the holster, he grabbed his sweatshirt. "I can't help it. It's urgent."

In fact, it was his informant, leaving him the code number they had worked out to let Derek know he needed to communicate with him. He couldn't keep the guy waiting. This particular informant was nervous and liable to bolt if Derek didn't keep in constant contact, always reassuring him.

Not that he could blame the guy for panicking a little. He was a top pharmaceutical chemist and sat on the board at Delco. He was privy to a lot of classified and sensitive information and when it eventually became clear he had ratted out his chums on the board, costing them millions and possibly sending them to jail, he was going to have a whole heap of enemies.

Derek knew what it was like to piss off your boss. He did that to Nordstrom on a regular basis.

Reese stop torturing the hotel pillow. "Oh, fine. Go save innocent lives and make the world a better place."

She smiled at him, apparently over her tantrum. Derek blinked in confusion. Dawn had never capitulated that easily, and had cornered the market on pouting. Reese just lay there naked and smiled.

He started sweating. Still semi-hard, he knew he couldn't walk out of there without making plans. Damn, he was in trouble here. One time and he wanted more—much, much more. "Can I see you again? Tomorrow?"

"I have this stupid wedding to go to tomorrow." She rolled onto her back, crossed her ankles, and laid her hand across her smooth stomach, which did interesting and perky things to her breasts. "Want to go with me?"

A needle in the eye would be more fun. "What is it, like a cousin or something? Is your family going to think I'm your boyfriend?"

She snorted. "No, it's not family. I won't know a single person there. It's for the paper. The daughter of a New Jersey senator is marrying a guy she met on a reality show, who happens to be rich and the heir to some big company."

Even worse than family. Self-important bigwigs flashing phony bleached-teeth smiles all night. It gave him a headache just thinking about it.

"Let me see who the guy is. . . . I can't remember his name."

Reese flipped up onto her knees, still completely naked, and crawled across the bed to her briefcase. Derek watched her smooth pale behind wiggle away from him, and nearly passed out. Her legs spread a little as she stretched forward, her hair tumbling down her narrow back, her breasts falling forward in tempting little mounds, and he found religion again.

As in *God, that was incredible.*

"Here it is." Reese waved a pile of papers at him over her shoulder and sat back on her feet. "His name is Phillip Chatterton and she's obviously marrying him for the money because he looks like a geek in these pictures."

Derek dropped his pager on the floor. Holy hell, she was going to the wedding of the son of Delco's CEO, Ashton Chatterton. The son Phillip also sat on the board, and both were knee deep in price-fixing.

"I'll go with you." The words were out of his mouth before she could go continue reading her file and put two and two together.

Obviously Reese had gone through his Delco envelope full of evidence, but it hadn't clicked yet that the large corporation connected to the Chattertons was the same one that the

FBI was trying to nail. But she would figure it out soon enough, and then letting Reese go to that wedding alone would be like sending a bull into a china shop. Subtle wasn't exactly her middle name.

Three agents on the case, six months worth of work, and all because of a nosy sexy reporter and the wrong rental car, this case could explode in the Department of Justice's face.

Or more accurately, in his face, leading to an unscheduled early retirement, minus his pension.

He bent and picked up his pager, stuffing it into his pocket.

"You will?" Reese stopped fooling with the papers and looked at him in surprise. Then her eyes narrowed. "Do you own a suit? You can't be looking scraggly, you'll make me stand out. I want to blend."

Of course he owned a suit. It was required for the job to have a closet full of boring, off-the-rack gray and black suits. Perfect for a wedding. "I can blend."

He sure in the hell didn't want to be drawing attention to himself with the Chattertons around. "But why are we blending? What are you supposed to be doing?"

"I'm supposed to report on the wedding for the paper. They've forbidden photographers and media, so I'm sneaking in. I'm now the third cousin of the fourth bridesmaid, who went to Kings High with my boss's son, and is more than happy to embrace me as family in exchange for a reunion date."

"You're kidding me."

"Dead serious. I told you I worked for a rag."

"I believe you now." Derek checked to make sure his keys were in the pocket opposite the pager and said, "What time tomorrow?"

"Be here at seven. You have some explaining to do about certain things I might have happened to see in that envelope when it slid open."

He just bet she'd accidentally seen a thing or two. When her fingers had ripped the envelope open.

Reese still hadn't bothered to cover herself up, and he loved the way she was so comfortable with her body. Loved it so much, he needed to get out of the room before he loved it right through to tomorrow. "You won't do anything until then?"

She shook her head, all wide-eyed innocence, which was hard to pull off with kiss-swollen lips and tight nipples, but she still tried. "I'll just watch pay-per-view and give myself a spa treatment. There are things I need to buff."

Christ. Derek backed up, his boner back and bigger than ever.

"I'd like to watch you buffing things."

"After the wedding, we can come back here and I'll buff whatever you want."

There was an invitation no sane and straight man on the face of the earth could pass up.

"Tomorrow. Seven," he managed to grunt, just barely remembering to grab his envelope of evidence before backing out of the room.

In the hall, he shut the door, leaned against it and gave his cock a hefty adjustment through his jeans.

This was stupid. Trouble. A big old horny mistake.

But he'd never let that stop him before.

Derek started down the hall to call his informant, walking gingerly and counting the hours until he could lie back and let Reese buff him.

When Knight left, looking like he'd undergone electroshock therapy, Reese pulled on a dorm style nightgown and flicked on the TV for background noise.

She set the dirty dishes and hot wings scraps out in the hallway for housekeeping and made a surreptitious run down the hall in her nightgown for the Coke machine, on the watch for people. When a guy in a plaid button-up stepped out of the ice room in front of her, she dredged up a smile and crossed her arms over her bra-less chest.

"Soft drink emergency," she told him and stepped to the side to let him by.

The guy retrieved his jaw from the floor and nodded, doing an admirable job of keeping his eyes off her breasts.

After inserting the ridiculous amount of two dollars for a can of Coke in the machine, she fast walked back to her room and cracked open the drink, taking a long swig.

She was dry from all that moaning when Knight had been there. Damn, that man knew his way around a clitoris.

Tomorrow night she was going to get to play with his piece.

But first she had to look at all the Delco evidence and strategize her next step. There was story there, and she was going to write it.

Knight was an added benefit, like a side order of fries.

An hour later she had picked her way through most of the documentation, having loaded the pictures onto her laptop from the digital camera.

The majority of it was documentation showing the high price of a variety of name brand prescription drugs Delco manufactured. Then papers showing the expired patents for generic versions of the drugs. Product plans showing competitive products not being launched.

A clear pattern that Delco, in collusion with two other manufacturers, was entering into agreements to not produce a generic version of their competitor's primary money-making pharmaceuticals and vice versa, thereby maintaining a high retail price for the brand name drug.

There was a pattern, but not necessarily any hard evidence, until Reese found the typed transcripts of phone and E-mail conversations between the CEO of Delco and that of Stanfield Laboratories, their main competitor. The half dozen transcripts showed clear intent to price-fix.

Hot damn. This was her ticket to freedom.

And there was something else.

The CEO of Delco was none other than Ashton Chatterton, father of the groom. *What do you know,* she thought. Knight had lied to her, right after she had given him an orgasm.

That took nerve. She felt cheap and used, completely ignoring the fact that she had lied to him repeatedly about the envelope. That in fact, he still had no idea she had copies of the documents in her possession.

Propped up against three pillows, she called her brother Riley, who was a doctor. "Hey, Riley, I need your brain."

"Nice to hear from you, Reese. Thank you, I'm fine, how about yourself?"

Rolling her eyes, she said, "I'm in Chicago and this is roaming charges on my cell phone. I don't have time for chit-chat."

She could hear him shifting the phone away from him and murmuring, "It's just my sister."

A catty female voice laced with insecure jealousy said, "Why would your sister be calling you at almost midnight?"

Reese glanced at the clock, surprised. Where had the time gone? Burned up in undulating waves of sexual satisfaction, that's where.

"If you let me talk to her, I could find out."

Riley gave a sound of annoyance into the phone and said curtly, "What's up, Reese?"

Distracted from her original purpose, she said, "Ditch the bitch, Riley. Ugh. You'll spend all your time explaining yourself."

"It's not that simple."

She didn't like that tone he was using, resigned and overwhelmed. It had been about a month since she'd seen Riley, and come to think of it, he'd been a little quiet then. "Why? Did you marry her? Knock her up?"

"Reese. What do you want?"

Fine. She'd call him back when the bitch wasn't around and get him to spill his guts. "I need to know what these drugs are." She read him the list of four prescription drugs.

"They're narcotic analgesics, or painkillers, usually given to people after surgery, or to terminal cancer patients."

"Are there generic versions of these? Are they expensive?"

"Very expensive. They're third tier drugs, meaning they probably run about three hundred bucks for a prescription before insurance. And the generic form isn't readily available."

Because Delco and Stanfield had rigged it that way. This went beyond price-fixing. This was insurance fraud, which explained the FBI's interest, as well. This kind of price-fixing and suppression of market alternatives would cost Medicare millions of dollars every year.

Reese thought about Knight's quick acceptance of her invitation to the wedding. He was clearly knee-deep in this case, given he had been sent to retrieve the envelope left by an insider at Delco. Did he plan on making a move on Chatterton at the wedding?

If he did, she was going to witness it, stuck to his thigh like a toddler to her mother. Not that it would be a sacrifice to cling to Knight all night.

"Why do you need to know about painkillers?"

"I'm chasing a story."

"Of course." Riley sounded amused.

Urgent whispering came from the woman. Not happy whispering. Reese wondered what exactly she had interrupted, then stopped her thoughts from driving down that dark alley. "Sorry I called so late, I didn't know what time it was. I'll let you get back to your grumpy girlfriend."

"Thanks."

Reese said good-bye and hung up her cell phone, tossing it onto the nightstand. Suddenly her bed felt large, cold, and empty, scattered with papers and generic white hotel pillows. The floral bedspread had her pinned beneath it, not an ounce of softness in its durable threads. She tugged on the rubber-looking blanket, the color of orange juice in concentrate form.

It was lonely and lacking a certain rigid male presence that had sprawled across the bed and her earlier. The memory had her yanking down the bottom of her nightshirt in restless anticipation.

Her panties were pulled too tight, nudging into her folds, the satin hot as she shuffled on the bed, crossing and uncrossing her legs. Her breasts were tender, her nipples beading as they brushed against the soft cotton, forcing her to press her hand against them to stop the fabric from shifting in torturous waves.

Grabbing the remote, she turned up the volume and grimaced at a talk show. She hit the up button and loud panting filled the room. A couple writhed on a bed, interlaced with one another, naked limbs sliding and melding as they sprawled across a bed.

Reese flipped the TV off and prepared to while away the night in sexual frustration.

On the plane earlier in the evening, sex had been the last thing on her mind. Now she could think of nothing else but bare sweaty flesh slapping together in mutual pleasure.

She turned on her stomach and recoiled instantly. God, that was ten times worse.

How could Knight have left her like this? He was probably fine, not suffering in the least, having compartmentalized his sexual needs like most men. On and off like a faucet.

Not on the verge of sliding his fingers down to appease himself the way she was.

Just fine.

The sexy jerk.

Chapter Six

Derek was a lot of things. Worried about this case, having just spent two hours trying to coax his whistle-blower into wearing a wire.

Tired, sleep avoiding him in the last few weeks.

And hungry, sharp pangs gnawing at the edge of his stomach, reminding him he hadn't eaten since he'd bitten that chicken wing and celery stick umpteen hours earlier.

As he turned the key in the lock to his apartment, he was very much aware that none of those were the first and most urgent need on his mind. Or in his body.

It was Reese and his deep, pulsing, biting desire for her that had him taut and frustrated, wound up and weary at the same time.

He wanted to be with her right now, burying into her, swallowing her moans and immersing himself in that satin hair that was the color of autumn leaves. The urge to turn back around, pick up a box of condoms, and go knocking on her hotel door was great, anxious, taking advantage of his fatigue and hunger to nudge him to do the unthinkable.

Maybe if he called first . . .

"About time you got in. A girl could grow old waiting for you."

Derek jerked in his doorway, reaching for his gun. Then he dropped his arm and sighed in relief when he saw his sister

Claire sprawled across his couch in pajama pants with teddy bears on them.

"Jesus, Claire, what the hell are you doing here?"

At close to three in the morning, chewing on what looked like a piece of licorice, reading a paperback book in her hand. Claire, a dozen years his junior, and the product of his mother's second, much happier marriage, was a perky, confident young woman who had just finished graduate school.

In the four months since her May graduation, she had been assessing her options, as she put it. Derek thought that meant she was taking time off to hang at the beach all summer before she had to chain herself to a job for life. Smart girl.

He dumped his keys in the little bowl on his minute kitchen counter and headed for the overstuffed chair. Maybe if he took his shoes off he wouldn't feel this tight throb everywhere, like his skin was too small for his bones.

"I can't stand my roommate. I moved out and I need a place to stay." Claire tore at the licorice with her teeth and chewed with her mouth open. She shook her straight blond hair back and sighed.

There didn't seem to be any further information forthcoming and as he sat down, Derek couldn't help but notice that a large corner of his living room had been given over to storage for suitcases and various boxes with markered labels like "School stuff", "Ex-boyfriend's crap" and "Alcohol—fragile."

"How did you get all this stuff up here?" He pictured her lugging box after box up the steps and couldn't quite reconcile it with Claire and her air-brushed nails.

"The guy downstairs, you know, the sort of weird-looking guy who picks the cigarette butts out of the potted plants in the front?"

Derek knew the guy. A little on the slow side, but a good guy, who acted as sort of a doorman slash janitor for the building.

"Well, he let me use the service elevator. And he loaded

everything up onto one of those dolly thingies. We were done in twenty."

"Oh. Great." He'd have to remember to tip the guy tomorrow for saving him from hauling all that junk up here himself. He unlaced his shoes and sighed. The gun went on the coffee table.

"Don't touch that," he reminded Claire.

She rolled her eyes. "What am I like twelve? I know not to play with guns. Where've you been?"

"Working." And sinking his fingers into Reese Hampton's wet and willing thighs.

"Well, I'm so bored I could scream. I guess I'll go to bed now, but I didn't want to scare the crap out of you when you came in."

"Thanks." Debating asking her exactly how long she planned to stay in his cramped one bedroom apartment, he watched her stand up and stretch.

"Want to hang out tomorrow? You could buy me dinner," she said with a smile.

"I have a date," he said before he remembered that Claire was a direct phone line to his mother. He braced himself.

"No kidding? Good to see you're not still pining over what's-her-name, like you were for *forever*. So where are you going?" Claire popped the last bit of licorice in her mouth and crossed her arms across the stomach of her tight tank top, revealing more of her breasts than he ever cared to see.

Wondering when exactly his baby sister had gotten so . . . *developed*, Derek rubbed at his mouth. "To a wedding."

"Whose wedding?"

"Phillip Chatterton, the heir to Delco Pharmaceuticals. My date is the bride's cousin." In a manner of speaking.

"Sounds like a rich people wedding." Her hand shot out. "Wait a minute. You are not going to wear that old tired gray suit, are you?"

"Yes," he said in suspicion, recognizing that shopping gleam in Claire's eye.

"No way, I won't let you do it. We'll go shopping in the morning and totally have you styling."

Over his dead body. "No. Forget it. You're not getting me to spend five hundred bucks on something that will make me look like one of Jennifer Lopez's backup dancers."

Claire snorted. "As if." Then she switched to speculative. "Think about how your date will feel if you show up looking like a million bucks. When was the last time you got some action, Derek?"

A couple of hours ago. "Claire," he said in warning.

"What? You show up looking suave and sophisticated, she'll be all over you like super glue. A woman likes a man who can dress for the occasion."

Derek rubbed his temples and considered it. Claire could be right. After all, Reese had made a point of questioning whether he owned a suit or not. While she might not ditch him at the door if he wore a cheap suit, she wouldn't exactly be bowled over, either.

He wanted her wowed. He wanted her soft and compliant and whispering brassy sexual overtures in his ear, making him sweat with need. After that wedding was over, he wanted to take her home and strip her, one piece of clothing at a time, taking it slow so he could touch and explore every little inch of her along the way.

Except Claire was going to be in his apartment as his new roomie. So they'd go to Reese's hotel room. Maybe he could pick up some wine and she'd drop her dress, nothing on but earrings, high heels, and a smile.

"You're getting a weird look on your face. Are you thinking or falling asleep?"

"Fine. We'll go shopping in the morning." He fell back into the chair and braced himself for the horror of trying on clothes and having little men with tape measures wrapping their arms around his chest.

Claire dropped her arms. "Dang. I can't believe you agreed that easily. She must be some woman."

That she was. He didn't entirely understand her and he didn't always agree with her. But she was smart, independent, and direct, and she tied his gut up in knots of sexual longing.

Reese Hampton was a woman worthy of a new suit.

Reese paced the lobby of the Crowne Plaza, glancing at her platinum watch for the twelfth time as she noted that Knight was now eight and a half minutes late. If he stood her up she'd track him down and force-feed him chicken wings until he was in ulcer agony.

If he ditched her and went to the wedding alone to bust Chatterton, leaving her wearing a hole in the aqua hotel carpet, she would likely kill him.

To think she'd run out this morning and bought an ivory thong and matching push-up bra. What a waste of good lace and sixty bucks. Sixty bucks. What the hell had she been thinking?

That Knight would drool when she took her dress off.

Reese muttered under her breath, "Fat chance."

A guy in his early twenties sitting in one of the lobby easy chairs looked over at her, wary.

"What?" she snarled at him.

He shook his head and stuck his headphones back into his ears, and pressed play on his disc player before studiously looking out the front window.

Annoyed at herself for getting worked up over a man she didn't even really know, Reese crossed her arms over her ivory dress and stared at the front door, willing Knight to walk through it.

But first, check out the hunk strolling through the doors. Reese fanned herself a little. Whew. Hot stuff coming through in a black suit, looking like he owned the hotel.

Only he had a slight stiffness to his left leg, and shoulders that were familiar, and why did that hair seem like an exact shade of caramel she'd seen before?

Knight turned and met her gaze, his lip curling up in the corner.

Reese grabbed the back of the nearest easy chair and whispered, "Honey, baby, come to mama."

And she had been worried that he didn't own a suit.

Not only did he own one, he filled every inch of the high-quality suit to perfection, broad shoulders straight and rock solid chest covered with a rich burgundy shirt, no tie. It was a risky move, not wearing a tie, the shirt's top button undone, but he looked at ease doing it, as if he were used to trendsetting. His belt was shiny black leather, the silver buckle taunting her, making her itch to undo it and move her hands into his pants.

Her cheeks flamed, her thighs twitched, her nipples shot forward in greeting.

And she hadn't even seen his butt yet.

Knight sauntered up to her. "Catching flies, Reese?"

"Huh?"

"Your mouth's wide open. I can see that you have three silver fillings and maybe a crown." He took her chin in his hand and peered into her mouth.

Reese snapped her jaw closed, jerked out of his touch, and glared at him. "I'm just in shock. I never would have guessed you could clean up so well."

He just smiled. "Thanks for the backhanded compliment. Now, shall we go?"

He offered his arm, which she took reluctantly, flustered at her reaction. Also, she was annoyed that he hadn't said anything about the way she looked. It wasn't easy walking in those stilettos—he could at least acknowledge that her legs looked good.

"You look incredible," he whispered in her ear. "But all I can think about is you naked."

Reese caught herself before she tripped in the toothpicks called shoes she was walking on. She swallowed hard and commanded herself not to look at him or to think about nudity in any shape or form. If she allowed her raucous thoughts to travel the path she wanted to, it was probable they wouldn't even end up at the wedding, but would turn around and head up in the elevator to her room.

"Are you wearing any panties?" he asked as they stepped into the revolving door together.

Reese stopped moving and the door thunked her butt from behind. He put his foot between her and the glass to stop her from losing the back of her heel to the relentless motion of the heavy door.

His eyes were dark, his left hand in his pants pocket. There was a predatory stance about him that made her nervous.

"Of course I am. They're big and plain white, with one of those stomach flaps on them to hold my gut in. Not sexy at all."

He had done something to his hair, trimmed it and slicked it back a little with hair gel, giving it that tousled model look. Reaching up, he brushed his bangs back and up with a little jerk of his hand.

"You're lying again."

Then that hand, that wandering, big, hard man hand, slid down her side and around between them to cup and squeeze her behind. Warmth flooded her ivory thong panties as she sucked in her breath and tried not to moan.

"See? I don't feel any panty lines at all." That hand moved over, over until his finger traced the dip between her cheeks, sliding down, low, floating back up until she was moist with need, her body tense.

A knock on the glass had Knight pulling his hand away. Dazed and disappointed, Reese turned toward the sound.

A man was standing on the street, holding his suitcase in hand and looking seriously annoyed.

"The thing about these revolving doors," the guy said with biting sarcasm, "is that you can't stop moving in them."

Embarrassed and horny, Reese pushed the door without warning, causing the guy to jump back. "Sorry," she said with a wobbly smile as he had to step out of the way for her and Knight to exit.

Charging ahead, no destination in mind, she was heading down the sidewalk when Knight grabbed her hand and pulled her to a stop. "Hey, slow down. Let's call a cab."

"Fine." She glowered at him.

He let out a chuckle and pushed her hair back over her shoulder. "What's the matter? You look like you might rip my head off."

"Is that possible?" she said testily.

"You want to explain why you're so upset?"

"Because it ticks me off that you look so good."

His eyebrow rose. "You'd rather I'd have shown up looking scruffy and unattractive?"

"Yes. No." She blew out her breath, making a raspberry sound with her lips. "I mean, with you distracting me looking like an FBI pinup, I can't concentrate on this case, which you failed to tell me involved Phillip Chatterton, by the way."

Knight dropped his hand, which he'd been hailing a cab with, and shot her a guarded look. "This case doesn't involve you, Reese, and it's a simple coincidence that you're going to Chatterton's wedding."

"Oh, right, how stupid do you think I am?" Reese covered her arms and rubbed. The late September wind was kicking up a little, raising goose bumps on her flesh. "You're going to bust him, aren't you?"

"Not today, for Christ's sake. It's his wedding." Knight turned and called the bellboy over, who had just finished loading a suitcase rack with luggage. "We need a cab, please."

The bellboy said, "Yes, sir," and hustled back to his post.

She stared at Knight. He stared back.

Knight broke the growing silence. "It's time for you to tell me exactly what you saw, Reese. I'm not playing around. This is a major investigation and you either tell me, or you tell my boss."

"You'd haul me in?" she cried indignantly, focusing on her

anger and not the fact that a not-so-subtle sex fantasy involving handcuffs had popped into her head.

"You can bet your little panty-less ass, I would."

"So this is what I get? And after I gave you some of the
best fifteen minutes of my life."

Knight's lip twitched.

The cab pulled up to the curb. He opened the door and
held his hand out to her. "If we're going, you're talking."

Reese ran through her options. She could walk away from
Knight, thereby getting herself hauled in by the Feds for
questioning. Sticky questions regarding certain photos she'd
taken with her digital camera would arise. And who knew
what the ordeal might entail besides vending machine coffee
and government gray walls. Were Feds authorized to strip
search?

She shuddered and moved on to option B, which involved
getting in the cab with Knight, and spilling her guts. She'd
have to trust him not to cut her out of the deal, that he would
let her have the story. That would require sticking close to
him, which was almost certain to ensure a great deal of personal sexual satisfaction.

No contest.

She got in the cab, scooting over to make room for Knight
and his gun.

When he sat down and shut the door, he gave directions
for the wedding to the driver, making her wonder how exactly he had known those little details, since she'd never
shared them.

His leg spread out as he got comfortable, knocking against
her knee. "Sorry."

Yeah, sure. And she was sexually disinterested.

His arm came up to rest on the back of the seat behind her
head. "As soon as we're alone, Reese, I want to hear everything. Not just about your tomboy childhood, but what you
saw in that envelope and what you plan on doing with it."

She stared at him, leaning forward to escape his touch as

she matched his tone for blandness. They could have been talking about the weather or the price of lattes for all the inflection in his voice. "I saw everything, and I already told you what I plan to do with it."

"This isn't a game, Reese." His eyes narrowed.

Her lips thinned. "I'm not playing. And this isn't just about me getting a story, the public has a right to know they're being fleeced."

"Yes, but not before a case can be made to take the perps to court." He was still using that calm, low, careful FBI voice that made her feel very tempted to rattle him.

"Of course not." She leaned back and flipped her hair, turning to the side to smile at him under her long mascara laden lashes.

He stiffened. "What are you doing?"

"Nothing," she said with exaggerated innocence, her hands fisting into the soft fabric of her skirt.

"You're trying to distract me." His hand went into her hair, tugging her head towards him.

She held her head back so he couldn't kiss her, which was clearly his intent. "No, I'm not. We can't talk about details here anyway, so we're done with this conversation for now. And I just wanted to show you something."

Reese took a glance at the front seat to make sure the driver wasn't paying them any attention. He was singing to Celine Dion and gesturing with his fist at the car in front of him.

"Show me what?" Knight tried to tug her to him again, but she wiggled back. He said, "Stop moving so I can kiss you."

"First I wanted to show you . . ." She eased her skirt up past her thighs and lifted her behind a little off the seat.

"That I really am wearing panties," she whispered, bunching the bottom of her dress around her waist, taking major pleasure in the shock that flooded Knight's face, followed quickly by a strangled gurgle trailing out of his mouth.

Derek blinked, his lips no longer working as he drank in the sight of Reese with her dress up past her hips. Her long creamy legs looked as soft as the dress she was wearing, and they went on and on up from the floor until he was treated to the sight of her reddish-brown curls covered by a scrap of ivory lace.

Two little teeny tiny strings went left and right, allegedly holding the triangle panties up, though he didn't see how it was gravitationally possible. The whole rig-up was about the size of a first class stamp.

Allowing him a long and lovely look at Reese's inner thighs, soft curving hips, and springy curls peeking at him invitingly. His hand shot out, ready to brush aside that lacy nothing, when her dress dropped down again.

He swore under his breath, but noticed that she didn't bother to push the skirt all the way back to her knees, and that her breath was just as ragged as his. Damn, she was a sexy, gutsy thing. Dragging his eyes off the shadows the dress made between her thighs, the narrow little alley that would lead him straight to the jackpot, he shifted in his seat.

His cock was so hard he swore he was light-headed from lack of oxygen to the brain. He had been hard since the minute he had walked into that lobby and Reese had been standing there, looking creamy and edible, wearing a classy ivory dress that reminded him of pearls. Beautiful, luscious, strong.

"Those didn't look big and white, with a stomach flap to control flab," he managed to grind out.

"I must have forgot what I put on," she said, looking every inch the naughty temptress that she was.

She had done something to her eyes, used some kind of black stuff that made them seem bigger, like she was always blinking at him in virginal innocence.

He reached for her, intent on ripping a little of that thinly veined satisfaction off her face. If he leaned to the side, his shoulders would block the driver's view of the backseat, and he could slide his hand up Reese's dress. Right into her thighs, where he would sink into her hot folds, the wet proof of her desire for him. He would make her come, biting her cries back, right here in the cab.

His thumb was under her skirt, Reese's hand grabbing the back of his wrist with a panicked gasp, when the cab stopped.

"Here you go," the cabby's impatient voice shouted back to them.

Sliding under her panties on one side, Derek fingered a few strands of her pubic hair, and watched her startled but excited reaction. He rubbed the warm curls between his thumb and forefinger before he gave a little tug.

She gasped, eyes rolling back.

"Too bad. I guess we'll have to wait until later." Pulling back his hand, he made sure she was covered before turning and opening the door.

The very tomboy word that came sailing from Reese's mouth made him laugh.

Chapter Seven

Reese watched Knight's gorgeous ass as he left the cab, and contemplated kicking it.

But she didn't want to leave a dirty footprint on those nice pants.

He paid the cab while she got out and then took her by the elbow and guided her towards the door of the hotel where the reception was being held. For about a split second Reese thought it was polite and well mannered of him, then realized it was more likely he wanted to keep her close to him.

Probably afraid she'd corner Chatterton and whip out a microphone.

"Who are we supposed to be again?" Knight asked as they entered the majestic lobby and followed the doorman's directions to the grand ballroom.

"I'm supposed to be the cousin of the fourth bridesmaid, Sharon Bismark. I'm still Reese and if they ask for a last name, I guess I'll be a Bismark, too. You can be Dan Mitchell."

She had pulled that name out of thin air and didn't think it was that bad. She rubbed her arms again. "Geez, what is the air-conditioning on? It's freezing."

"Maybe you should have worn a dress with, I don't know . . . sleeves."

They turned a corner and had to stop as the wedding

guests clogged the reception line to the ballroom. Knight said, "And I don't like the name Dan, by the way."

"What's wrong with Dan? It's not like Derek is so great."

"What's wrong with Derek?"

"Nothing." She smiled to soothe him. "But I'll stick with Knight, if you don't mind."

"You know, I don't need a fake name. Chatterton has no idea who I am. He doesn't know my name or what I look like." Knight eased her forward as the line began to move again.

Trying not to inhale the obnoxious cloying perfume of the woman in front of her, Reese turned to face him. "Okay, fine, you stay Knight, then. Don't go all PMS on me."

Whatever response he was going to make was lost as they both heard a high voice exclaim, "Derek? Is that you?"

Knight winced and turned toward the voice with a very fake, hardly convincing smile. "Dawn. How are you?"

Reese followed his gaze and just a few feet away spotted a blond with upswept hair moving in on them fast. She was also pregnant and accompanied by a staid-looking guy in his forties with gray at the temples.

"My ex-wife," Knight whispered, his mouth still twisted in that serial killer smile.

"Oh, how fun." Reese moved in closer to Knight, feeling an undeniable grip of territorial possession sweep over her.

Which was stupid. All Knight was to her was a good story and a couple of orgasms.

He lived in Chicago and she had a life in New York. A few days of fun, nothing more.

But she didn't like the looks of Blondie wearing her Pea In The Pod five hundred dollar black maternity dress. Reese wrapped her arm around Knight's and snuggled up so her breast was brushing his bicep.

"Derek, what a surprise to see you at something like this. You were never one for big social events."

Dawn reached out and took his hand in a big show of intimacy, as far as Reese was concerned. So she'd been married to Knight. Big whoop. She wasn't now.

Reese inched in closer to Knight.

Derek thought if Reese got any closer to him, they were going to be sharing DNA. While part of him was arrogantly pleased that Dawn was seeing him with a gorgeous woman like Reese on his arm, the other, more rational half, just wanted to get the hell out of there.

"Reese's cousin is in the wedding," he said, and hoped he could just leave it at that.

No such luck.

"The bride's side?" Dawn asked.

"Yes."

"I thought so." Dawn laughed, a repelling and shrill sound that made him wonder how she could have changed so much in the last eight years. This was not the woman he had fallen in love with.

When Reese looked at her blankly, Dawn added, "You have that Jersey look to you."

Oh, shit. Knight squeezed Reese's elbow, praying she wouldn't cause a scene.

To her credit, she merely spoke in a neutral voice. "I'm Reese Hampton, by the way. And you are?"

Dawn patted him on the arm again, like he was a pet she'd once had a fondness for. He felt his anger start to build and searched the room for an escape. They were still trapped in the reception line, but at least Dawn's current husband looked like he was suffering equally, if that wince was any indication.

"I'm Derek's first wife, Dawn Lansing. This is my husband, Bill."

The wording further annoyed Derek. She was his ex-wife, not his first wife, since he'd never gone on to take a second wife.

"Have I met you before, Reese? Aren't you one of Claire's friends?"

Now that was really uncalled for. He wasn't sure if the barb was meant to indicate he was old, or that Reese was young, but either way he didn't like it. Dawn made him feel like a pervert for being with Reese, who was definitely all woman and then some. And Christ, he was thirty-six, not even halfway through a normal life span. He was not old.

"No, she's not one of my little sister's friends. She's a journalist. If you'll excuse us . . ." he tried to hint, but Dawn cut him off.

"Have you been dating long? Is it serious?"

Bill roused himself from his squirming long enough to say, "Dawn, dear, that's a little personal. Why don't we head in? The line's cleared a bit."

Dawn wasn't going anywhere, and neither was Reese. Derek recognized the challenge gleaming from Dawn's eyes and it would have scared the shit out of him, except that Reese's face had already accomplished that.

Reese looked like she was smiling, a wide-open perky beauty pageant smile. But her eyes glowed like one of Satan's assistants. Derek was considering taking a step back when she spoke.

"I don't mind you asking about our relationship. But the truth is, I'm actually in it for the great sex."

He about choked on his own tongue.

Oh, my God. Where was a camera when he needed one?

Dawn was slack jawed and ogling, while Bill had let fly with a loud snort of laughter. Derek had to bite his lip not to laugh, himself.

This was great. A hot woman bragging about his sexual prowess to his ex-wife.

Reese just continued to smile.

Finally, after a good thirty seconds of showdown silence, Dawn let out a forced chuckle. "How cute. And appropriate. Just what Derek's always wanted. Zero responsibility and a young sex toy. I'm surprised it took him this long to figure it out."

Hold it. His amusement evaporated. That wasn't a damn

bit funny. Derek clenched his fists and willed himself to calm down. He had never shirked responsibility, his whole damn life was wrapped up in the responsibilities of his career.

So he hadn't wanted to start a family. Maybe the timing hadn't been right. Maybe he'd wanted a family, just not with Dawn.

And he didn't like the cracks about Reese being nothing but a sexual diversion.

Even if it were true.

Something ugly was about to come out of his mouth. He was going to insult his pregnant ex-wife. Reese's cool hand slid into his and squeezed, steadying him.

Dawn said, "Well, we're going to see if there are any waiters running around this place. I'm just dying of thirst, and I have to keep this little baby happy, you know." Dawn ran her hand along her stomach.

Reese glanced down at the slightly rounded belly. "When are you due? In a week or two?"

Just when he thought it couldn't get any more uncomfortable. Derek coughed into his hand and considered turning his gun on himself to get out of this encounter.

Color leached from Dawn's face. "Not until Christmas Eve, as a matter of fact."

Which by his calculations was about twelve weeks away.

"Oh." Reese took another long pointed glance at Dawn's stomach, her eyebrows raised.

Dawn suddenly turned on her heel and left, leaving Bill to trail after her obediently. Derek almost felt sorry for the poor guy, predicting that Dawn would take out her distress on Bill. He'd felt that cool breeze quite a few times in their marriage.

Derek looked down at Reese, who was sporting an unholy grin, and frowned. "You knew she was only six months pregnant. I told you that."

Secretly he thought it was borderline hilarious, but he didn't really think he should encourage her. God only knew what she'd do if she thought she had his permission to be brassy.

"It slipped my mind." Reese shrugged on the blatant lie. Then she wrinkled her nose. "Oh, alright, I knew. But I couldn't help it, Knight. She was asking for it."

"She's an expectant mother."

"So? She still just about called you a dirty old man and me a gum cracking bimbo from Jersey."

"That's exaggerating." A micromillimeter.

"If you want to defend your ex-wife, that's fine. It doesn't mean anything to me." Reese sniffed and removed her arm from his. "Though I have a hard time picturing you with her."

"She's changed a bit."

"A bit?" She flipped her hair back over her shoulder and scanned the room. "Well, I still don't think she could have ever been your type."

As a matter of fact, he was starting to figure that out himself. Dawn had always been more of a social climber than him. He'd been leaning toward the apple pie–baking, homemaker type in the last year or two, and had been coming up short as well. It was occurring to him now that maybe he liked the bold, sassy, tomboy types.

For tonight, anyway.

"Yeah, I like women who look sexy in heels or jeans, who know how to have a career and how to play sports." He took her slim hand in his, and tugged her until she was flush up against him, ignoring the crowd milling around them.

Reese smiled, obviously knowing where he was going with this.

That sexy ivory dress rustled across his arms, calling up images of it crumpled next to the bed. His bed. Burying his hands in her hair, he stared into her passionate gray-green eyes and said, "And knowing how to arm wrestle and spit doesn't hurt, either."

"Hmmm." She placed her hands on his chest, and fiddled with the button on his shirt. "Sounds like someone I know."

Joking, he said, "Maybe you could set me up with her."

Reese ran her finger across his bottom lip, making him wish this stupid wedding was over and they were naked. On a tropical island.

Then she said, "Don't try funny, Knight. It doesn't work on you."

When she laughed, he couldn't help but laugh with her. He was fascinated by her, drawn to her quirky personality and unexpected responses. It was tugging at him, this desire, this deep, quenching interest, until he was distracted from everything but her and the way she laughed, the way she smiled, and the look of passion in her eyes when she met his stare.

Christ. He did not need this distraction right now.

Reese felt Knight pressing into her thigh, and it wasn't his gun. It was a little unnerving, this flammable passion between them, the way he could glance down at her and she wanted to drop her dress to the floor and do the naked tango.

It wasn't that she had never been a sexual person. She was young, healthy, and had always enjoyed her sex life, except for that first time, which was a paranoid blur. But since then she had no complaints, even if she'd been going through a minor dry spell. And the college years had been especially good to her.

But with Knight it was more than that. It was . . . fun. She liked being with him. He kept her on her toes, and he took her rough edges in stride.

He held her head with his hand, in a gesture that made her feel soft and sexy. Lips hovered over hers, those chocolate eyes darkening as he moved closer. He was going to kiss her, and she was going to let him. She didn't care if everyone in Chicago and his mother was watching them, she couldn't resist his gruff charm.

The kiss never came. His lips moved past to her ear and he said, "Remind me never to piss you off."

Forgiving him for the tease, she laughed. "Words to live by, Knight."

"Let's go into this damn wedding," he said as he turned around and started towards the door, his hand still in hers.

That fabulous behind taunted her as he walked, looking sophisticated in those suit pants. The jeans were still orgasm-inspiring, but this was a total package. He looked like a model, like an actor, like a very fuckable FBI agent.

Reese reached out and gave his ass a quick squeeze.

He jumped, turning to look at her in shock.

She liked that she could shock him.

"What?" Defiance and innocence she was good at, having perfected them during the many escapades of her childhood.

"Knock it off."

"Knock what off?"

"You grabbed my ass."

"I did not." Guys weren't the only ones who knew how to deny.

He looked ready to argue, but they had reached the receiving line and Reese was eager to meet the Chattertons. Not to mention she had to meticulously record for the *Newark News* which designers the bridesmaids and mothers were wearing. Her camera was in her clutch and she was hoping for a snapshot or two.

"You forgot you were supposed to be Reese Bismark, by the way."

"Whatever. Your ex-wife is not going to run around and tell everyone." Reese peered around the line into the ballroom.

There were approximately four hundred guests if she was counting the tables right, each with elaborate floral centerpieces in a russet autumnal theme. Whew. Reese was mentally tabulating the cost of a sit-down dinner for four hundred and could only come to the conclusion that the Chattertons had done well in the drug price-fixing business.

Maybe her outrageously expensive allergy medicine had financed a portion of this wedding. A centerpiece, maybe.

Then she remembered Delco was price-fixing painkillers for terminally ill patients and somehow that seemed even worse. Someone dying in pain had paid for this exercise in overabundance.

"And who is this beautiful young lady?"

Reese found her palm grasped between two firm, eager, masculine hands and looked up, startled. Lovely. The father of the groom, Ashton Chatterton himself, was leering at her over his tuxedo tie. While she had been gaping at the opulent room lost in her thoughts, she had inched forward in the line and Knight was standing behind her, waiting for her to introduce them.

"I'm Reese, cousin of the bride."

Shit. She was supposed to be the bridesmaid's cousin, not the bride's. She had always been such a good liar, but trust her talent to fail her right when she needed it most.

Knight coughed.

"And this is my fiancé, Derek Knight." She might as well torture Knight, too, in the process. Besides, if he knew she was engaged, maybe Chatterton would release the hand he was currently holding hostage.

No such luck. He just squeezed harder. "Oh, of course! Jeannie's cousin, Reese."

Ashton Chatterton was a little on the short side, heading towards bald, but he had a command of presence about him that Reese recognized immediately. He dripped authority and stood straight and proud, a man used to getting what he wanted. A wealthy man, who wore a tuxedo as comfortably as if it were jeans.

"Good looks obviously run in the family," Chatterton was saying. "And you got more than your fair share," he added with a wink that reminded her of Uncle Hal back in Brooklyn when she'd been growing up.

Uncle Hal hadn't been anybody's uncle, he had only wanted girls to call him that. Before he dropped his pants and showed them Mr. Happy.

That wink was followed by a lean that brought Chatterton firmly into her personal space.

Yeesh, Ashton Chatterton was coming on to her. With her fiancé standing right next to her. Who wasn't really her fiancé, not even her boyfriend, but just a sexy pseudo-stranger who knew how to hit her g-spot like his thumb was a homing device.

But Chatterton didn't know that. The nerve.

She added gross lecher to his list of crimes and tried to pull her hand back. His middle finger stroked across her palm in a sign language invitation and rude gesture she remembered from sixth grade. And it didn't mean *meet me on the playground later.*

Maybe she was overreacting. Giving a light laugh, she said, "Oh, thank you, how sweet."

Chatterton raised his eyebrow, gave a slow smile, and stroked her again. "I meant every word. Save me a dance, Reese. I'm looking forward to getting to know you better. Much better."

Even more reason to nail the guy and send him to prison.

"Lovely," she murmured and moved down the line. Before they reached the bride and groom she ditched out of the line, yanking Knight with her, wondering if anyone would notice if she pulled out her camera and took a picture of the table settings.

Her boss would kill her if she didn't come back with something good after he had sent her all the way to Chicago for this wedding.

Knight, who had shaken her hand off his arm, said in a harsh voice, "I don't want you dancing with that creep."

"What?" Distracted, Reese opened her clutch. The camera took up the entire purse, and she reached in carefully to tug it out. She kept an eye peeled for anyone looking in her direction. *Just getting a lipstick here, no cause to think I'm a media spy.*

"The guy is a prick. I don't even want you near Chatterton and I definitely don't want him touching you."

"Why? You think I'm going to blow your cover for you? Or start asking price-fixing questions while we dance to 'When a Man Loves a Woman?' " Reese wasn't going to blow his cover, or hers, for that matter, but if she was going to be forced to dance with Ashton Chatterton, she might as well see if she could find out anything interesting.

Like what kind of an idiot his wife was, since he was clearly a philanderer.

Reese answered her own question.

His wife was a rich idiot. Money could make you ignore lots of things, she imagined.

"I'm not talking about the case, I'm talking about the fact that the guy was undressing you with his eyes and is old enough to be your father."

"Hey, the bride is wearing Vera Wang. Remember that. Not that I know how to describe that thing, my God, it's got like gobs of fabric on the bottom." Reese finally got the damn camera out and added, "Block me."

As Knight moved to her side and pulled his jacket open briefly, she took a quick shot of the table.

"Oh, my God. You've got to get a new job."

Where had he been? That's what she had been telling him for twenty-four hours. "I know. That's why I need this story."

Satisfied with the shot, she dropped the camera back into her purse and grabbed a glass of champagne off a passing waiter's tray.

"Is the whistle-blower here, at the wedding?" She'd been wondering about the guy who was letting the FBI wire him so he could rat out his coworkers.

His name wasn't in the transcripts and she only had the sketchy idea that he was a fellow board member, given his access to the meetings. She wondered why he had come forward when he stood to lose so much.

"No, he's not here. He and Chatterton aren't close. Chatterton doesn't really trust him, I don't think."

"With good reason, I'd say." Reese inspected a passing

bridesmaid. Straight line, antique gold. Skirt and bodice separate.

"Hey, this guy is risking a lot, Reese. By giving us this evidence, he's going to right a wrong that Delco has been committing for three years."

"But why is he doing it? For the good of the American public?" She'd like to think someone would do it for the right reasons, but people so rarely did, she couldn't help but feel cynical.

Knight studied her. "Something like that."

He was holding out on her, she could tell. "So when do you have enough to prosecute, or to raid their offices, or whatever?"

"We need one or two pieces to fall into place."

"You need a meeting on tape between Delco and the other company, don't you? Where they actually use words like cooperate and setting the price and withholding patents."

"That would help." He glanced around the room, his hands in his pockets.

"Are they planning a meeting?"

"It's possible."

If he gave her another cryptic cop remark, she was going to hurt him.

"Thanks for opening up to me, Knight, I feel like everything is crystal clear now." Reese drained her champagne, wondering why the waiter had only filled her glass a quarter of the way. Now she was going to have to find another one.

Those fudge eyes just gazed steadily at her. His chiseled jaw clenched and one finger came up and brushed along his ever-present whiskers.

"You'll get your story. Don't worry."

Somehow, that wasn't convincing. "Don't hold out on me, Knight, I'm telling you."

He dropped his hand and smirked a little. "Are you threatening me?"

"That wasn't a threat. This is. You'll regret it if you cut me out."

Reese was tempted to bend his thumb back to add oomph to the threat, but restrained herself. That would be childish even for her.

Chapter Eight

Of course he was going to cut her out. He didn't have a choice.

There was too much at stake here. First and foremost, he wanted to nail these guys and send them to jail. Innocent people were being ripped off, paying astronomical prices for prescription drugs so they could line Chatterton's pockets. And ripping off Medicare cost every single American money in the long run.

A case like this would send a clear message to other corporate CEO's that the Justice Department wouldn't tolerate price-fixing and corporate monopolies.

All of that was the most important factor in this case, and he couldn't risk jeopardizing it.

Then there was his own career.

He'd always been something of a rule bender, aggressive, out to get the perp at all costs.

That kind of attitude had earned him a broken kneecap and another federal agent a bullet in the arm.

It hadn't seemed like a big deal at the time. He had stumbled across some money laundering during a prior investigation. It had seemed like such a small op, a car rental franchise, that he had thought he could handle an office raid with just Sam Barker with him.

He should have waited, he should have followed procedure. That little op was really a front for the mob, and before the day was done, he and Sam had both been injured and the middlemen running the op had fled.

A total disaster. A screw-up as big as the fucking Sears tower, Nordstrom had called it.

Sam had left the field temporarily, his arm too stiff to hold a gun steady. And Derek himself had an arthritic knee that he had lied to his boss about.

Just fine, he'd said. Good as new.

So Reese needed to be cut out. He had to protect this case and he had to protect her. Keep her far away from Chatterton.

An hour and a half later he had come to the conclusion that protecting Reese was going to be by far the most frustrating op he'd ever done. She was manipulating circles around him.

All with a smile on her face.

During the whole Maine lobster, asparagus, and squash dinner she had driven him nuts with her exploring fingers under the table. All while telling every single person they'd talked to a different story about who they were.

He couldn't remember if he was supposed to be a prize-winning French scientist or a rancher from Texas named Ridge. Either way, she might well say he was mute, too, since he couldn't do accents for shit. His rancher had sounded like Elvis drunk.

Now he was standing in a corner watching her dance with Chatterton. Somehow her quick trip to the ladies' room had resulted in her firmly hooked in Chatterton's pervert paws, doing a bastardized version of the waltz.

As an FBI agent working a case, he didn't like it.

As a man who was rapidly developing a thing for this woman, he *hated* it.

Reese danced by him, her light laughter making him wince, Chatterton's hand so close to her ass that he swore out loud.

"You used to look at me like that."

Derek glanced over, embarrassed that he'd spoken out

loud. Dawn was watching Reese and Chatterton, Reese's auburn hair swinging around as Chatterton spun her a little wildly.

Derek said ruefully, "What . . . in horror?"

Dawn cracked a small smile, but it didn't reach her eyes. "No, I mean like you couldn't get enough of me. That even when you were across the room from me, you had to be watching me."

That wistful, regret-laden trace of something in her words made him uncomfortable. He couldn't think of anything to say and so said nothing.

Nor did it seem like he could remember far back enough to a time when the sight of Dawn had filled him with passion and possessiveness. Too much time and divorce papers had made it impossible to stand in his old shoes.

"She's gorgeous." It wasn't delivered as a compliment, but as a begrudging admission.

"Yes." Just where in the hell was this conversation going?

"She's got claws, too. That was a good one about my due date."

Derek raised an eyebrow and she laughed.

"I guess I deserved it. I was being just a little bitchy."

A little? "Why?"

Dawn shrugged, her dangling earrings shaking back and forth. "Like I said, I've never seen you look at a woman like that, except for me. A little reactive jealousy, I guess."

"You left me, remember?" He spoke casually, not interested in an argument. Not caring anymore why Dawn had left him. He was done psychoanalyzing her, had done enough of that in their marriage to call himself Freud.

Now he was more concerned with wresting Reese from Chatterton, whose short hairy fingers had dropped another inch, coming perilously close to the curve of her ass. His ass. The ass that he wanted to be touching. Right now.

Tonight.

For hours.

"I know I left you." Dawn clicked her tongue. "And I got everything I wanted, but that still doesn't mean I want you falling in love and getting remarried."

That pulled his attention off Reese's ivory satin covered backside to gape at Dawn. "Hold it. First of all, Reese was telling you the truth. It's a casual relationship. Second, you can't leave me, remarry and start a family, and then get pissed if I do the same thing. It doesn't work like that."

Her fingers went up to smooth her perfect salon-created hair. "I'm selfish, you know that. And part of me wishes I'd never left."

With that little gem of a parting comment, she walked off, leaving him catching flies with his wide-open trap.

Christ. He really didn't want his ex-wife expressing regrets for their divorce. Not when he didn't have any at all.

Reese touched his arm, her breathing hard as she tucked her hair behind her ears. Her cheeks were two bright spots of color, and the strap on her dress had fallen over onto one shoulder.

"Well, that was a waste, not to mention disgusting. Chatterton didn't want to talk about anything except having me spend the weekend out in the country with him."

Fanning herself with her hand, she said, "Where's the waiter? I need a drink."

She turned towards him and frowned. "What's the matter with you? You look like you saw a Christina Aguilera video. Stunned and horrified."

"My ex-wife just said she wished she hadn't left me."

Reese took it with great aplomb. "She wants you back? *Why*?"

No chance of his ego inflating around Reese. "You don't need to act so damn surprised. Some women appreciate my many fine qualities."

Not her, apparently. She shrugged, looking baffled. Then she fixed her dress strap and said, "Well, she can't have you back until I'm done with you."

"You make me sound like a movie on DVD."

It wasn't meant as a joke. He was feeling a little put out and sick of this whole day . . . year, whatever.

But he suddenly felt a whole lot better when Reese moved closer to him. Her finger toyed with her bottom lip, before she nibbled on her fingernail.

The sight of her pink tongue, dampening her finger, perked him up.

"As long as you're rated R. For sexual content."

That really perked him up. "And nudity."

"Perfect," she said, her gray-green eyes hooded. "Are you ready to go, then? I'm tired, and I want to just curl up on my bed and . . . watch."

His hand spasmed, his heart raced like he was running up the side of a mountain, and his mouth dried up like a worm on the sidewalk in July.

"You do that, Beautiful. You just lie back on the bed and watch me getting you off."

A little "oh, *yes,*" slipped past her lips.

He took her elbow to guide her out of the crowded and stuffy room and to a cab before he dragged her into the coat-room and slid into her standing up.

She walked with confidence, with a seductive roll and sway of her hips, a toss of her hair. A shoulder was raised, and she glanced back at him over the creamy flesh, mouth open on a minxy smile.

"I told your ex-wife I'm in this relationship for the great sex. You'd better prove me right."

Oh, he would. Or die trying.

Reese wondered why the cab driver was only going sixty-five miles an hour. Surely at this time of the night, with light traffic, he could be doing at least eighty.

"We could go to your place this time if you want," she said, then regretted it. Knight probably had one of those cop apartments, all black lacquer furniture and empty Pop-Tart boxes. A lumpy bed with no headboard and a bathroom that hadn't seen the receiving end of Lysol in months.

She wanted an orgasm from Knight, not a toenail fungus from his dirty shower.

"We can't go to my place." Knight was sitting back in the cab seat, relaxed, his arm up stretched out behind her head. "My little sister Claire moved in with me yesterday because she had roommate problems."

Since the idea of living with other women gave Reese hives, she could understand. "How old is Claire?" The ex-wife had asked her if she was one of Claire's friends, she recalled.

"Twenty-four."

Reese laughed. "That was a good crack, then, on Dawn's part. She was calling you old. Geez, that's funny."

Knight wasn't laughing. "Yeah. Hilarious."

Reese leaned against his arm and dropped her hand onto his thigh. "Oh, don't pout. If I thought you were old I wouldn't be in this cab taking you back to my hotel room."

"You're taking me? I thought I was taking *you* back to your hotel room."

The contours of his face were shadowed in the dark cab, but she could still see the strong set of his jaw, the hot desire banked in his eyes.

It swirled in the cool closed air around them, mutual lust and a faint power struggle. They both yearned for control, they both deemed their careers and personal lives unsatisfactory because they were lacking in that control.

They approached each other both wanting the upper hand, and Reese enjoyed that ever-present pull between them. She liked that Knight was older, experienced, had spent his life fighting for justice and truth and the American way. She enjoyed his rather brooding moodiness and the fact that he was willing to arm-wrestle a girl.

"How about we take turns taking each other?" she whispered, allowing her finger to creep northward along his hard thigh.

His hand closed over hers, stopping her seductive trail. "I go first. I'm taking you."

Oh, baby. First she'd found herself turned on by a gun, now alpha male domination was getting her hot.

But she wasn't going down without a fight, no matter what her nipples thought about it. "Want to bet?"

"I'll take that bet."

Without warning, his mouth covered hers, cutting off any protests she might have made had she not been drowning in horny hormones.

It was a taking kiss. A demanding, selfish, who's-your-daddy kind of kiss that filled her mouth with burning breath, hot tongue, and urgent need.

Pushing on the floor of the cab with her heels, she opened her mouth to him all the way, let him cover her with his lips, his hands, his leg as the wave of passion pulled her under.

She told herself it was the suit.

Any man filling a shirt and pants the way he was right now would draw this reaction from her. It didn't have anything to do with Knight himself.

And she made her Christmas cards with rubber stamps and ribbons a la Martha Stewart.

Puh-lease.

For some unknown reason, this guy did it to her. And instead of trying to figure out why, she decided to just enjoy it.

She broke the kiss, needing oxygen that hadn't been in his lungs first.

"I'm taking you," he repeated.

Shivering from excitement, Reese scooped up her purse as they pulled in front of the Crowne Plaza and gave him a cocky grin. "If I don't take you first."

She didn't wait for Knight, but got out of the car and stepped onto the sidewalk. The September night was cool and balmy and the breeze from the north brought a faint fishy smell of the lake, making her wrinkle her noise. Give her exhaust fumes any day over that briney odor. At least in New York all the bad smells were man-made.

Knight joined her at the door as she went into the hushed lobby of the hotel, the only sound the low voices of the desk clerks speaking to guests, and the constant ding of the elevators.

Reese had always felt the urge to swat men off her like irritating insects when they latched onto her arm or elbow or the small of her back. But when Knight did it, she didn't mind. It was a promise of pleasure, a reminder that he had large masculine hands that were soon going to be all over her body, stroking her mindless.

As his fingers pressed into her dress, right above her thong panty line, he told her, "You're forgetting I'm an agent. I have a lot of experience with take-downs."

She had a button on her body that read *Get me off,* and Knight seemed to know exactly where it was. And he wasted no time in pushing it frequently.

"How is that relevant here?" Reese stepped onto the elevator and hit the five.

They were the only people on the elevator, a fact she was very aware of when the doors closed, leaving them in a small enclosed space where no one could see anything they might happen to do.

Knight took a step towards her, stalking. "That's why I get to do the taking first. Because I can."

The sensual game of words left her breathless, clinging to the wall of the elevator with her hand, thighs rubbing together in agony.

"I'm not a perpetrator, though."

"Yes, you are. You're so damn sexy it should be illegal."

He was in front of her, surrounding her, shirt rustling across her bare chest above her cleavage. His scent filled her nostrils, a rich, deep exotic smell of aftershave, musky soap, and expensive clothes. It was different from the way she remembered him the day before, earthy and casual. Gritty at the end of a long day.

"You can't arrest me for being sexy." Reese dipped her nose into the hollow of his neck and sniffed again, running her lips along the collar of his burgundy shirt.

"Yes, I can."

The elevator shuddered to a stop, the doors opened, and Knight stepped away from her.

Reese slipped past him and said, "You can't if you can't catch me."

Then with a laugh, she sprinted down the hall towards room 517, the heels slowing her down a little, her purse falling off her shoulder. When she heard him give chase, she kicked it into third gear, delighted that he was going to play with her.

Derek couldn't believe he was in hot pursuit of his date, instead of a suspect. Reese sure in the hell made him work for it.

But he wasn't ticked off. He wasn't even mildly annoyed. The thing was, he liked Reese's sharp tongue and her little betting games. He liked chasing, and her running, because he knew in the end they both wanted her to be caught.

It made him feel alive. Young. Excited to be in the game, the rush of something new and different and not-standard-procedure.

He had eaten up the distance between them, and was about to overtake her, when she reached the end of the hall and her room. Skidding to a stop, she shrieked when he caught her by the arm.

The turn-on of her delighted smile was so great, he barely even felt the twinge in his knee from racing down the hall like a track star. They ran for a medal and glory.

Derek got Reese as his prize.

"Ma'am, this could be considered resisting arrest."

With a gentle touch on her waist, he turned her around so

she was facing the door. Her breath hitched as he took first her left hand, then her right, and placed them flat on the door above her head.

All the doors to the rooms were in a little alcove with the room next door, giving subtle privacy from the hall, but not totally eliminating the chance of being caught.

But Derek didn't care.

"Spread your legs," he told Reese.

Her answer was a low sensual chuckle, before she complied, moving her legs apart until the skirt of her dress was taut above her knees.

"I'm going to frisk you," he said as he slid his hands down her waist, over the bump of her firm behind and down.

He wanted his hands on her bare thighs, he wanted to feel her softness, hear her whimpers, and push himself to the edge of sanity with how much he could touch and still not take.

"I don't have a weapon, Agent Knight," she said, her voice husky and muffled as her head dropped against the door, a soft metallic thunk reverberating in the quiet hallway.

"I still have to check."

Bending over, he ran his fingers over the smooth flesh on the backs of her knees and moved up, taking her dress up with him. It pooled along his forearms as he moved his thumbs around her inner thigh, stroking, always moving higher.

His mouth was hovering over the small of her back, where bare skin from the plunge of her dress tantalized him. Unable to resist, he placed his lips on her, sucking her flesh a little before retreating.

Reese made a low murmur deep in her throat. "I don't think you're concerned about a weapon. I think this is an excuse to get your hands on me."

He had a momentary image of Reese ripping the balls off any guy who tried to grope her without her permission. It made him angry that as a woman she could ever be vulnerable, and he almost halted their play-acting right there. The last thing he wanted was to make her uncomfortable.

But Reese added, "If you're going to frisk me, maybe we should go into my room where you can be more thorough."

Derek relaxed, reassured she was enjoying the game. He had never been one for fooling around in the bedroom, he was more of an in and out kind of guy, but he had to admit, his heart was racing and his blood had all gone south.

He ached to be inside her, and every minute, every touch pushed his desire farther and farther until there was nothing else but him and Reese and their bodies blended in mutual pleasure.

"Don't want your neighbors to see you getting arrested?" he said as he stood, hands climbing until he reached her ass.

He found it bare, nothing but warm hard flesh waiting for him to explore. With a groan, he cupped her cheeks with both hands, giving a soft squeeze. Where the hell were her panties? He'd seen them when she'd flashed him in the cab, but he wasn't feeling them now.

"They can see me getting arrested, but I don't feel like having them see me come."

"Why would you come? I haven't even touched you yet."

"Then you better get working on that."

Damn. Derek dropped his hands. "Turn around."

He wanted to taste her, to lick and suck and rub against her like a fucking cat.

Arms still over her head, Reese rolled across the door and turned until she was facing him, her legs crossed at the ankle.

"Yes, sir."

The rise of her breasts, straining behind the satin cool fabric of her dress, beckoned him. Leaning forward, Derek placed his tongue right between into the dip of cleavage, gliding back and forth until her skin was soaked and they were both panting.

Careful not to rip the dress, he shifted it so her breast was exposed, ready to flick his tongue across her ripe nipple. Only there was no nipple, ripe and pink and ready for him.

Instead it was covered with what looked like a white drink coaster.

"What the hell?" He touched the cup shaped *thing* tentatively. It was soft paper.

"It's a pastie," Reese said. "I can't wear a bra with this dress, but I didn't want my nipples showing."

Which was all fine and good, but what the hell was he supposed to do with it?

He plucked at the edge of it with his fingernail. It didn't budge.

The stupid thing was between him and paradise and he had no idea what his next move should be.

Christ. He had never been trained to deal with a situation like this.

"Does it come off?"

Chapter Nine

Reese blinked. Oh, Lord, Knight was looking at her like he was faced with a bomb he had thirty seconds to defuse.

If her pleasure was derailed by a pastie, she was going to sue somebody.

"Of course it comes off. You just pull it." What did he think? She was going to spend eternity with a piece of cotton stuck to her boob?

Reluctantly letting her hands drop from over her head, she reached into her dress. She had kind of liked that cop/suspect thing they'd had going on. With little patience or finesse, she stripped the pasties off her skin and tossed them on the floor.

Knight winced. "Jesus, doesn't that hurt?"

Not as much as wanting to have sex with him and instead standing there doing nothing.

"No. Now, what were you saying before that?" To make her point clear, she put her hands back up over her head and licked her lips.

Knight drew his gaze from the abandoned pasties on the floor and went wide-eyed. That was good. Right back where she wanted him.

He might think he was a federal agent in charge, but she knew better. He wanted her bad, which was just right.

"I have no goddamn idea what I was saying."

Then his mouth covered her breast, and his warm wet

tongue tickled across her nipple. She squirmed against the door, wanting way more than that. Knight had tugged until her dress was under the swell of her breast and he held it in place while his fingers rushed along her sensitive skin and his mouth covered her more fully.

"Keep talking," she murmured, only to give a cry of disappointment as he pulled back.

Small kisses rained down her ribs and abdomen over her dress as he bent down. Reese reached for him. "Where are you going? Come back up here."

He took her hands and pressed them back against the wall, next to her thighs. "Ma'am, you're interfering with a federal investigation. Just stand still, please."

As if she could move a muscle. Not when every one in her body was a squishy mass of orgasmic anticipation.

"What are you looking for?" she asked, focusing on the top of his head, trying to keep her eyes open, noticing the little swirl of darker hair he had at the crown.

"I want to know what happened to your panties."

His hands were under her dress, inching upward until his thumb and forefinger touched the front of her lace panties, stroking back and forth. Reese gripped the door and tilted her legs together as desire shot through her, ripping into every inch of her body and flooding her inner thighs with moist heat.

"Nothing happened to them, except they're a little warmer than they were before." Hot enough to melt plastic, in fact.

"I saw them before . . ." Knight was inching her dress up over her hips as he spoke. "Then when I felt your ass, they were gone, and now they're back. How is that possible?"

Reese wanted to explain the mysteries of the thong and the desire to eliminate unsightly panty lines in clinging cocktail dresses, but her mouth was too full of saliva to speak without gurgling.

Besides, given the way he was studying her, hands all over her thighs, mouth sliding along her skin to . . . ohmigod, he was bound to figure it out on his own.

"Wait a minute."

When he pulled his lips back from the front of her panties, Reese tried not to cry.

Then strong hands twisted her back around until her backside was towards the hall—towards him—again, only this time her dress was up around her waist and she was sure he could see everything that God had given her. Left and right side.

"A thong," he said, voice thick and low. "Christ, that's a beautiful thing."

Her face was smushed against a cold hotel door, the peephole pressing into her cheek and her bare behind was stuck out for Knight and anyone who happened to walk by to see, but when one rough finger ran down the lace line of her thong, she didn't give a flying fig about anything.

Anything but his hard warm hand, plucking the little string forward, and slipping down, down, between her cheeks and around, where he stopped.

"Look what I found," he murmured, his mouth by her ear, his chest brushing against her back.

Reese wiggled, wanting him to move, to fill her with his fingers like he had the day before. Her breast was still out of her dress, the fabric shifting and bunching, her nipple randomly hitting the cold door as she rocked. The surprise of cool metal against her hot flesh made her gasp.

Knight pushed her thighs apart with his wrist, then dipped inside her with his finger. He wasted no time, setting a quick rhythm of sharp thrusts that had her clinging to the door and panting, ready to let a quick orgasm overwhelm her.

Then the door next to them opened.

Knight heard the sound before she did and he pulled out of her with a quick jerk, while his other hand yanked the skirt of her dress down. She wasn't that quick. Reese was still clinging to the door and moaning when a nice-looking, older couple stepped out of the room next to them.

"Honey, I can't find my key," Knight said. "Let me get the other one out of your purse."

She could feel him bending over to retrieve her fallen purse, felt his hip knock against hers, and she struggled to peel herself off the door and at least attempt to look normal.

Given the twin expressions of shock on the couple's face, she guessed she wasn't succeeding.

But then Knight said, "I think my wife ate bad chicken. All of a sudden her stomach hurts and she's flushed."

The woman's hand went to her chest. "Oh, poor thing. You'd better get her inside quick."

Reese moaned again, keeping her left side turned to the door, suddenly aware that if she stood straight up, her breast would be waving at the nice couple. Knight stepped in front of her, shielding her as he stuck the key card in the slot.

The green light blinked, Knight turned the knob, and the couple started down the hall. And Reese felt the overwhelming urge to laugh, a wheeze squeezing past her clamped lips.

Knight shot her an amused look as he pushed the door open. The door had barely swung shut behind them when his arms were around her, and his mouth was rushing towards hers.

"Wait, you'd better not kiss me. I've had bad chicken." She put her fingers on his lips to stop his progress.

"Ha, ha."

His tongue reached out and flicked her fingertip, all that moist heat, slick and intimate, creating a comparison to another part of her she wasn't likely to misunderstand.

It seemed Knight had figured it out, too. Already he was lowering himself to his knees, right there in the entry to her room, the coat closet behind her and the mirror—holy hell, the *mirror*—right in front of her.

Unable to look away, fascinated and flushed with pleasure, Reese watched the back of his head, and the taut pull of his suit jacket as he yanked up her skirt again.

He didn't bother to take her panties off, just pushed the lace to the side and spread her soft hair with his thumbs. His shoulders tensed, one knee on the floor, the other bent as he studied her, breath blowing across her clitoris. Reese dared to look higher in the mirror, to confront her own image, and her hand fell to his head for support.

Curling her fingers in his thick hair, she took in her own disheveled hair, the bright pink spots on her face, the cherry lips, and one breast pushed up out of her dress. Bad chicken, her ass. She looked like she'd been caught in the act. Plain and simple.

"I want to taste you."

When his tongue gave a light dart across her, she tightened her hold on his hair and pulled, the strands curling around her anxious fingers. Her knees bent, weakening under the onslaught of pleasure tearing through her.

Knight took another slow lick, sliding from one end of her hot labia to the other, and she shuddered. His hands snaked around to her bare backside, and holding her tight, he drew her forward, bumping her against his tongue, driving her insane with need, burning aching need that was every kind of pleasure mixed with tight pain.

Back and forth he went, up and down, while his nose knocked into her, and his thumbs stroked the underside of her ass. Reese held on and gave in to it, feeling an orgasm building, hot undulating waves of desire rushing up to consume her.

When they did, she jerked hard in her intense satisfaction, falling back against the closet door. But Knight held on, fingers squeezing hard in her thighs as he kept his tongue roving over her, questing, pleasing, while shudders coursed through her body. Eyes half closed, she still managed to catch their reflections in the mirror, her body pressed up against Knight's, her taut hold on his head, his movements slowing as she relaxed.

When he leaned back and gazed up at her, she nearly

blushed. Geez, was she easy, or what? The arrogant satisfaction on his face didn't help. So she shoved his head none too gently, letting her fingers unfurl from his soft caramel hair.

Most men would have been offended. It was a rude gesture. But Knight just laughed.

"You like to go first, but then it pisses you off that you're finished first, doesn't it?"

Maybe. Yes. So, what of it?

Reese raised her arms and tried to tug her dress up over her hips. Nothing moved and she wiggled to get a better hold. "I'm not finished. Get a condom and I'll show you."

Knight's head hit her thighs. Startled, she dropped her arms and looked at him buried in her crotch, groaning. "What?"

"I never bought condoms. Last night I was up working until two, I got home and my sister was in my apartment, and then this morning—" he pulled back and pointed to his head "—I got a haircut. I forgot to get the condoms."

That was possibly the worst thing she'd ever heard.

"Do we really need them?" he asked, a hopeful pleading in his voice.

Reese cuffed him on the head. "I can't believe you just said that."

"Okay. Sorry." He stood up and stuck his hand in his pocket. "But I just meant that if you're on the pill . . ."

She knew what he meant, but women who have sex every three years do not need to be on the pill. She suddenly wished she had suffered from cramps and irregular cycles. But no such luck, she'd never needed the pill for that, either.

"No, I'm not." But she was glad he'd gotten the haircut. He looked really hot. Not that he'd been hurting before, but in the suit, with the hair . . . yowsa.

She wanted to take that jacket off him. Right now. Forgetting about her uncooperative dress, she reached out and ran her hands along his chest, scraping her nails over the smooth crisp fabric of his shirt. She could feel his hard muscles tightening beneath her touch and she explored up and down, shoving his jacket to the side.

"Are you frisking me, now?" he asked, staying aloof with his hands still in his pockets.

"I'm looking for your gun." Reese closed the remaining distance between them and rolled her head back when his erection nudged her. If he had been aiming for the target, he couldn't have done better. Bull's-eye.

Still wet from her orgasm, she squeezed her thighs together. Like that had ever helped.

"I don't wear my gun when I'm off duty."

She dropped her hand to his pants and said, "You could have fooled me."

"Reese." Knight's stance was no longer casual. "Shouldn't I go to the store?"

Kissing the corner of his mouth, she murmured, "You can't leave me here alone. Who knows what I might do, given how desperate I am."

"Shit." Hard hands stole up and grabbed her arms, trying to urge her back.

"And you wouldn't even be here to see it." She flicked her tongue across his bottom lip, tasting the moist saltiness of his mouth.

On a groan, he stopped shoving her, though he gave one last token objection. "But . . . the condoms," he said, even while his thumbs found her nipple and his mouth dipped into her neck to lave kisses behind her ear and down to her clavicle.

"We'll just have to *feel* our way around the situation." And she stripped his jacket down off his arms, stepping back as it fell, to take him in.

Hot damn. He was gorgeous, every inch of bronzed, muscled, charming, put-together man enticing her, thrilling her.

"Not bad for an old guy," she said in a husky voice.

Undoing the buttons on his shirt, he quirked an eyebrow up. "I'll show you 'old guy.' "

"Please do." She'd seen his chest the day before, but now, with the dress shirt sliding down his arms, she gained new appreciation for it.

Maybe it was because she suspected the sight of Knight in dress pants was a rare treat, but he looked divine standing there bare-chested. He undid the black leather belt on his pants and unzipped them.

Then started towards her.

"No, finish the job. I want to see you." Reese took a couple of steps back to maintain her view.

"You are so demanding." But he did what she asked, pushing his pants down and stepping out of them.

Reese kicked off her high heels as she drank him in, every hard, golden inch of him. His black briefs were straining against his erection.

"Oh, my. Somebody wants to come out and play."

The urge was overwhelming, then, and she knew what she was going to do. She didn't just want her hands on Knight, she wanted her mouth on him. To taste him, have him fill her, let him hold her head and grind his teeth in pleasure.

"Will you play with us?" Derek grinned, gripping the band of his briefs, ready to drop them but waiting for her answer.

He wasn't entirely sure it was a good idea to be stripping naked when they didn't have any condoms, but those reservations weren't enough to stop him.

"I am definitely going to play with you."

Reese's eyes dropped to his briefs, her mouth open a touch, and Derek couldn't resist. He shucked the briefs and stood up straight, feeling a bit like a proud peacock, emphasis on the words proud and cock.

"Mmmm," she said, bubble gum pink tongue slipping out and wetting her plump lips.

"Come lie on the bed," she added, lifting her dress up over her head and sending it sailing over the dresser to land in a heap on the ice bucket.

With the pasties gone, she was wearing nothing but the thong, and his brains turned to scrambled eggs. She was thinner than most women Derek had dated, but she still had that womanly swell to her hips and belly, and full rounded breasts that bounced just a little as she climbed onto the bed. With a naughty smile in his direction she slid the panties down and kicked them off.

Everything about her was smooth and soft and real, honest and totally lacking in artifice.

And this might be his only chance to be with her. In the next day or two she would go back to New York and he would probably never see her again.

The thought had him sitting on the bed next to her, reaching for her, wanting to touch and taste everything he could while he still had the chance. Reese turned to him, melting towards him, her mouth open, eyes shining. He opened his own mouth for the kiss he thought she was about to give him.

Instead, Reese ducked down at the last second, her head bending over his lap, her soft lips closing around his cock. The intense pleasure rocked through him and he placed a hand on the bumps of her spine arching in front of him as she took him deep into her mouth on a long, slow, hot stroke.

"Reese." He shuddered, one hand staying on her back, the other reaching around between their bodies to find her breast and pinch her nipple.

He felt like every muscle in his body was about to snap, that he couldn't stand the torture of her warm slick mouth covering his cock over and over in a languid skilled rhythm. With each lift of her lips, each flick of her tongue over the tip of his engorged head, his need built, straining, pulsing, desperate desire growing.

Needing to hold, to pull, to squeeze, he ran his hand up

her back to her glossy hair, burying his fingers in it and tugging. Her head jerked back, her mouth slid off him, her lips shiny and wet, her gray-green eyes sparkling with desire and determination.

"Lie back," she said, pushing on his chest.

Releasing his hold on her hair, he did as she asked, the stiff hotel pillow causing a lump behind his shoulder. Without taking his eyes off her, he reached behind him and ripped the pillow out from under the bedspread. He tossed it to the side, where it tumbled off the bed and onto the floor.

Reese lay down next to him, her hip next to his shoulder, her feet pressing against the headboard as she leaned back over him, reaching for his cock. One hand squeezed the length of him, the other cupped his balls, and her mouth closed over him again.

He groaned, clamping his eyes shut, reaching back to grab the headboard, needing something to hold on to. Reese's tongue moved quicker this time, dancing across him, while he fought against the need swamping him. He didn't want to come. Not yet. Not when it felt so damn good.

Turning his head, his nose collided with her thigh and he realized how tantalizingly close she was to him. With a little nudge of her knee . . . yes, he could see everything. Her swollen peach folds, her dusting of auburn curls, the curve of her backside.

Hauling her leg over his shoulder, he buried his head between her thighs and sucked on her clitoris. Reese's mouth jerked on his cock, and he heard her little pants of excited pleasure that she couldn't contain before her lips closed over him again.

He met her stroke for stroke, his tongue moving as possessively and quickly as hers did, just as wet, just as eager until it swamped him, sending his hot come into her mouth in great pulsing shudders of pleasure.

Before he could think to move, apologize, groan his way through the last jerks of his pleased body, Reese's thighs clenched. He dipped his tongue inside her just in time to feel her muscles spasm, her hips lifting off the bed.

Her hands were still on him, his on her, mouths and wet tongues pressed intimately against each other as they shattered and came back down, one shudder at a time. Reese's fingers relaxed first, then her thighs settled back down on the bed, her heavy breathing the only sound she was making.

Derek held on still, tense, shocked, pleased, wishing he had the right words to say, something to express his total enjoyment of her, his gratitude that she made him feel alive and in control again. But there were no words in his testosterone-flooded brain and he sank back onto the bed, releasing his death grip on her thighs.

Bright red marks marred her pale skin where he had been squeezing her, and he caressed her, wanting to rub the bruises away, struggling to catch his breath.

"I like the way you play," she said, arms slung over her head as she rolled onto her back.

And still he just lay there like a dolt, unable to think of a single thing to say, a boneless, brainless mass of male idiocy.

A soft touch feathered across his knee.

"Does it hurt?"

Rousing himself, he looked down and watched her gently tracing the scar from his surgery, her lips placing a light kiss on his kneecap. Things shifted in his chest, as if he had indigestion. A strange pain settled in behind his ribs.

"Not all the time. It's kind of like arthritis, some days are worse than others." He was surprised it didn't hurt now, after his sprint down the hall. But all he felt was deep, abiding satisfaction in every inch of his body.

Reese listened to Knight's husky low voice, felt his fingers still stroking on her thighs, and feared for her heart. This guy was kicking down the walls she had erected around herself one by one. She never wanted to lose herself in a guy, risk her heart, her money, or her self-respect.

She wanted to be in control, call all the shots and be the

master of her own destiny, even if that destiny currently sucked rocks. At least she could blame it on herself, she could take chances, she wasn't tied to another person and their capricious desires, needs, and whims.

A war was waging in her. She wanted to be with Knight and she didn't. She had fun with him, but he wasn't a good candidate for continual mindless commitment-free sex. He was a good guy, not terribly selfish and a little bit of a loner.

If she had wanted a casual affair, she had picked the wrong guy. She should have gone after one of those egocentric types, who waxed his car every Saturday and lost interest in women after three dates and penetration. But she hadn't wanted one of those guys.

She had wanted Knight.

And now she was stuck. If she left tomorrow on her flight like she was supposed to, she was going to lose the story and the chance for some more naked fun. If she stayed, she was going to have to go hard and fast for this story, possibly alienating Knight and eliminating the chances of sweaty sex anyway.

Or he would let her in on the story, and in the off hours drive her to new heights of pleasure. And possibly make her fall for him, leaving her with a news scoop, a broken heart, and a high standard for penis size by which to judge all subsequent men.

And she hadn't even had actual sex with him yet. That would probably kill her.

"Do you like your job?" She withdrew from his knee and brought her legs around, so she was lying in the same direction as him. Her face was now next to his abdomen and chest and she couldn't resist giving him a little nip, wanting to taste his salty skin.

"I love my job. I love helping people, doing my small part to right a wrong."

Reese had noticed he liked her hair. Whenever they were together, he found reasons to dig into it, to smooth his rough hands along her long satin strands, and he was doing it now. She liked the feeling and felt for the first time ever that she could soothe someone, be a little tiny bit nurturing in her own way.

Nurturing had never come easy to her. She had grown up with no guide on how to do that. And then when she might have figured it out herself, she had rebelled against it, not wanting to be under male control any longer after the twenty years of her father and brothers' well-meant dictatorship.

"That's what I want to do, Knight. I want to write stories that matter, not pass on gossip and meaningless trash."

"So do it."

Stroke, stroke, he kept moving over the back of her head, and she nestled into the crook of his arm, indulging herself since she knew this opportunity would probably never arise again.

"I'm trying to. That's why I want this story."

His hand stilled. "Are you leaving tomorrow, Reese?"

She already knew she wasn't. She couldn't. Ralph would have a fit, but screw him. Well, not literally, since the thought of that made her want to have her stomach pumped. But she couldn't worry about Ralph.

It would only be a few days, long enough to do a little more fact gathering.

Only she knew just as clearly that despite the way he made her feel, Knight was devoted to his job as special agent, not her. She didn't trust him to keep her abreast of the case.

And she didn't trust herself not to fall head over heels for him.

"Yes," she lied, waiting for a bolt of lightning to come out of the sky and zing her on her bare ass. "I'm leaving tomorrow. Two o'clock flight."

It wasn't a lie if there was a reason for it.

That's what her brother Ryan had always told her, and she thought it made perfect sense.

Chapter Ten

Reese had lied to him. He didn't know why. He wasn't even entirely sure about what. But he just knew she had.

Her eyes opened a little too wide when she lied and a sort of cocky swagger sent her shoulders arching up, which is exactly what she had done in bed with him when he had asked her if she was leaving.

Derek nursed his tepid coffee, stretched his legs in front of him, and tried to focus on Nordstrom droning on and on in his ear.

It was Monday morning, nine A.M., and Reese was back in New York. Or so she said.

Derek felt cranky, on edge, and a little bit like he missed her. Sleeping on his couch alone last night while Claire slept in his bed had been a stark and lonely contrast to the night before, when he had slept with Reese snuggled up next to him, naked.

Neither one of them had mentioned going to the store for condoms again, but had simply gone to sleep after talking. Derek suspected that they both knew sex would be too much, too intimate, and that they might be facing regrets about Reese leaving if they took that step.

Not that he wasn't facing regrets anyway, because he was.

And what they had done had been pretty damn intimate.

The way Reese's mouth had wrapped around his cock, her tongue lapping him up . . .

Derek shifted in his chair and stuck his hand in his pocket. He was back to wearing a cheap suit this morning, his old gray one, and he had to admit he liked the new one better. He liked the look in Reese's eye when she had caught sight of him. Lust. Heavy, wet, dripping, raging lust.

Christ. He shifted again.

"Are you listening to me?" Nordstrom said sharply, perched on the corner of his desk.

No. "Of course I am, sir."

Special Agent Maddock, seated next to Derek, looked over at him curiously, his eyebrow quirking up in question. Derek shook his head a little and focused on Nordstrom, whose receding hairline was tinting a soft pink as his blood pressure shot up in anger.

"Then why the hell are you just staring at me? Can you get Markson to wear a tape recorder or not?"

Derek knew the case was coming to this. He had delivered the documents to Nordstrom on Sunday and they had spent the better part of an hour this morning discussing the holes in the evidence.

Essentially, price-fixing was hinted at in the documents, which were various E-mail transcripts and financial records of profits from the abnormally high-priced drugs in question.

But in order to prove their case, the Justice Department needed actual conversations between executives where they discussed slicing up the market share, deciding who would patent which drugs, and what each price would be.

The FBI, and Derek in particular, needed Markson to wear a wire anytime he was with other board members and hope he could coax admissions of guilt out of them. And they especially needed him comfortable recording his coworkers before the big price-fixing meeting scheduled for two weeks down the road, in New Zealand, where the three companies in question would actually sit around a table and divvy up the market for the products in question.

"Markson is a skittish CW. It's going to take some coaxing." The chemist, who was also a products division executive, had made Derek nervous since day one when he had contacted the FBI on his own and claimed knowledge of illegal price-fixing.

In his fifteen years on the job, Derek had never seen that. Witnesses don't just stroll into the FBI field office and offer to bite the hand that feeds them. It made him suspicious of Markson's motives. The man claimed he just wanted to do what was right, that the guilt of ripping off consumers in need of meds kept him up at night.

Derek had seen too much to avoid being a little bit cynical about Markson's explanation.

But there was clearly illegal activity going on in Delco and Markson was their only in. He was the only way they had to get insider information and hopefully actual documented conversations between the executives making the price-fixing decisions.

"So coax him. Hold his damn hand for all I care, just get it done." Nordstrom straightened his tie and dared Derek to defy him.

"Knight's right," Maddock said. "I've been there twice with him when he met with Markson and the guy is a loose cannon."

Maddock was a nice guy, about five years younger than Derek, and always ready with a quick grin and a joke to defuse tension. The women around the office adored him, and the men all thought of him as a buddy, the kind of guy you want at your back.

Nordstrom was the only one unaffected by Maddock's charming smile. "All the more reason to hurry. Knight, get an FD-473 ready. The minute the guy agrees, you can hand him the form and give him the recorder."

Derek wasn't sure that pressuring Markson was the way to go. "I don't know. This guy is going to freak if we whip out an authorization form to carry a recorder on his body and then wire him up right on the spot."

It wasn't the right thing to say. Nordstrom stood up and hovered over Derek. At six three and two hundred and eighty pounds easy, he was old, cranky, and intimidating. Not to mention that prior to the FBI he'd been a marine.

"We don't have time to dick around, Knight. This meeting is taking place in two weeks and after that there won't be another one until the next fiscal quarter. I've got three agents on this case, and nothing happening. We don't have the goddamn budget for you to spend the next three months playing with yourself."

Well, when put like that.

Derek really didn't know how he managed to piss Nordstrom off so regularly.

No one moved in the small airless room with government gray walls. As chairs squeaked and Nordstrom breathed hard, Derek was formulating a response, wishing Maddock or the other agent in the room, White, would rescue him.

They didn't, but another agent popped his head in the door to Nordstrom's office and said, "Reeder wants to see you, sir."

Thank God.

Nordstrom started towards the door. "Get me something on tape, Knight. And don't hang around my office all morning, I'm expecting someone at ten."

Derek let out a sigh of relief as his boss left, and lifted his suit jacket a little to let his armpits air. He was sweating like a pig.

Maddock gave him a light clap on the shoulder. "Hey, don't worry about it, man. Nordstrom's just got budget concerns and stuff that we don't have to deal with. You'll be able to talk Markson into wearing a wire." He grinned and shot a look at White, a female agent who was as unaffected by Maddock's charm as Nordstrom.

CJ White, a serious and quiet agent, always had her hair scraped back into a ponytail and her body covered in loose ill-fitting pants and sweaters. She never wore makeup or jewelry and looked like she could take down a hardened criminal just by piercing him with a cold stare.

For some inexplicable reason, Maddock seemed to pick on her, and Derek thought it was because she was the only woman under fifty who didn't flirt with him. An ego blow for the charming Maddock.

"Well, if you can't talk him into it, maybe White can do it. Come on, White, we'll slap you in a dress and you can go come on to the guy."

Derek buried his face in his hand. Jesus. What the hell was Maddock doing? The guy wasn't normally such an idiot.

He was about to reprimand him, when White spoke.

"I heard Markson was gay. So maybe we should send you, Maddock. You could pass for gay easily."

Derek laughed as White left the room, a faint smile on her face. Maddock sat up straight, his mouth wide open. Then he scoffed and laughed along with Derek, but was obviously still annoyed.

"I think White has a thing for me, that's why she's such a bitch to me."

Derek wasn't about to feed that delusion. He said, "More like she thinks you're an asshole."

Maddock sighed, gazing towards the door White had gone through. "Probably," he agreed.

They sat there for a minute, Derek's mind wandering back to Reese. They had said good-bye Sunday morning, had exchanged E-mail addresses and phone numbers and she had left.

Just left. And he missed her. Her laugh, her feisty smile, her soft satin hair.

She hadn't even suggested they keep in touch for any reason other than the case, and she hadn't so much as mentioned ever seeing each other again.

It shouldn't matter. It didn't matter. It was two nights out
of his life. She and her incredible legs had intruded into his
job and personal life for less than two days, then popped
back out. That's all it was. A fun weekend.

Then why did he feel so damn depressed?

"I thought I understood women," Maddock said into the
brooding silence. "But it seems like there's always one that
turns everything you think you know upside down."

Maddock turned to him. "You know what I mean?"

Did he ever.

Reese hung out on the sidewalk with the pigeons and wondered if she should walk into the FBI building in front of her,
or if she should just go back to the Crowne Plaza. Or back to
New York.

She hadn't been this indecisive since voting in the last election.

The wind was kicking up, flapping the bottom of her olive
green suit jacket, and dipping down her ivory shell to chill
her skin. Fall had come early and she was getting cold. A pair
of jeans and a soft cable knit sweater would be better suited
to the weather, but she hadn't planned to extend this trip
when she had packed, and she had no other clothes. This was
the same suit she'd worn on the flight in.

Sunday she had spent rereading carefully all the Delco
documents, trying to determine how close the FBI was to an
indictment. Then she had researched price-fixing on-line and
found out what she could about Delco Pharmaceuticals.

Followed by canceling her plane ticket, writing the story
on the Chatterton-Bismark wedding, which she had E-mailed
to the *Newark News* office, and a really hideous phone conversation to Ralph she'd prefer not to think about.

Given that she didn't want to print the Delco story in the
Newark News, she had been forced to lie to Ralph, claiming

she had a roaring case of the flu and couldn't fly. He had been less than thrilled, and she had cringed through the lie.

She had never lied so much in her life.

And she still wasn't exactly sure why she had told Knight she was leaving when she wasn't. If she wanted to pursue this story, she had to be in touch with him. Of course, it was possible she had been thinking that touching was a bad thing, and staying in contact by phone was much more the way to go as far as Knight was concerned.

He had a way of distracting her with his rippling muscles and heartfelt sighs of impatience. Not to mention his tongue and what it could do to her.

It had seemed like a smart move just to get away from him.

A panhandler approached Reese, wavering slightly, smiling a toothless grin as he asked her for spare change, anything she had for a man down on his luck who needed to eat.

Reaching into the bag she was clutching like it was holding her afloat, she pulled out a roll and handed it to him. "Here, have some bread."

The man looked at her like she'd lost her mind, but he took the roll and thanked her before wandering off.

Reese looked up at the stark concrete building in front of her and wondered what her problem was. She'd never been such a wet noodle and she didn't like it now.

So what if Knight would be ticked at her for lying about leaving Chicago? Who cared if he didn't like her showing up at his office unannounced? She'd brought him lunch, hadn't she? Ulcer-sensitive potato soup.

She'd never brought another man soup. If he didn't appreciate it, she'd drop it in his lap.

The truth was, she needed his cooperation if she were going to write this story. And she wanted to make love to him, to ease herself down onto his impressive penis and engorge herself on pleasure.

It was the thought of that that sent her up the stairs and through the heavy doors.

*   *   *

Derek was filling out an avalanche of forms, waiting for Markson to call him back when the front desk security called him.

"You have a visitor," the bland voice told him, before disconnecting.

A visitor? Derek started, wondering if Markson would be stupid enough to show up here. It didn't seem like a move the CW would make, but then you never knew with these guys. And Derek wasn't expecting anyone else.

It was the laughter that tipped him off it wasn't Markson.

He could hear it the minute he stepped off the elevator. Rich, feminine laughter coming from a woman who met life on her own terms. A woman who made him insane with lust and occasionally annoyance.

Reese Hampton.

Leaning over the guard's front security checkpoint desk, holding a big brown bag, one leg bent, foot kicked back, tips of her toes pressing into the marble floor. Torturing him.

When she saw him walking towards her, she smiled and said, "Oh, hi. I brought you lunch."

Like she hadn't left him without so much as a see you later. Like she wasn't supposed to be halfway across the country by now, planning a layout in the *Newark News* for the wedding photos.

He was equal parts thrilled and scared. He knew that smile. It meant somehow she was about to complicate his life. Again.

"Hi Reese. What a surprise." A big-ass, huge, what-the-hell kind of surprise.

She grinned. "Are you hungry?"

"Sure." He was trying to stay cool, in control of the situation. He should approach this calmly, see what she wanted and why she hadn't gone back to New York.

Instead, he was besieged by carnal images of backing her up against the nearest wall and sinking himself into her.

"Where should we go to eat?"

"I guess my office would be fine." With a little luck, no one would notice Reese.

She shook her hair back over her shoulder, and he decided that was a futile wish. No man with blood running through his veins could not notice her.

"Cool. You can give me a tour of the place, then."

So she could pinch pens and flirt with his coworkers? Screw that. He was keeping her behind his cubicle walls until he could figure out just what in the hell she was doing here.

It was a long way to come for lunch and Reese didn't strike him as one for social calls. She would have a purpose behind this little visit.

He gestured for her to get on the elevator in front of him and said politely, "Can I carry that bag for you?"

She shook her head, eyes sparkling. "No, I've got it."

When the door closed behind them, she reached over and placed her hand square on his ass, giving a squeeze. He didn't move a muscle, just looked at her steadily, as if he were unconcerned. Well, one muscle moved, betraying him by swelling with interest.

Reese noticed too, damn her.

"You're mad at me, aren't you?" she asked, the gleeful tone clearly indicating she wouldn't mind if he was.

"Of course not. Just curious as to what you're doing here when I thought you were flying back to New York."

If she didn't take her hand off his ass, he was going to lose it. Those little strokes were driving him nuts, making the dingy elevator stifling, and his mouth dry, hands itching to touch her.

He'd thought he wouldn't ever see her again and here she was. In the flesh. Alone with him. Touching him.

"Would you believe I didn't want to leave you?" Her hand stopped moving, but still rested on his backside.

He forced himself to relax certain muscles, which were clenched tight. "Not really, no."

"It's true," she insisted, turning towards him, the bag of food between them. "Don't I even get a hello kiss?"

Given his suspicions about her motives, it wouldn't be in his best interest, but he ached to anyway. "If I kiss you now, I'm not going to stop," he told her, keeping his hands resolutely to himself, wishing he had the willpower to take a step back away from her. He could smell her, a light lotion and shampoo scent.

"Would that be such a bad thing?" Reese went on her tiptoes and brushed her mouth over his.

That soft feathery touch that brought her breasts against his chest and her hair sliding across his shoulder did away with any fight he had thought to put up.

"Reese," he breathed, leaning forward to nip her bottom lip, to draw her to him, his hand possessively around her waist.

She maneuvered her hand from his ass to his shoulder, gripping the lapel of his suit. "Ugly suit," she murmured between kisses.

"Thanks." Derek took the bag of food, shifting it behind her back so that he could feel her breasts more fully, could twist and pinch her nipple through her silky thin shirt and lace bra.

Their kisses went deeper, harder, his temperature spiking and his cock throbbing. Reese moaned.

Derek walked her back, one step, two. He wanted up her skirt, wanted to glide his hands along her thighs and feel her tremble with anticipation. His mouth met hers again and again, wet and frenzied and hot, their teeth knocking together and fabric rustling as their bodies crushed together.

The elevator door swung open. Derek was only vaguely aware of the fact until he heard someone clear his throat.

Then he jumped back from Reese like he'd been caught with his hand in the cookie jar. Or up a woman's skirt.

Turning around, he squeezed Reese's hand and prepared to drag her off, avoiding meeting the eyes of whoever was waiting in front of them.

"Knight."

Shit. Derek broke his plan not to look and snapped his head up, staring in horror at his boss.

"Good to see you're hard at work," Nordstrom said, voice dripping with sarcasm.

His hard-on shriveled up and died. Nordstrom was the most effective birth control around. Nobody could possibly think about sex with him in the room.

"It's my lunch hour, sir."

Derek pulled Reese off the elevator and stood aside to let Nordstrom on. The older man just gazed at him without blinking. "Aren't you going to introduce me to your girlfriend?"

And let Reese open her mouth? Hell, no.

Too late.

She already was.

Reese said, "Oh, I'm not his girlfriend. We've just been having sex."

Derek had a heart attack. Or at least that's what it felt like when his chest spasmed in pained shock.

There was an eternal moment of frozen silence, then Nordstrom laughed, a dry, rusty, hacking laugh that sounded like a lawn mower starting up. Derek stared at his boss in amazement. No one had ever heard Nordstrom laugh. The other agents had all decided that since he was a robot, he was incapable of feeling human emotion.

A laugh was downright amazing.

And Reese had caused it. It figured.

"That's funny." Nordstrom shook his head, still chuckling as Reese smiled widely back at him.

Derek winced as Nordstrom clapped him on the shoulder. "Hang on to this one, Knight. Not every woman can make you laugh."

With those words of wisdom Nordstrom got on the elevator and the door swung shut. Reese was looking around curiously. Derek was standing still, his ulcer sending forth a slew of angry stomach acids.

"Where's your office?" she asked, taking the bag of food back from him. "You're going to spill this. You can't hold it crooked like that."

"Down the hall. Fifth cubicle on the left." Derek started walking, intent on getting Reese fed and out of the building so his ulcer could settle down.

"Is it private?" She winked at him. "We could finish what we started in the elevator."

He was too horrified from the close encounter with Nordstrom to feel even remotely turned on. "No, it's not private."

Reese licked her lips, her hips swinging seductively as she walked in her high heels. "Even better."

Okay, he was turned on again.

But as they walked into his cubicle, he knew he had to establish a few facts first before he indulged further in Reese's body. Reese started pulling out little Styrofoam bowls and setting them on his desk, glancing around his three stark white walls.

"Don't you have any pictures or anything to hang up? This place is depressing."

He wasn't the kind of guy to tape Dilbert cartoons clipped from the paper up onto his cubicle wall. If he had a wife and kids, he would put their pictures on his desk, but since he didn't, the desk was empty. What was he going to put a picture of there? His mother?

"Reese. Tell me why you didn't go back to New York." He leaned against the wall and pinned her with his best investigative stare. The I-know-you-know-something stare.

She sighed as she pried the lid off a bowl and stuck a plastic spoon in the soup. "Sit down and eat your soup and I'll tell you everything. I'll bare my soul and talk about my dreams and aspirations."

"No need to be soul-baring." Derek reached for the bowl and picked up the soup and sniffed. Potato. He took a bite. "Just explain to me what's going on."

"Okay, here's the deal." Reese leaned against his desk, ripping open a pack of crackers. "I lied to my boss, told him I had the flu. I E-mailed in the wedding story so it could go in the Wednesday social section. And I stayed because I need to write this story, and I want to be here when it breaks." Her words were laced with stubborn determination. "I need you to talk to me, tell me when you think it's possible you can get an arrest."

Derek glanced around, fighting the urge to clap his hand over her mouth. "Shh. We're in the middle of the office, Reese. Jesus."

"What? Are we being recorded or something?" Reese snorted, but damn if she didn't look a little excited by the prospect. She dumped her crumbled crackers in her soup and looked around his cubicle, like she expected to see microphones jutting out from the file cabinet.

"Listen." Derek set his soup back down on the desk, his appetite gone. "Why don't we make plans for tonight? We'll talk all you want, somewhere where there aren't half a dozen agents milling around all the time. Okay?"

Reese flipped her spoon over and licked it clean, slowly. "Can we do . . . other things, too?"

Given that gleam in her eye, he knew exactly what other things she was talking about. Making a mental note to stop at the drugstore for those long overdue condoms, Derek nodded. "Whatever you want."

"Mmm. Carte blanche. I like it." She tapped the clean plastic spoon on her bottom lip. "I guess we should meet at my hotel again, then. How about seven?"

"Fine." That gave him half a day to pretend he was actually getting some work done.

She smiled. "Great. Now eat your soup like a good little boy and maybe I'll let you have some dessert."

Chapter Eleven

Reese contemplated opening the door for Knight naked, but then nixed the idea. She really did need to get him talking about Delco and how far along the case was. The whole naked thing would probably distract him.

Her other clothing options weren't all that palatable. She had her suit, which she'd taken off the minute she'd gotten back to her room after lunch. She and panty hose didn't get along.

There was her cocktail dress from the wedding. But how stupid would that look sitting around in her hotel room? Very stupid, she decided.

There was a pair of pajama pants she had packed for downtimes, along with a white tank top to wear with it. They weren't flannel and three sizes too big like she'd told Knight the first night she'd met him, but they were loose fitting gray cotton. Not at all sexy, but comfortable. And if she wore the tank with no bra, that should counter the sex-less effect of the shapeless bottoms.

Pulling the pants on, she rolled her eyes, singing along with the music of a car commercial playing on the TV. Knight was making her go to a lot of work. Maybe sex wasn't worth all this effort. Then she remembered Knight's tongue pushing inside her while she closed her mouth over him, and her body twitched in response.

Oh, yeah, sex with Knight would be worth a little clothing crisis.

The knock came as she was pulling on the tank top. "Coming!"

She ran to the door and promised herself she would not leap into his arms, under any circumstances. Business first, then pleasure. Though he looked very delicious, all folded arms, and well-worn jeans, he appeared to have the same idea.

Without even a greeting, he strolled into the room and said, "Okay, lay your cards on the table, Reese. What the hell do you want from me with the Delco case?"

She matched his brisk tone. "I want to know how close you are to an arrest."

"I can't tell you that."

"Don't give me specifics. Just give me vague. Tell me what's going on in hypotheticals." Why was he making this so hard?

He didn't say anything for a minute. Then he sighed. "Here's the thing. To make an arrest in a price-fixing case you need to have irrefutable proof, usually a tape recording, of executives from the companies involved actually agreeing on a fixed price and on production volumes from each company." He stopped in front of the bed and yanked his black fleece sweatshirt off over his head.

Trying to ignore the muscles and the gun in its holster, Reese said, "And you don't have an agreement yet?"

"I can't answer that."

"I'll take that as a yes. So what's the problem? You get your witness to tape their meetings. How hard could that be?"

"You have no idea of the legalities involved. We can only tape if a consenting person is present, and our guy can't be at all the meetings. And he's nervous, so we haven't approached him about being wired yet." Knight ran his fingers through his hair. "Look, get your story ready based on what you've read in the files. Go back to New York. When things break, I'll call you. That's all I can promise. I can't tell you anything about the investigation right now."

"Can you tell me who the cooperating witness is?"

"No."

"Can you tell me which executives are involved in the price-fixing?"

"No."

Reese groaned in frustration. She applauded his ethics for his job, but it only made it all that much harder for her to do hers. Given what she'd seen in the notes the witness had taken of several meetings, Ashton Chatterton was more than aware of the price-fixing scheme. He was ordering it, he was negotiating with the competitors for volume, he was sending his top executives when he wasn't present at meetings.

An idea was forming. "I can help you. If you can't get your witness to tape, I could do it."

Knight blanched in horror.

Reese hastened to reassure him. "No, I mean, I could get a job at Delco as an executive assistant or something. Then I could tape their meetings."

Knight undid his gun holster and tossed it on the dresser. "You've lost your mind. Why would Delco hire you? It would take weeks to go through the whole resume/interview process, and then you'd wind up as secretary to some dweeb in accounting or something. They don't give new inexperienced secretaries to the big boss. And," his finger went up to tick off the point, "they wouldn't talk about price-fixing while you're serving their coffee."

Clearly, they were not going to agree on this. Reese thought he was underestimating her considerable powers of persuasion. She said, "You're very negative. And cranky tonight."

He walked towards her, stalking, hands fisted at his sides. "Because you insist on poking your pretty little nose into this case, jeopardizing a six-month-long investigation. And you're talking about it again, when all I want to do is lay you flat on that bed and sink into you."

As Reese tried to think of something to say besides *take me*, Knight reached into his back pocket and emerged with a row of three condoms.

Oh, yeah. Desire hit her below her belly, hard, heavy, aching want. Without her brain even being involved, she tugged at the waistband of her pajama pants and let them drop to the carpet.

His nostrils flared.

"You went to the store." Smart man.

"On my way home from work," he agreed, taking another step towards her.

The room was hot and the backs of her knees were sweating. But her inner thighs were burning, wet liquid heat rushing in anticipation, dampening her panties.

Knight's pager beeped.

Reese froze in the act of tearing her tank top off.

Knight swore. "Reese . . . shit, I've got to go. My witness needs to talk to me."

She pulled her top back down to cover her breasts and took a shuddering breath to regain her sanity. Knight must be as rattled as she was, since she couldn't imagine he would have offered info about his witness otherwise.

He was strapping his gun back on, the condoms back in his pocket. "Can I come back when I'm done?"

She should tell him no. Who did he think she was? Some sex slave, always available to him? She wasn't going to just hang around waiting for him to grace her with his presence.

Except she couldn't worry about her affronted dignity when she was this aroused. If he didn't come back, she was going to suffer through a long and lonely night. Besides, she had every intention of following him to find out who his witness was.

It only seemed right that after that little bit of deception, she should sleep with him.

Aware that something sounded a little strange about that whole line of reasoning, nonetheless she said, "Yes. You can come back."

He leaned towards her like he was going to kiss her, then jerked back at the last second. Looking uncomfortable, he gave her arm an awkward pat. "I'll see you later, then."

"Bye." Reese smiled and waved, pulling her pants back on.

The minute the door closed behind him, she dove for her purse and shoes. Except she couldn't exactly wear brown pumps with pajama pants. Afraid she'd lose him, Reese shoved on her fuzzy white slippers, grabbed the sweatshirt Knight had left on her bed and stepped into the hall, peeking first to make sure he'd gotten on the elevator already.

Reese sprinted for the stairs. By the first floor her thighs were burning, her lungs collapsing, and her slippers sliding off. But when she burst into the lobby, sucking air like a vacuum, she saw Knight step through the doors to the hotel parking garage.

In another minute she was in her Ford Taurus rental car, following Knight as closely as she could without risking him noticing. If he discovered her, she didn't think it would be pretty. Likely it would involve handcuffs. Not part of a fun-sex-game handcuffs. But you're-heading-for-the-slammer handcuffs.

Twice she worried that he had spotted her, given the sharp lane changes he made, but he never stopped and he never seemed to glance in his rearview mirror.

She concluded he was simply a lousy driver, allergic to his turn signal. Twenty minutes later he pulled into the parking lot of a Holiday Inn in a modest neighborhood. Knight got out of his car, walked over to a black Toyota Avalon, and got in on the passenger side.

Derek debated making a quick detour to strangle Reese first, but decided he really wanted to get this Delco case indicted before he was jailed for murder.

Once his blood had redistributed to his brain from his cock, Derek had known almost immediately Reese was following him. But after two efforts to lose her, where she had displayed a frightening ability to weave in and out of high-speed traffic, he had decided it was better just to let her follow him.

The woman was nuts enough to get herself plowed over by a semi trying to keep up with him, and he really didn't like the idea of her flat as a pancake on the highway.

If she stayed in her car, parked three spots away, everything would be fine. Reese was reckless, but she wasn't stupid. She would know to stay out of sight.

"Hi, Stan," Derek said when he had closed the car door and looked over at his CW.

"Hey. Hey there, Derek. How are you?"

Derek took the opening, studying Stan. The man looked as he always did, thin, pale, dressed in an expensive suit, his glasses slipping a little down his nose. He fidgeted, as was his usual custom, drumming his thumbs on the steering wheel, a thin sheen of sweat on his upper lip.

"Well, Stan, I'm not so great. My boss is getting antsy. You've been helping us out for months, now, and that's great, but the antitrust lawyers say we don't have enough."

Markson sputtered. "But I gave you everything! I risked getting caught and gave you all the patents, all the agreements, all the numbers. I have E-mails from Chatterton. I've risked my job. I have a wife and two kids, Derek. What more do you guys want?"

Derek tried to soothe him. "I know, I know. And you've done great. But it's still your word, and your word won't hold up in court. We need tapes, Stan."

Stan's eyes darted around nervously. "I can't do that. I just can't. These are my coworkers."

"Who are doing something illegal, that affects hundreds of thousands of people every day by charging them more for drugs than they should be paying." Derek kept his voice low, calm, not wanting to spook Stan.

"Explain to me again why you need the tapes."

Derek tried not to sigh. They had been over this dozens of times. Leaning against the car door, he settled in for a long, persuasive chat with his cooperating witness who wasn't being very cooperative these days.

Reese tried not to fall asleep. This was about as exciting as watching grass grow. Knight had been in that car jabbering for over an hour.

She couldn't even see the witness, and now that she'd rushed to get herself here, it occurred to her that seeing the guy wasn't going to do her a damn bit of good. She still didn't know his name.

What a great investigative reporter she had turned out to be. She couldn't investigate her way out of a paper bag.

Feeling grumpy and unsure of what to do, she stared at a flower bed attempting to camouflage the Dumpster. The marigolds and petunias were hanging tough despite the chilly fall nights, and the leaves on the burning bushes were just starting to turn red.

Wondering how her single green plant was doing without water in her apartment back in New York, she wasn't paying the least bit of attention to Knight in the black car.

When her passenger door suddenly jerked open, she jumped, hitting her head on the ceiling of the rental car. Clutching her chest with one hand, she fumbled for the doorknob, ready to throw herself out into the night and escape the intruder.

"You know, if you're going to follow me, you should at least *try* to be discreet."

She knew that voice. Crap, Knight had caught her. Swallowing the scream in her throat that she'd been about to unleash, she turned to see Knight climbing in beside her.

"Oh, hi," she managed to choke out. "Fancy meeting you here."

Dragging in a huge breath, she whacked his arm. "Yeesh,

you scared me! I've probably got half a dozen gray hairs now."

He stared at her without blinking, running his eyes over her chest, taking in her tank top and PJ pants. His head went slowly back and forth. "My God, I do not understand how I can feel this way."

There were so many ways that could go, she decided to nudge him in the right direction. "Wowed by my beauty?"

He didn't take the bait. "You could cost me my job, you could compromise a federal investigation, you're reckless and unpredictable, yet when I look at you, all I can think is how much I want you."

"It's a gift," she joked, feeling just a little embarrassed at her foiled stakeout. Not one of her better ideas.

There was no answer but the sound of his ragged breathing and her nervous gulping breaths. Her nipples were hardening in her tank top, brought about by his steady, probing stare. Maybe he had mind-control powers and he had ordered her nipples to bead.

She liked that better than the idea that one glance from him and her insides were lusty oatmeal mush.

"Ever done it in a car?" he asked, pulling the condoms out of his pocket and tossing them up onto the dash.

Sam Hill, was he serious? "Just one failed attempt senior year. We couldn't quite figure out the physics involved."

Patting his thighs, he said in a coaxing voice, "Come sit on my lap."

He was serious.

"You know, Knight, we're in a hotel parking lot. It's barely even dark out and there's a huge streetlight shining right on us."

"Chicken," he taunted.

Oh, like that was going to work. She was way too mature for that kind of tactic. Sort of. Reese clenched her fists and tried not to give in. They could not have sex in a car in a parking lot.

"No, we're not doing this."

Knight unzipped his jeans.

Mama. Like she could resist that blatant invitation.

Pulling her legs up, she scooted over across the gearshift, squeezing her side against him in the quarter inch space he'd left her.

"Move over."

"No, I want you to get on my lap."

"I was going to take my pants off first." Reaching down, she grabbed her slippers and tossed them on the driver's seat.

"Nice slippers," Knight said, his lip twitching.

"I was in a hurry." Reese was wiggling against Knight, trying to shove him over with her hip, about to push down her pants.

A knock on the window made her scream. "Aah!" Heart pounding, eternally grateful she hadn't dropped her drawers yet, she turned to see who it was.

Knight's big head was blocking her view.

"Derek? Is that you?"

"Shit." Knight cursed, trying to get the window to go down. "Reese, turn the car back on, the window won't open."

She did, all while craning her neck to get a glimpse of the person standing outside. She strongly suspected this was the cooperating witness, and she wanted a good look at him.

After Knight sent the window down, he said in a low voice, "What is it, Stan? Everything okay?"

Stan. Reese ran through the list of names she'd seen in the Delco documents. Stan something-or-other, a chemist in charge of the new products division. Bingo.

"Who's with you?" The man was upset, jumpy.

Knight zipped his pants back up. "It's just my girlfriend. Let me step outside the car."

It figured. He was the picture of discretion when it came to his work. But this time she could forgive him because she was too busy being preoccupied with his wording. Girlfriend. He had said girlfriend. *It's just my girlfriend.*

She had no idea how she felt about that.

There was a lot of time to think about it, since Knight stood over by the Dumpster for fifteen minutes talking. Yet she couldn't come to any sort of conclusion. Except that she liked Knight. She really liked their sexual by-play.

But that didn't mean they could or should be girlfriend/ boyfriend. She lived a thousand miles from him. Besides, Knight struck her as the kind of guy who'd want a domestic wife, cooking and cleaning and never complaining about his weird hours.

She was too selfish for that.

Without a female role model growing up, she had never learned the art of cooking. Some men cooked. Her father hadn't. The way Reese had learned to sustain herself was by microwaving things that came out of boxes in her freezer.

Knight probably wanted a wife who would bake him chocolate chip cookies. She wasn't baking anybody chocolate chip cookies. That's what the bakery across the street from her apartment was for.

Of course, Knight had probably just used the most plausible explanation for her presence. They had been sitting just about on top of each other. The use of the word girlfriend was probably just to reassure the witness.

Probably she needed to get a goddamn grip.

Derek couldn't believe what he was hearing. After months of indecisiveness and stubborn refusal, Stan had agreed to wear the wire to tape price-fixing meetings at Delco with Stanfield Laboratories.

This was it. A couple of good tapes and they could finally hand this case over to the lawyers.

Trying to stay calm and not alarm Markson, Derek said, "This is great news, Stan. I know you'll be glad you've decided to cooperate. Why don't you meet me here at the hotel again in the morning and we'll have all the equipment."

"Equipment? Isn't it just a tape recorder?" Stan was the

most nervous Derek had ever seen him, pacing back and forth behind the Dumpster, running his hands through his thin hair over and over.

"It's a little more high-tech than that. It's a recorder worn on your back, that doesn't need batteries and doesn't need to be turned on or off by you. It's got some kind of microchip."

Stan perked up. "Oh, okay." He laughed nervously. "Like a spy or something."

"Yep." Derek chuckled with him. "So I'll see you here at nine A.M. tomorrow? I'll call you to let you know which room I'll be in."

"Okay." Stan took a deep breath and nodded.

Derek took his hand and shook it, clapping Stan on the arm in reassurance. "You'll do great. Thanks."

After Stan had gotten back into his car and pulled out of the parking lot, Derek walked back to Reese's car, triumph surging through him.

They weren't there yet, but this was a huge step forward. Nordstrom was going to be thrilled.

Derek wanted to celebrate. The best way he could think to do that was with Reese naked in his arms.

He strolled up to the window and leaned in, noting it was still open. He had counted on that, figuring Reese would try to listen, which was why he'd taken Markson behind the Dumpster fifteen feet away. She would need elephant ears to hear what they'd been talking about.

Then again, he wouldn't put anything past her.

"Well, you're grinning like the village idiot," she said, her leg propped on the dash, her slipper tapping to the beat of the radio. "Things go well?"

"Yep."

"Good for you. Now I'm leaving, before I slip into a coma. Thanks for one of the most boring nights of my life." She dropped her leg and started shimmying over to the driver's side.

Derek slid his hand along her bare shoulder. "You followed me, remember? I left you back in a nice cozy hotel room."

"Obviously not one of my better ideas." She paused halfway across the gearshift.

"No, definitely not." He squeezed her arm lightly. "Can I follow you back?"

He was asking out of politeness, but her answer was irrelevant. He was going to go back to Reese's room and finally get to have all of her, every luscious inch, inside and out.

Not that he expected Reese to say no. She had it for him just as bad as he had it for her. They couldn't be together five minutes without passion flaring between them. And Reese had a little trouble keeping her hands off his ass, he'd noticed.

Not that he minded. It only added to his desire. As did the lusty gleam in her eye right now. Her teeth nibbled at her bottom lip, tugging, pulling, making him want to push hers aside and replace them with his own teeth.

He played with the strap on her top, flipping it until it fell down her arm, giving him a flash of creamy flesh above her breast. If he were a little closer, he would lean forward and suck hard right there, marking her, tasting her until his mouth left a red stain on her flesh.

But he was still half in the window and she was too far away.

"If you *don't* follow me to my room, I'll hunt you down and kill you," Reese said.

He loved a woman who knew what she wanted.

Especially when what she wanted was him.

Chapter Twelve

Reese didn't even mind the humiliation of having to follow Knight back to her hotel. She had no clue where she was since the only thing she'd been paying attention to on the drive over was keeping Knight in her sight. She supposed if she had actually managed to stay undetected, she would have just called Map-Star to get herself back.

The whole night was a disastrous waste of time. Knight was right, she could have just been waiting for him at the hotel, chips from the minibar in her hand while she watched a movie.

But at least he wasn't mad at her.

There wasn't going to be any information forthcoming from him on the Delco investigation, but she still thought it was worth it to stick around for a day or two. One simple phone call to Ashton Chatterton wouldn't hurt, and she wouldn't tell Knight about it unless she was successful.

Meanwhile, tonight was knocking boots time. Or knocking slippers, in her case.

Knight waited for her in the parking garage, hands in his jeans pockets. She hitched her purse over her shoulder and tried to sail past him, acting like she always went out in her pajamas and slippers.

The elegant act was hard to accomplish when she had to shuffle to keep from stepping out of her slip-on slippers.

Knight rubbed his head like he was in pain. "So are we agreed that in the future you should not attempt to follow me for any reason?"

"Well, I can't make any guarantees," she said airily, then squawked when her slipper stayed behind and her foot kept going, landing on the filthy dirty concrete of the garage floor.

"Come here, Cinderella." Knight bent over and picked up her foot, jamming her slipper back on.

His hair was falling in his eyes and she watched him in amusement. "You don't look like a prince."

It was a joke, but he didn't laugh.

He looked up at her and said, "If you're looking for a prince, you'd better start looking somewhere else. I'm more like the village peasant."

He was no brawny potato farmer. "No, you're the castle guard, ready to defend to the death. After all, your name is Knight."

Now he did laugh, his hand stroking her ankle. "And you're the princess who has an affair with the guard?"

Yeah, right. She would be an embarrassment to her kingdom. "No, I'm more like the not-so-buxom maid who has an affair with the guard."

"And the guard is enjoying it a whole hell of a lot." Knight's hand roamed up her calf, under her pant leg, raising goose bumps on her skin.

That look on his face was wicked, amused, full of sexy intent, and she felt her nipples respond, her breath hitch, her thighs ache.

It was unbelievable but true. Knight could turn her on in a parking garage. A parking lot had been bad enough, but a parking garage? Where the smell of exhaust fumes clung in the air and the temperature resembled that of a cave.

She was about to protest, make a sarcastic remark about them already having a room, when Knight leaned forward and pressed his lips right on her. Just between her thighs, dead center over her clitoris, pressing her panties against her restless body, and sending his hot breath searing through the thin cotton of her PJ pants.

"Upstairs. Now," she croaked.

"Gladly." Knight stood and tugged her hand towards the lobby door, while she trailed behind in a boneless fog.

This time when they got upstairs there were no games, no chasing, no teasing. Knight was in an aggressive mood, taking the key card from her fumbling fingers and opening the door.

He tossed the key in the direction of the dresser, not stopping to pick it up when it fell on the floor.

Then his hands were on her, everywhere, sliding, demanding, rough and pushy hands that wanted her, that stroked and squeezed until she was crying out. He had her tank top up, her pants half down, all while covering her mouth with deep penetrating kisses.

She lost her grip on her purse and it landed on his foot. He didn't notice or didn't care, and broke the kiss to suck hard on her nipple, leaving her gasping and tugging at his head.

Then he shifted his mouth and bit her, a light nip on the tender flesh of her breast, his teeth skimming over her before sinking in, and she called out some garbled illogical word that could have passed for Klingon.

While his mouth went to her nipples, shifting back and forth from one to the other, his hands worked her pants down to her knees, along with her panties. A finger slid inside her and she clung to him, mindless with need, grateful for the wall behind her that was holding her up.

Reese heard the sound of his zipper going down, saw him give a shove at his jeans. She rolled her head back as he kissed her on the mouth again, sucking her bottom lip. Rough hands gripped her cheeks, forcing her eyes open.

"God, I want you so much."

"I want you, too." Like she'd never wanted anything. Not even a byline in the *New York Times*. Right then, she wanted nothing but him, to feel his hands and mouth on her, to come at his direction, to shudder onto his fingers and to taste his tongue with hers.

Knight had pulled a condom from his pocket, had torn it open viciously and was rolling it on. Reese couldn't move, couldn't draw her eyes away from the sight of his bulging erection, throbbing and rocking as he put on the condom.

Yes, she thought. *I want that.*

When he was ready, Knight moved his hands over her belly, up to her breasts, brushing each nipple, his tongue teasing along her bottom lip. His cock was nowhere near her and she wanted him to nudge, to bump and grind and tease her swollen clitoris, but when she rocked forward he evaded her hips and clenching thighs.

"Knight."

Burying his hands in her hair, he met her gaze and said, "You're gorgeous."

Then without warning, he pushed forward hard and sank into her, all the way to the hilt, ripping the air out of her lungs and shattering her with pleasure. She came in little jerks of desire, her inner muscles gripping him as he filled her completely.

She felt wonderfully full, slick, engorged with him, his chest pressing against her breasts, her bursts of pleasure like ripples on a pond, rolling out of her.

As she came back down, he pulled out a little and thrust again, lengthening her orgasm and dragging another moan out of her. There was no time to recover, no time to sink against the wall and relax in stillness.

Knight was moving, hard, fast, thrusting so deep that she was lifting off her feet with each entry, and she had to hold onto his shoulders for support. He gripped her waist, pulling her hips forward to meet his, their skin slapping together and heat building inside her all over again.

Derek was lost, out of control, his excitement and pleasure

so intense he was nearly in pain. Reese's inner muscles clung to him, quivering, and she fit tightly around his cock, her body still slick with desire.

He had meant to wait, to take it slow. To lead her through several rounds of foreplay before sinking into her soft and slow on the bed. But the minute he had had her alone, he couldn't stop himself. He had waited too long, wanted her too much, and he had taken her, right there four steps from the door, on the wall next to the closet.

There should be regret, he should stop and do this right, but it felt too good to stop. Her orgasm had surprised him, pushed him on, to plunge deeper inside her and to sink his hands into her satin hair, cover her mouth with sliding, gasping kisses.

Never had sex felt like this, this total urgent oblivion, where nothing mattered but Reese and him, joined together in mutual pleasure. That pleasure built, swelled, rocked through him until it spilled over the edges, bursting from him along with a throaty groan.

"Reese." He dropped his head onto her delicate shoulder and closed his eyes as he shuddered into her, the sensation reverberating throughout his body.

A little laugh tickled across his ear, and he became aware of her thumbs trailing across his shoulders.

"Jesus, I'm sorry. That wasn't even five minutes, was it?" For all his bragging, he was no better than the boy who'd taken her virginity.

"It's all about quality, not quantity," she murmured, her lips brushing against the scratchiness of his chin.

Derek tried to push himself back a little, aware he was pressing her against the wall like a trash compacter. He buried his nose in her hair, breathing in that fresh, floral smell of her shampoo.

For thirty seconds he refrained from asking. Then he couldn't help himself. "So how was the quality?"

God, what a dork thing to ask. Did he need her reassurance so much? A pat on the back, an A on his report card, an Excellent sticker slapped on his dick?

It would serve him right if she teased the hell out of him or refused to answer.

But she just sighed, a low, deep sigh of satisfaction, her arms wrapping around his neck. "Mmmm. I've got no complaints."

Well, that wasn't too bad, then.

He forced himself to stop leaning on her, straightening up. The sudden sharp pain in his knee caught him off guard, and he winced before he could hide it.

"What's the matter?"

"Nothing, just a twinge." Annoyed, he tried to bend his knee a little without her noticing. Reese's eyes were half closed, so maybe he could manage to loosen it up without drawing attention to himself.

That's all he wanted was for Reese to think he couldn't even handle sex without crippling himself. He was older than her, but he wasn't *old.*

What he didn't count on was Reese displaying any sort of nurturing instincts. After hitching his pants back up onto his hips, he walked slowly to sit down on the bed where he could rid himself of the cumbersome jeans. Reese hovered over him making distress noises.

"You're limping!" she accused.

"No, it's called walking with my damn pants undone and about to fall off."

He noticed she had pulled her own pants back up and covered her breasts with her tank. He had to fix that immediately. There was no way in hell he was finished with her.

"You sit down and rest your knee. I'll get rid of the condom." Hair falling over her face, Reese reached out.

Derek grabbed her hands before they could close over him. "No! Hell, no." He was not letting her touch his used condom. God, how humiliating was that?

"Don't be a baby," she scolded.

"I'm not a baby." But before he let go of her hand, he yanked the condom off with his other hand, biting his lip when it snapped at the end with a fierce sting. There. Let's see her get it now.

Shaking her head at him like she'd seen right through him, she said, "Let's take your pants off." A second later she was on her knees and tugging at his pants.

"Now you're talking." Though it felt suspiciously like he was five and being undressed for an early bedtime.

"Then I'll call 911."

"What?" He dropped his feet flat on the floor, preventing her from removing his pants any further. Had she lost her mind?

"Knight, if you reinjured yourself, you shouldn't fool around with that."

"It twinged. How is that reinjury?" Derek wanted to pull her into his lap and show her how *not* injured he was, but he was still holding the freaking condom.

"I don't know! You could have yanked, or pulled, or torn something. What do I look like? Nurse Hampton?"

That was more like the Reese he knew. Not this weird let-me-take-your-temperature-with-my-lips Reese.

"Nothing's wrong with it that a little sex won't cure."

Reese sat back on her haunches, still clutching the bottoms of his pants. She seemed to be debating her next move, so he let go of the condom, and pulled his shirt off, balling it up and giving it a good throw towards the TV.

Thinking about sinking back into her welcoming body, Derek felt his semi-hard erection swelling back up to full capacity.

Reese noticed too. She swallowed hard, her eyes widening. "Are you sure you're alright?"

This time when she tugged on his jeans, he let her strip them off him until he was naked, and aroused all over again.

"I'd be even better if you sat on my lap."

Reese didn't hesitate, but stood up and dropped her pajama pants to the floor, pushing off her panties at the same time. "If I'm on top, then you'll technically be resting then, right?"

"I won't exert myself at all," he promised, mouth dry in anticipation.

"Can I trust you?" she said on a slow smile.

"If it hurts, I'll stop." Her belly was tantalizingly close and he reached out with his tongue and dipped into her belly button.

"Where are the condoms?"

"Pocket of my jeans." He nuzzled her skin, loving the way she tasted, fruity and floral and slightly sweaty, the tangy scent of her desire filling his nostrils.

Shoving the tank top out of the way, he kissed along her flesh, sucking on her hipbone, holding onto her smooth firm ass.

After several seconds of exploration and Reese breathing hard, she pulled back and retrieved another condom. Derek let her put it on him, tugging at a strand of her hair with his lips as it cascaded in front of him.

"It's really nice of you to offer to let me take it easy."

"I'm a feminist," she said, wrapping her legs over his thighs. "Men shouldn't have to do all the work."

"How liberated of you." Derek spanned his hands over her waist, enjoying the contrast of his large, ruddy hands against her soft pinky-pale skin, dipping into an hourglass shape at her narrow waist.

Reese's soft opening pushed down on his cock, before retreating. "Equal opportunity orgasms, that's my motto."

"It's a good one," he ground out, sweat breaking out all over him as she teased, easing down again.

When she let her feet leave the floor, she sank down on him, and they both moaned. He wasn't even fully sheathed inside her yet and he wanted to come again. Reese was stretched tight from the position, her breasts close enough for him to lean over and suckle, her hands digging into his shoulders.

She moved up, then down, Derek watching her narrow hips picking up speed as she found her rhythm, her gasps of pleasure intensifying his own. His fascination with her grew with each stroke, his deep yearning needing, pulsing and multiplying until he could no longer sit still.

The hard thrust sent her pitching up, her cry of ecstasy making him break out into a sweat, his teeth clenched. He wanted to own her in pleasure, to push her into desperate mindless passion that no other man had given her.

With one hand he gripped her smooth ass, using it as leverage as he pumped into her. Then with the other, he found his way down between their merging bodies and ran his finger across her engorged clitoris.

"Dammit," she breathed into his ear on a pause, a still moment of anticipation before she came, jerking up, nearly toppling off him as her body convulsed with passion.

Derek held her in place, continuing his thrusts, enjoying the pulses of her inner muscles on him, the wild digging of her nails into his shoulders and the gasps she gave.

"Knight," she breathed, head lolling back. "You rock."

It was such a Reese thing to say, but it turned him on even more, which he wouldn't have thought possible. She made him feel like no guy had ever fucked her quite so good, and it was that surge of triumph that sent him groaning through his own orgasm.

And it was the smile on Reese's face, that pleased, seductive, I-did-that-to-you smile that made him swear in agonized ecstasy, his mouth finding her nipple and sucking hard.

As his body relaxed, he moved his wet lips off her and pressed a worshipful kiss on her shoulder. She was amazing. Absolutely amazing.

"You moved," she accused.

"Oops." His knee felt fine. And the rest of him felt like

Superman on a beach vacation after saving the world. Powerful, relaxed, and damn satisfied.

Reese loved watching Knight's face. Most of the time, he had a cop poker face, sort of tight and drawn, hiding, revealing nothing but what he wanted to in his own sweet time.

But now, even more so than the two previous nights, he was relaxed, wide open to her and looking smug and satisfied. It made her feel sexy, feminine, triumphant. She'd put that look on his face.

They were so relaxed, breathing against one another, boneless, that neither moved. Reese rested her head alongside his, wrapping her hands around his neck, rubbing her lips against his rough chin.

He was still inside her, and if she had more energy she didn't think it would take much to arouse her all over again. His hands still held below the small of her back, a protective gesture to keep her from pitching to the floor.

Then her stomach growled, shattering the comfortable silence of the room. Knight laughed, a deep low chuckle.

Reese sat up. "It's time for my nine o'clock feeding."

Knight shifted, pulling out of her. With a sigh, Reese let go of him and lay on the bed next to him, curling up on her side.

"You're not serious, are you?" Knight pulled off the condom and stood up.

She watched him walk to the bathroom, enjoying the view of his fine behind, feeling the inexplicable urge to land her hand on it with a resounding smack.

Geez, she was turning into a dominatrix.

"Yes, I'm serious. I think I'll order more chicken wings. Want some?"

Scooping his briefs off the floor, he said, "So you're ready to call 911 about my knee, but you'll kill me with chicken wings?"

He had a point. "So order a salad or something."

The bathroom door slammed shut on a grunt.

Reese flopped back onto the bed, staring at the white speck-
led ceiling trying to remember exactly why she was in Chicago
in the first place. Three days ago she had stepped onto a plane,
ticked off that she'd drawn the short straw and the lousy assignment yet again.

Thanking the Fates that Knight's witness had put the documents in the wrong rental car, she did a quick assessment of
her life back in New York.

Crappy job. Lousy apartment. Zero sex life.

Yet here, for the last seventy-two hours she had been chasing a major story, eating room service, and having hands-
down the best sex of her entire existence on earth. Going
home right now seemed about as fun as an extra forty pounds
suddenly adhering to her ass and thighs.

That wasn't fun. This was fun.

The decision wasn't all that hard to make. By the time
Knight reemerged, wearing his briefs and running his fingers
through his hair, she had formulated a plan.

Sitting up, she reached for her pajama pants, forgoing the
panties. "So do you want a salad?"

His sigh was heartfelt. "Okay."

Not seeing her tank top, she headed for the phone without
it. "Don't sound so enthusiastic about it."

Knight stopped dragging his jeans on to stare at her.
"Would you get excited about rabbit food? I don't see you
ordering a big old bowl of water and roughage."

With good reason. Still, she took pity on the guy. It must
really suck to suffer every time you ate something that tasted
good.

"You want me to eat a salad, too? I can eat a salad." As
long as it was followed by a slab of cheesecake.

"You're not going to eat a salad."

"Yes, I am." Every last crouton.

"Bullshit."

Picking up the phone, Reese dialed room service. "Yes, I'd
like two house salads with ranch dressing and a piece of

cheesecake." Then she panicked. After all that lettuce, she was going to need something to purge it from her system. "And two Bud Lights and a slice of carrot cake. Thank you."

Knight was smirking. "Couldn't do it, could you?"

"I can't help it. The only thing green I ever ate growing up was Jell-O."

He shook his head. "And I can't believe you just ordered room service topless."

She glanced down at her bare breasts. "It's not like he could see me. And you're topless, too."

"That's a little different, Reese." He climbed onto the bed, stalking towards her, on his knees like a lion towards his prey. "Not that I mind. Trust me, I do not mind."

Before he could grab, kiss her, and touch her bare breasts like she was hoping, he stopped short and ran a finger along her hipbone.

"You're bruised. Did I do that?" He looked mortified.

Reese glanced at the purple splotches dotting her left hip right above her pants. Just the sight of them reminded her of his rough hands holding on, squeezing, pressing hard as he thrust into her over and over again. Feeling her face flush with heat and desire, she licked her bottom lip, her nipples jutting forward.

"It's okay. They match the scratch marks I gave you on your upper back."

His expression changed, shifted from horror to speculation. "I have scratches on my back?"

Yep. She'd seen them when he walked into the bathroom. "Oh, yeah."

He grinned. "You're lethal with those hands, aren't you?"

Waving them at him, she said, "You know it. You better watch yourself."

"You don't scare me." Knight reached forward and gave a loud smacking kiss on each of her hands.

Then she did it again, the girl thing she had thought was eradicated from her personality forever. She giggled. Yikes.

Next thing she knew she'd be using hairspray and buying a Madonna CD.

"I can't spend the night, Reese."

Even as disappointment surged through her, she knew it was for the best. She had a busy day tomorrow, all in accordance with her brilliant plan devised five minutes ago.

It was hard to manage a shrug, but she pulled it off. "That's fine. I've got to get up early tomorrow anyway."

Still on his knees, he searched her face. "That's why I have to go. I have a really important meeting in the morning. It will help move this case forward and I want to be well rested. If I stay, I sure in the hell won't be sleeping."

"I understand." Snaking down his chest, she covered his bulge with her hand. "Want to tell me what the meeting's about?"

"Nice try, Woodward and Bernstein." He sat up. "But I'd like to come over after work tomorrow if I could. If you want me to. If you're still here in Chicago."

Wouldn't he be surprised when he found out she was *here* indefinitely?

"Yeah, I'll be here, but why don't we go out somewhere? I'm getting a little sick of the walls in this hotel room."

That grin he was giving her made her wonder why in the hell she hadn't put a shirt on. He looked like sin on a spoon, and her breasts were dying to be touched.

"Then tomorrow night you can lie on your back while I fuck you, and look at the ceiling instead of the walls."

He couldn't have shocked her more if he had stood up and performed Riverdance naked.

"Knight!" He was such an ethical, by-the-book kind of guy, but when it came to sex, Reese was discovering he liked it rough and raw.

That worked for her.

"I should cancel your salad after that remark."

"Oh, hurt me, baby," he said sarcastically.

There was a knock on the door. Knight stood up and

tossed her his T-shirt lying on the dresser. "Put that on and get under the covers or something. I don't want the room service guy checking you out."

Even though it was a little high-handed, Reese found herself obeying, smelling the scent of him on the shirt as it passed over her nostrils. She was snuggling under the covers, propping herself up with three pillows when the same deliveryman as two nights before brought their food in.

He nodded to her with a grin.

Five minutes later, Knight was on the bed next to her, sprawled out on top of the bedspread eating his salad drowned in dressing while they watched an action movie.

The plot, which mostly involved grinning men and explosives, wasn't hard to follow and Reese was enjoying the lazy relaxed atmosphere between her and Knight.

Reese ate several pieces of her lettuce. Even more went into her balled up paper napkin until it looked like an origami interpretation of the surface of the moon. Round and full of craters.

Knight didn't notice.

Flicking her finger over a crouton, she picked it up and pouched it in her cheek squirrel-style. Maybe it would be more exciting if she sucked on it instead of biting it. A second later it was soggy and gross and she hid it in her napkin with the growing compost pile already there.

"Do you need my napkin?" Knight asked, startling her into dropping her fork.

"Huh? Uh, no thanks."

"Because yours looks about to burst from all that lettuce you've stuffed in there."

She grimaced. "How did you do that? You weren't even looking at me. How could you know I was hiding lettuce in my napkin?"

"Nothing gets by a Fed. We're trained to notice everything." He bit a cherry tomato.

"Well, do you notice me getting annoyed with you?"

Abandoning pretense, she tossed the salad on the nightstand and reached for the Bud Light and the cheesecake.

"I notice you like me more than you want to."

"Pff." Her fork dipped into the cheesecake. This was a much better use for a utensil than stabbing a broccoli floret.

If Knight wanted her to gush about her feelings, he'd picked the wrong girl.

"You going to save any of that cheesecake for me?"

Was he nuts? Reese attacked the back end, wanting more of the graham cracker crust. "You can have the carrot cake."

Maybe. If he was quick.

"Actually, I should probably go in a minute."

His hands were in her hair, brushing and smoothing along the strands, tucking behind her ear.

It was such a simple gesture, but so intimate, that she balked. This was not what she was here for, and there was no such thing as a happily ever after.

What she wanted was a well-paying prestigious journalism career and a chance to see the world outside of Brooklyn. Not maternity stretch pants, a mortgage, and a husband who could be killed any day on the job.

Not that Knight was leaping that far ahead. But the more they were together, the softer the look in his eyes, and it scared the hell out of her.

Because sometimes, for a split second, in the back of her sex-fried mind, she didn't think it seemed all that bad.

God help her.

Chapter Thirteen

Derek was waiting for Markson in the Holiday Inn at seven-thirty A.M. Maddock was lying on the bed, his suit jacket off, flicking through the TV channels. CJ White was pacing, tossing Maddock a look of annoyance every few seconds.

"If there are too many of us here, he might balk," CJ said. "Why doesn't Maddock leave?"

Maddock snorted. "I've met the guy before. He likes me, he trusts me. Maybe you should leave."

Derek sighed, tossing the consent forms he'd been clutching down on the table. These two were driving him nuts. Every time they were in a room together, tension rose about three hundred percent.

"No one is leaving. Now let's not be bickering when the guy shows up, alright?" He wasn't about to admit it, but Derek was nervous. Or scared shitless, if that's how you wanted to put it.

The whole damn case hinged on Markson agreeing to wear this wire, and taping price-fixing meetings. They were so close, but still had nothing to give the prosecutors that could be considered hard evidence.

There was a knock on the door. Maddock sat up straighter on the bed and flicked off the TV as Derek went to answer the door. Stan Markson was there, looking nervous, sweat on his brow.

But he took a deep breath and said, "Hey, there, Derek. How's it going?"

"Good, Stan. How you holding up?" Derek ushered him into the room.

"Okay, I'm okay. I think I'm doing okay. This is the right thing." He nodded up and down, hard, as if to convince himself of the words.

Derek clapped his hand on Markson's shoulder, hoping to reassure him. "You remember agents CJ White and Wyatt Maddock don't you?"

"Sure, sure, guys, yep, I remember you."

As he watched him shake the other agents' hands, Derek hoped like hell Markson would calm down by the time he showed up at Delco for the day's round of meetings. Right now he looked and sounded like a guy wearing an illegal wire.

"I just need you to sign these forms indicating that you've agreed to cooperate with the federal government by wearing an electronic taping device on your person, alright?"

When Markson nodded and accepted the pen, Derek let out part of the breath he was holding. When Markson signed the papers, he expelled the rest. Step one done.

"Now if you'll take off your jacket and shirt, we can attach the recording device, okay, Stan?"

"Sure." Markson carefully laid his blue suit jacket on the bed and then began unbuttoning his shirt.

The rather nervous glance he sent in CJ's direction had Derek giving her a nod. She understood his directive and went casually over to the table, sitting with her back to Markson as she flipped through the stack of forms sitting there.

For the next step, Derek tried not to grimace. He'd lost the coin toss to Maddock on this one. He figured there were a lot of undesirable things he'd been forced to do over the years as an agent, but he still couldn't help but be big-time uncomfortable over shaving another guy's chest.

"Sorry, Stan, but we've got to do this." He held up the can of shaving cream and a razor to show his intention.

Markson blanched but then nodded.

Derek went as fast as he could without severing an artery. But they both gave a sigh of relief when the job was done. Derek explained how the recorder worked as he attached it to Markson's back, running the wires around to his chest and taping them in place.

"We'll program the recorder to run all day. Give me a quick call when you want to go to lunch and I'll turn it off." He handed Markson his shirt.

"You might want to go to the john then, since you probably don't want that recorded," he said, hoping to lighten the tension rolling off his CW.

Markson gave a brittle laugh. "Yeah, that would make my wife proud, wouldn't it?"

Maddock said, "Of course, you never know. Major deals can happen in the men's room. Chatterton might open up to you when he's taking a leak."

They all laughed except CJ, who rolled her eyes.

Maddock stopped laughing and frowned at her.

Christ. Like Derek needed those two having a playground fight right now.

"Now, I want you to act completely natural, Stan. Don't say anything you wouldn't normally say, try to relax. Who do you normally sit next to during these meetings? How far are you from Chatterton?"

"Oh, it's informal. We sit where we want, except for Chatterton, who always takes the head seat."

That was good news. "So do you think you can try and snag a chair close to Chatterton without it looking suspicious?"

"Sure." Markson buttoned his shirt up, looking a little calmer.

"Great. So all you have to do it show up and do what you always do, Stan. No big deal."

"Okay."

Derek shook his hand again, handing him his suit jacket. "We'll see you back here tonight about six, then."

"See you then. Have a nice day, guys," Markson said, heading for the door.

As the door closed behind him, Derek breathed a sigh of relief. Step two done. Now he hoped that Chatterton said something, anything of importance in this meeting.

"That guy's a wreck," CJ commented. "I hope he doesn't crack before we get something we can use."

That was Derek's big fear as well.

"He'll be fine," Maddock scoffed. "Sure, he's a little nervous, but he just agreed to record everything his boss says. That would make anybody a little nervous. Don't go borrowing trouble, White."

"And you shouldn't go around acting like everything's peachy keen all the time," CJ shot back.

"Peachy keen?" Maddock let out a bark of laughter. "Yeah, that's exactly the words I'd use to describe myself. Peachy keen. Shit."

Derek started stuffing papers in his briefcase, adjusting his holster under his suit jacket. His stomach burned, his ulcer dumping anxiety acids into his gut.

"If the fruit fits . . ." White said, her biting words baiting Maddock as she'd no doubt intended.

As Maddock spluttered and flushed and protested, Derek felt in his pocket for his antacids. As he popped two in his mouth, he realized between this case and Reese, he was going to need to buy more.

Easy as pie. That's what it had been. First thing Monday morning, Reese had put in a phone call to Ashton Chatterton, dodging a few assistants along the way, before she had finally been put through to him directly.

Chatterton had recognized her name, he'd said, as the charming young woman he'd met at his son's wedding.

After that, it had simply been a matter of explaining to him that she had lost her job, split from her fiancé, and was in dire straits. Did he have a job, anything, something horrible if need be, that she could do?

In discussing her fabricated qualifications, it had been mutually agreed upon that she should work as a personal assistant to the assistant to Chatterton's assistant. Her responsibilities would include making copies, fetching coffee, and best of all, acting as a runner in all of Chatterton's meetings.

If someone had a phone call or a message or needed a copy of something, or if the oj and muffins needed replenishing, she would be there to take care of it. Listening to every single word Chatterton and the Delco board were saying.

Starting today.

Knight would be amazed at her ingenuity. And possibly pissed off. But he would get over it.

She hoped.

This was her chance to *do* something, instead of just waiting around hoping for Knight to toss her a bone every other week about the case.

With Phillip and Jeannie Chatterton off on their honeymoon, there wouldn't be any reason for Ashton to discover that she wasn't really Jeannie's cousin. By the time the happy couple got back from the south of France, Ashton would be well on his way to being indicted.

At nine A.M., she was rubbing her hands on her thrice-worn suit, which was getting a little ripe, she had to admit. She was going to have to hit the mall and grab a few mix and match office items to wear.

She nodded. "Sure, I've got it. No problem." Jennifer Magic, the assistant to Chatterton's assistant, and her new boss, was looking at her sternly.

"Are you sure you can handle this? The gentlemen's demands can come fast and furious in these meetings."

What, like she couldn't handle dumping coffee into their cups and fetching them markers to draw their dumb charts? She'd gone to college.

Piece of cake.

Two hours later she wanted to throttle every last idiot on the Delco board. If more one guy asked her for coffee, a copy, or a phone number, prefaced by the term sweetie or honey, she was going to kick him.

This was why she'd never gone into food service. She hated people.

It didn't escape her attention either that she was the only female in the room. There wasn't a single female executive at Delco Pharmaceutical. At least none that were being included in this meeting.

"Reese, sweetie." Ashton flagged her over to the head of the table. "Can you ask Jennifer to send lunch in?"

"Sure." Reese squeezed her lips together and hoped it resembled a smile.

Her feet hurt from walking back and forth across the room twelve thousand times as various executives snapped and waved her over, and she had to go to the bathroom so bad she just knew she was causing future bladder damage. Which was amazing, since she hadn't had a sip of anything to drink since seven that morning and was probably on the verge of total dehydration.

Never again would she complain about interviewing reality show cast-offs. This fetch and carry servitude was much worse.

Which would be fine, if she was actually learning anything useful, but so far they had discussed nothing but quarterly profits. Even the subtle wink she'd given the CW to let him know she was on his side had been met with a blank stare.

Heading for the door, she called out to the room, "Does anyone else need anything while I'm gone? Tell me now before I go."

There was a stunned silence, then someone laughed. "I'm

fine." Then he turned to Chatterton and said with a smirk, "Like the new assistant, Ashton."

"Reese is a family friend who needed a job. We take care of our own here at Delco, don't we?" Chatterton's voice was full of innuendo and Reese wasn't exactly sure what he meant by it.

The only thing she was sure of was that when the Feds came to haul Ashton Chatterton off, she wasn't going to be the least bit sorry.

Derek had spent a nerve-racking day filling out 302 reports of that morning's conversation with Markson, hoping the guy hadn't choked in the meeting, or acted suspicious. Or worse, gotten caught.

When six rolled around, he was waiting anxiously for him at the Holiday Inn again, pacing and looking out the window for a sign of his CW every five minutes. By the time Markson knocked on the door, Derek felt five years older.

But Markson smiled, came inside, and said, "I've got the tape. Everything went without a hitch."

"That's great, Stan. That's great. Good job."

Markson was already removing his jacket to have the tape taken out by Maddock, and Derek heaved a huge sigh of relief. Step three accomplished.

Now with a little luck, in the coming weeks there would actually be something useful on these tapes. Enough to justify the Bureau following Delco to New Zealand for the big price-fixing meeting that was scheduled in two weeks' time.

Given that the FBI would need the cooperation of the New Zealand government and the hotel the meetings were taking place in, they would need these Delco tapes to show intent to price-fix at that meeting.

Derek was convinced that's what the meeting was all about. Knowing the strict nature of the U.S. antitrust laws, it would make sense to meet outside the country when it came time to discuss actual prices and market share.

Maddock already had the tape set to listen to as Derek escorted Markson to the door. "Okay, let's meet tomorrow in the parking lot here by the Dumpster and you can just give me the day's tape, okay?"

"Sure, sounds good."

"You did great, Stan."

Markson left, looking relieved and tired.

"Markson said there's a full eight hours on this tape," Maddock said. "Are we going to try to listen to the whole thing tonight?"

"I think we have to. If there's nothing there, we're going to have to lean on Markson to guide the conversation around to New Zealand. We don't have much time." Derek thought about Reese and their plans for that night and experienced a big wave of regret.

It wasn't the first time his job had interfered with his personal life, but he'd never felt it so acutely. In his pants.

And if he was honest, he was disappointed he'd have to miss her company. Reese made him laugh, something he hadn't been doing a whole lot lately.

Maddock reached for the phone. "Then I'm ordering a pizza."

"Sounds good." Maybe, with a whole boatload of luck, they would find something early on in this tape and he could still make it to pick Reese up at eight, according to plan.

No such luck. Even fast-forwarding as they munched on greasy pizza, Derek and Maddock weren't even a third of the way through the tape an hour later. The only thing they'd discovered was that Delco executives liked to talk. A lot. About nothing.

"Jesus, this is boring," Maddock complained. "And where the hell is White, by the way? How did she get out of this?"

"She had a previous appointment. Something personal." Derek listened to Ashton Chatterton rambling on and on about how he was satisfied with profits, but there was room for growth.

"What? Did she have like a date or something? You let her off the hook for a date?"

Derek rubbed his temples and looked across the table at Maddock. What the hell was this all about? "I don't know if it was a date. She said she had an appointment." He pinned Maddock with a hard stare. "So what exactly is going on between you and White?"

Maddock leaned back in his chair, tipping it off the floor. "Whoa! Nothing. Whoever said there was anything going on between me and White? I don't date women who want to pretend they're men." He wiped his fingers on a paper napkin and looked really guilty.

Derek grinned. "Nobody said anything about you two dating, you ass. I just meant you're always at each other's throats and I was wondering what gave. But now I've got it. You have the hots for White."

"Shit." Maddock took a swill of Coke and looked annoyed. "I don't have the hots for her. I can't stand her. She's one of those man-haters."

Laughing, Derek threw his own balled up napkin in Maddock's direction. "Yeah, right. You can't stand that she thinks you're an idiot."

Maddock didn't laugh with him. "Yeah, you wait. You'll get your turn with some woman who annoys the hell out of you."

"I already have. I'm divorced, remember?"

Then his laughter cut off as he heard a really familiar voice sail across the tape that was playing, clear as a bell and full of sass.

". . . else need anything while I'm gone? Tell me now before I go."

Jesus H Christ. "Play that back again!" He swallowed the wad of pizza clumping in his mouth and prayed he was hearing things.

"What?" Maddock reached for the tape player. "What's the matter?"

Only everything. Heart thumping, hands squeezing the end of the table, stomach in throat, Derek waited for the voice again.

"Does anyone else need anything while I'm gone? Tell me now before I go."

That voice belonged to Reese Hampton. The woman he was going to throttle, slowly and with total enjoyment. Just what in the hell was she doing in the room with Delco executives?

"Like the new assistant, Ashton."

"Reese is a family friend who needed a job. We take care of our own here at Delco, don't we?"

"Oh, my God!" he exploded, jumping out of his chair and jamming his hands into his pockets.

"What's the matter?" Maddock asked. "Who is that woman?"

"That," Derek pressed a hand to his chest, wondering if he was having a heart attack. "*That* is my girlfriend."

"Oh, shit," was Maddock's stunned reply.

Which about summed it up.

Reese checked the clock impatiently, glaring when she read eight o'clock. If she had known Knight was going to be so late, she would have run to the mall and bought some clothes. Instead, she'd showered and washed her thong in the sink. Now she was starting to get annoyed. And hungry.

The phone rang. "Hello?"

"I need to talk to you."

"Where are you? It's eight o'clock. I'm dying of hunger, my stomach is digesting the lining of its walls."

"I thought we said I'd pick you up at eight."

"I don't remember eight. We never said eight."

"Reese, we have more important things to talk about than what time it is. I'll be over in half an hour." His voice was tight.

Whatever he wanted to talk about couldn't be as important as her suffering through another day of wearing the same pajama pants. "Swing by your apartment and get me some clothes, will you?"

"What?"

"I have nothing to wear and I want to go out to dinner. Grab me a pair of your jeans or something and a T-shirt."

There was a long silence where Knight's strangled breathing filled the phone. He seemed a little tense.

"What's the matter? Did you have a bad day?"

"You could say that."

"So let's make it a better night." One or two, or a thousand different ways to do that popped into her head. All involving her and Knight naked.

"I'll be over as soon as I can."

Derek had started to suspect he'd lost his head over Reese, now it was confirmed. She had gone behind his back, infiltrated Delco Pharmaceutical, potentially compromising his case, and yet he was standing in front of her hotel room holding a bundle of fresh clothes for her to wear.

Insane, that's what he was.

He pounded on the door vehemently.

Reese opened it, standing in her pajamas. "Good, you brought the clothes! You're so nice."

Nice was not what he was feeling. Handing the bundle over to her, he stepped into the room. He said carefully, trying not to yell, "Would you care to explain to me what you were doing in Delco's board meeting this afternoon?"

Reese halted in her tracks in front of the bathroom door. "You know that already? Geez, that was fast. How did you know?"

Derek's blood pressure shot up. She sounded so nonchalant, he found himself saying in exasperation, "Your voice on the tape was a dead giveaway."

Reese broke into a smile. "You're taping the Delco meetings? That is so cool. Did you get anything good today?

Because I didn't hear anything good. They just run on at the mouth as far as I can tell."

Well, he had walked right into that trap. Now Reese knew what they were doing in the investigation, something he had never intended to tell her.

"I can't tell you, Reese." There were only so many ways he could say that, and yet she persisted in trying to pump him for information.

She shucked her pajama pants and shook out the jeans he'd brought her. And despite how totally pissed he was at her running into this investigation headlong with New York attitude flying, his mouth went dry at the sight of her in her panties, long smooth legs touching distance from him.

"That's why I had to take matters into my own hands. So I called Chatterton and he gave me a job. Now I can gather evidence for my story and for you. If Markson trips up, I can help out. I'm your insider now, Knight. Isn't that great?"

If that was her idea of great, he'd hate to see bad.

His hand automatically went to his pocket for his antacids. But when he'd gone home, he'd changed into jeans and had left them in his suit jacket.

"Reese, honey, babe, that is not a good thing. You can't be a reporter and my girlfriend and working for Chatterton, all while being aware that meetings are being taped. There's about half a dozen different ways that would be a conflict of interest and probably illegal."

She paused while pulling his jeans onto her narrow hips. "I'm your girlfriend? Since when?"

That's what she had pulled out of that whole explanation? "Since we started seeing each other every day, taking meals together, and sharing a bed. I think that would be called dating by most people's standards."

Reese zipped the jeans, buttoned the button, and let go. They promptly slid back down to her hipbones, where they came to a saggy rest. "Give me your belt," she said, holding out her hand.

Derek did as he was told, undoing his black leather belt and silently handing it to her.

"Because you know, I'm not sure that I ever *agreed* to be your girlfriend. That implies exclusivity and a commitment to continue seeing each other."

He could not believe they were having this conversation. "So what are you saying? You want to have sex with someone else? You don't want to see me anymore?"

Cinching the belt on the last hole, she frowned. "Well, no."

The breath he'd been holding let go with a whoosh. If she had said she wanted to let some other asshole put his piggish hands on her gorgeous body, he would have punched a hole in the wall. "Then you're my girlfriend. End of story."

Her eyebrow shot up. "Well, aren't you getting all caveman."

Nothing was ever easy, and this only confirmed that maxim. He rubbed his temple. "Look, I've had a long day and I'm not exactly sure what we're even talking about."

Her belligerence disappeared. "Oh, I'm sorry." Her hand patted his cheek. "Let's go eat, then. You look tired and hungry. But you know, I just think I object to the phrase girlfriend."

Sticking her arms in one of his long sleeve button-up shirts, she added, "It's just so outdated or something."

Watching the sleeves swallow her, he reached over and rolled one up, then the other, tugging the ends together more over her tank top. "What should I call you, then? My lover?"

Still gripping the shirt, he could feel her breasts beneath the soft fabric, pushing against him, her nipples taut and teasing. He had stepped into her space and was leaning over her, leg inserted between her thighs, and the fresh smell of her shower enveloped him. This close, he could see her hair was still damp, not as wet as it had been that first night he'd met her, but damp underneath, where it caressed her skin.

"How about just your friend?" Reese looked up at him

from beneath those mink colored lustrous eyelashes, a dusting of freckles beneath each eye noticeable on her makeup-free face.

Burying his head in her neck, he kissed her, trailing his tongue downward, leaving a wet path of possession behind him. "Friends don't do this."

He dragged her tank top down and covered the rounded top swell of her breast with his mouth. Then he sucked. Hard. Wanting to mark her, to claim her, to say yes, no matter what the hell she wanted to call it, for as long as she was in Chicago, and as long as they both wanted it, she was his. Exclusively his, and he was hers. They wouldn't be with anyone else, and they would date, and they would spend each night they had together, pleasuring each other until that explosion of lust they felt in each other's presence was gone, eradicated, saturated, satisfied.

"Oohh," she said, eyes drifting shut.

His jeans were so loose on her that his whole hand fit between her stomach and the pants, and he reached down inside and cupped her mound, sliding across the satin of her panties. Heat met him, pouring out from the center of her, spilling into his hands, and he pushed against the panties, sliding his finger an inch or so inside her despite the barrier.

Thoughts of dinner disappeared. "Let's stay here and order room service."

"No," she murmured. "I want to go out." She gave a half-hearted tug at his hand down her pants. "Stop it, Knight."

"Okay." He stopped and went to remove his hand.

"Shit, don't stop!" Reese grabbed his elbow and guided him back down.

He laughed. He loved her honesty, especially when it was what he wanted to hear.

"Okay, Knight, let's have a competition. If you win, we'll stay in." Reese spoke while moving his hand up and down, rubbing him against her.

Derek gripped the back of her head with his other hand,

aching for her, turned on by her desire for him. There was nothing shy about Reese and how she wanted him, and he couldn't imagine anything sexier.

"If I win, we'll go out."

"What's the competition?" He figured he would agree to just about anything at this point.

He pressed again, sliding her panties into her, his finger coming back wet, hot from her moist heat.

"It's simple." She clung to him, rocking herself onto his questing, stretching, reaching finger.

"Whoever comes first loses."

Given the way she was responding to him right now, Derek nearly laughed out loud. "This isn't like arm wrestling. I'll win this one, Reese."

Without warning she squeezed his rock solid cock with one hand, yanking the zipper of his jeans down cleanly with the other. "Don't bet on it."

Her fingers moved at the same time his did, and Derek decided there was no such thing as an easy win.

Chapter Fourteen

Reese didn't know why the hell she had just set herself up to lose, but it no longer seemed to matter. She could eat room service chicken wings twenty-four/seven if it meant Knight would keep stroking her into oblivion like this.

She wiggled back and forth, wanting him to move her panties out of the way, wanting her breasts bare against him, but he held her tight in place, running his finger over and over her clitoris through the satin panties, teasing her by dipping a little inside, then drawing back out. The jeans were pulled forward hard to accommodate his arm down them, and the back seam drew up, sending the string of the thong digging into her and the denim brushing against her bare behind, further arousing her.

Not that she was going to go down without a fight. He was grinding against her hand, and when she pulled the length of him out of his briefs, he groaned.

This hadn't been her plan when he'd shown up for the night. But then he had babbled on about the case and she had watched him, so cute, so stressed out, so perfectly moral and sexy, that she had felt that now-familiar tug between her thighs.

Then he had called her his girlfriend, which had both freaked her out and turned her on. She had never really been good at being a girlfriend, but they were only talking short-term, while she was here in Chicago, maybe a month or so at the most. It was perfect, low-risk, a great way to indulge in fabulous sex without guilt. She had never really had what could be called an affair, but she suspected this was one.

And she was going to enjoy it. Even if that meant repetitive meals and bad outfits.

She loved the way he felt, the way he filled her hand with his hot throbbing cock, the way his breath hitched and caught when she touched him. The way they leaned into each other, their fingers picking up speed together, her hair spilling over her face and his chest, muscles tightening, hands holding onto each other.

Racing forward, meeting for a grinding teeth-knocking kiss, Knight's hand finally, blissfully tearing aside her panties and sliding into her, gliding across her slick burning flesh, pushing between her swollen folds.

"Yes, yes, yes," she chanted softly, arching against him, her own fingers frantic and frenetic over his cock.

He had big fingers, and when he went deep, she could feel the rounded hard edges of his fingernail scraping across her, an arousing contrast to the soft milky wetness of her own body.

She felt that difference everywhere, her rounded breasts pressing into his hard chest, her curvy hips flush against his solid ones, her slender pale fingers on his darker remarkably firm cock. When his finger slipped out, and circled around her clitoris, she let the orgasm sweep over her, rocking onto him and squeezing her fingers over him tightly. Eyes closed, she shuddered as the pleasure ran over her like a semi-truck, knocking her out with its breathless intensity.

The final jerk she gave made her tug on him, her fingers almost flying off as she stroked fast and hard, and then he was joining her, panting his way through his own orgasm, murmuring her name with such ecstasy that Reese smiled, a deep sense of satisfaction stealing over her.

They stayed motionless, hands still on each other, her head

resting against his, while Reese tried to even her breathing and remember why she was even in Chicago. Why she was even alive for any reason other than to touch and be touched by Knight.

Retrieving his hand from her pants, he said, "I guess we stay in."

"Why?" She still wanted to get out of this hotel room, and she wasn't going to let a little thing like losing interfere with that.

"You came first. That was the deal, remember?"

Pressing a kiss on his shoulder, she tried hard to sound innocent. "I didn't come."

"What?" Indignation ripped through his voice.

He forced her chin up so she had to look into those double chocolate fudge eyes that made her just want to slip a dollar into his jeans in gratitude.

"You came, Reese. I felt it."

She gave him a slow grin. "You can't prove it."

Understanding dawned in his eyes. "You are such a cheat."

"Of course I am. I have four brothers. Cheating was the only way I was ever going to win anything."

"Well, then, I didn't come, either. So we'll have to have a do-over."

Reese looked down between them, where the unmistakable evidence of his orgasm was on his shirt. "Uh, in your case we have proof."

She laughed as he grimaced, and finally muttered, "Fine, we'll go out. But I have to change my shirt, now."

"Here, just put this back on." Reese slipped off the shirt he had given her. She would just put on a bra with her tank top and the heck with it. She was starving.

Derek couldn't believe he was sitting in a restaurant with a woman wearing white fuzzy slippers.

It was only a casual Mexican restaurant, but he still was

going to take a wild guess that Reese was the only one who had terry cloth on her feet. Yet she looked adorable, strolling around wearing a tank top and his jeans. They kept sliding low on her hips, exposing her midriff, and she had rolled the bottoms up above her ankles so she wasn't walking on them.

Derek was starting to get a bad feeling. That he was forgetting to think of Reese as temporary. Fun while it lasted.

He was enjoying her company too much and was having trouble concentrating on anything other than making her go weak with pleasure in his arms. He needed to regain control, drag himself back into reality and remember what exactly was at stake here.

His career.

Long after Reese trotted back off to New York and resumed her life, he had to live here in Chicago, working for the Bureau for the next twenty years. He had no interest in spending that time pushing papers or taking an involuntary transfer to Podunk, Georgia.

That case had to work out. Delco needed to be indicted.

"So, tell me again exactly what your plans are for the next few weeks?" He bit a tortilla chip and forced himself to relax back into the booth.

"You know there's a giant maraca over your head?" Reese was looking above him as she sipped her enormous margarita that was the most horrifying blue color he'd ever seen.

Nothing could make him drink something that looked like toilet bowl cleaner.

As he tilted his head back to check out the hot pink and tan maraca swaying behind him, he realized she had effectively distracted him again.

"Reese. Forget the maraca. Tell me your plans."

"Well, you know, Knight, sometimes we need to just go with the flow, you know? Well, that's what I'm doing."

"What the hell does that mean?"

"It means I quit my job with the *Newark News* and I'm planning on staying here until the Delco story breaks."

Of course. What had he been thinking? "Working for Ashton Chatterton?"

"Yes."

He needed a beer. Flagging the waiter over, he said to Reese, "What happens when Chatterton figures out you're not the bride's cousin? If he looks into your background, you could jeopardize this case."

"Oh, give me a flipping break. If Chatterton figures me out, then why in the world would he connect a reporter from the *Newark News,* small-time East Coast rag, with the FBI investigating Delco for international price-fixing?"

She had a point. But the whole thing still made him nervous.

After ordering the beer, he said, "Yeah, but you can't be involved in the investigation, so why bother? If you want to still stick around for the story to break and you need money, you can be a waitress or something."

Given the narrowing of her eyes, he suspected she wasn't pleased with his suggestion.

"I don't want to be a waitress! And why can't I help you in this investigation? I could speed things up, I know I could. Or at the very least conduct my own independent journalistic investigation."

"You could screw things up, is what you could do."

"You trust that geek, Markson, but not me?" Her voice rose and he panicked.

"Christ, keep it down. You're yelling out the name of a CW in a public place!"

She snorted. "No one gives a crap. They're all stuffing their faces with burritos after a miserable Monday back at work. There are no corporate spies lingering around the guacamole at Amigo's."

"This is why you cannot be involved in this case. You have no sense of discretion."

"Uhh!" She gasped and set her margarita down, sending the blue liquid sloshing over the sides. "I am so goddamn discreet, I'm practically invisible. And don't you dare take that patronizing tone with me. You can't forbid me to work for Chatterton."

Not at the moment. But Derek was sure if he thought about it hard enough, he could figure out a way to do that. But did he really want to make an enemy out of Reese? God only knew what she was capable of doing when she was angry. And she knew a lot about the Delco case, thanks to Markson's rental car goof.

"Look, don't get so upset. I'm not forbidding you to work for Chatterton."

The soothing tone didn't seem to placate her. "You know, Knight, I'm not one of those Betty Crocker types and I wish you would just figure that out once and for all. I told you right off the bat that I'm a straight-talking ex-tomboy, and you said you liked that about me. But the truth is, that's not what you want. You want one of those soft-spoken agreeable women who will greet you at the door wearing an apron, the kids all pink from their baths, and smiles on their faces."

She had lost him. Completely and utterly lost him. How had they gone from Delco to his fictitious wife and kids?

"I have no clue what you're talking about."

She went on like he'd never spoken. "Which is fine, because you're entitled to want what you want. But the thing is, I don't like being compared to a pie-baking paragon who doesn't even exist, and I don't like you implying that I don't have the brains or the professionalism to assist this investigation."

Derek opened his mouth, not at all sure what was going to come out of it.

But she kept going, the pause apparently just for air. "So the thing is, you have to either accept me just the way I am, unable to boil water and working for Chatterton, or the whole thing is just off. Off."

Reese took a sip of her drink, waiting for his response. She didn't want to stop seeing him, but she had to make her point

clear. There was no way she would ever be Holly Homemaker and she didn't even want to try. And it didn't matter
because they both knew their relationship was only temporary, but she didn't want any misunderstanding and she did
not want him talking to her like she was slightly dense.

Knight just stared at her, a blank look on his face. Then he
said, "Does this mean you're not going to spend the night
with me?"

Brought up short by his question, Reese thought about it.
Not sleep with him anymore? She really didn't think that's
what she had meant at all. There was no actual good reason
they couldn't keep seeing each other as long as he understood
the score—that this was just a short-term thing and that he
could not force her to leave Delco.

Besides, she was finding out that Knight was like potato
chips. Once you tasted one, you wanted the whole bag. She
was pretty sure she'd only made a small dent in the bag so far
and she wanted to keep eating until she was full.

"Well, no, not exactly. We can still do that as long as you
understand I'm not quitting the Delco job." She quickly
added, "And that I'll never cook anything for you. Ever."

Knight stopped peeling the label off his beer bottle. "How
about you agree to stay out of my job and I'll agree to stay
out of yours?"

He grinned, a slow, cocky grin that turned her insides into
spicy salsa. "And that when I hand you the scoop for this
story, like I've been promising since day one, you will bake
me a pie from scratch."

If he wanted to throw up, that was his business. Besides,
she'd never completely believed that he would give her the
story. If he did, she'd gladly bake him a pie. "What kind?"

"Pumpkin."

"Fine." By the time this case wrapped, every store in town
would have pumpkin pies for Thanksgiving. She'd just buy
him one and fake it.

"And I get to watch you making it."

Dammit. He knew her too well.

"Fine," she said, significantly cooler this time.

Knight laughed out loud.

Derek was sitting in his cubicle, listening to the day's tapes from Markson. CJ and Maddock were next to him, taking notes as they plowed their way through hours of corporate double-talk. Markson had told them that after the lunch break on Tuesday, Chatterton had asked him how the arrangements were going for the upcoming meeting in New Zealand.

Maddock had wanted to skip right to that segment of the tape, but Derek had insisted they listen to everything.

Now he was damn sorry he had.

Every time he turned around, he could hear Reese's voice on the tape, attending to various needs around the room. She appeared to have become quite popular in the course of her day and a half on the job. All the execs called her Reese and teased her jovially.

It made Derek insane with jealousy.

"Can you have copies run of this report, Reese?" he heard Chatterton say on the tape.

"Sure, Ashton. But it will have to wait until after lunch. I'm starving."

Derek hung his head. Aside from the fact that she was the only secretary he'd ever heard call Chatterton by his first name, Reese was also telling the head of the company to wait for his request.

Maddock snorted. "Your girlfriend is about the worst secretary I've ever seen, Knight."

They heard three or four men chime in, offering to take Reese to lunch.

CJ said, "Something tells me they don't mind."

That's what pissed him off the most.

"You know, Knight, you've got to tell Nordstrom." Maddock dropped his usual clowning demeanor.

Those were the words Derek had been dreading hearing.

He knew Maddock was right, but he didn't know how in the hell he was going to explain this to his boss.

"I know, man, I know. But what do I say?"

"How about . . . my girlfriend got a job at Delco without my knowledge?" CJ asked. "You can't control what another person does. And some people are just selfish."

Reese hadn't done this to be selfish, Derek knew that. She had done it for the story, to take charge of her life, to feel a sense of control. He knew her whole life men had been calling the shots for her and she wanted to be successful on her own, without interference. And here he'd tried to go and take that away from her.

His head hurt.

He wanted Reese to be successful. He wanted her to trust him to deliver her the story. He wanted this case to be successfully concluded and the only concern on his mind to be which room in his apartment he would take Reese in that night.

Of course, if the case were over, Reese would be gone.

Christ.

"But I can't claim that Reese didn't know we were investigating Delco, because she does. She saw a file with their name on it." That was the very narrow condensed version of what had actually happened. He was skirting the truth there a little, but he wasn't about to reveal the entire breadth of his mistake if he didn't have to yet.

And to make it all the more embarrassing, Nordstrom had caught him making out with Reese in the elevator. If Nordstrom even had a hint of the fact that Reese was a reporter, he was going to assume Reese was manipulating him and remove Derek from the case.

"Can you trust her?" Maddock asked. "Does she know enough to jeopardize this case?"

"I trust her. She wouldn't jeopardize the case." Not on purpose, anyway.

Maddock gave him a hard stare. "Is that your head talking or your dick?"

"Come on, Wyatt. You know me better than that." He looked around the office nervously. There were only a few random agents hanging around, but he did not want anyone hearing this.

"I've known you for two years, Knight, and I've never known you to even really date. Now you've got this woman in your life, she's young, pretty. Better men than you have fallen for that."

"What are you saying? That's she setting me up? Sleeping with me to gain access? That's prostitution, for Christ's sake!" Derek didn't know what made him angrier—the fact that Maddock had suggested it, or that part of him deep down wondered if there might be a grain of truth to it.

"No, it's having sex to gain something. People do it all the time. I'm just saying be careful."

Reese wouldn't do that. He was sure of it.

But then again, she was ambitious. She wanted out of that rag newspaper, had even quit her job now. He knew she enjoyed sex with him. No one could fake it that well. Of course, she had said herself that you could never really tell with a woman. There was no way to prove it.

His blood went cold. And even if she did enjoy it, that didn't mean she wasn't enjoying it at the same time she was using him.

It wasn't a pleasant thought. More like a kicked-in-the-gut thought.

"What do you think?" He turned to CJ.

She looked him straight in the eye. "I agree with Maddock. I think you need to be careful. And you need to tell Nordstrom."

Maddock let out a whistle. "First time you've ever agreed with me on anything, White."

"That's because you're usually wrong."

Maddock grimaced.

Then as Derek brooded, they all heard Chatterton's voice come over the tape, which had continued running throughout their discussion about Reese.

"So is the meeting all set for New Zealand for October the sixth?"

"Yes, sir, it is." It was Markson, sounding calm and natural.

Derek was pleased with his casual, things-as-usual tone of voice.

"Are Stanfield and Ricould both going to be there?"

"Yes, sir, and the agenda is set to discuss which companies will be renewing which patents."

Damn, that was good. Markson was leading the conversation, steering Chatterton into actual admittance of patent-fixing.

"Good, good. We're all set to play hardball with these guys, then. We'll show them that it's in all our favors to work together and agree to divide the market like we have been for the last three years. But we still want the most profit since we're the largest company."

"Of course."

Chatterton laughed. "I like the way you say that. Of course. That sums it all up. We're going to make a lot of money this year, Markson."

Then another executive interrupted and the conversation turned.

Derek stopped the tape. "That's it! Damn, that was great. That's exactly what we've been looking for. It should be enough to take to Justice to prove we need to go to New Zealand for this meeting. This could be the big one."

Maddock shook his head, grinning. "Geez, these guys are so bold, aren't they?"

"It makes me nervous," CJ said.

"It just makes our job easier," Derek assured her.

"I just can't believe that the price of a prescription drug is determined by half a dozen guys sitting around a room saying who gets to make what and how much they get to charge. It's unreal. It's wrong."

It sure in the hell was. "That's why we're sending Chatterton and the rest to prison."

This was why Derek loved his job. Putting the bad guys away.

The only interesting thing to happen in two days and Reese had missed it. She didn't even know what it was, since Knight wouldn't tell her, but she knew it was something because he was excited when he called her on her cell phone, his voice rushed, his energy high.

She either didn't know what she was supposed to be listening for at Delco, or she was going to have to stop going to the bathroom so she wouldn't miss a word.

But the day hadn't been a total waste. She had met Knight's sister Claire, that morning when Claire had returned to his apartment after spending the night with a friend. Reese had been impressed with the order and cleanliness of Knight's apartment when he had brought her there after dinner the night before, and she was really impressed with his sister.

After Knight had gone off to fight crime for peace, justice, and the American way, she and Claire had gone shopping. Claire had immediately understood her dilemma of trying to live on three outfits and had offered to show her where to grab a bargain. Reese had called Chatterton and told him her tale of fashion woe, that she had left all her clothes in Jersey, etcetera, etcetera.

He couldn't have cared less and happily agreed to let her arrive an hour late to work. It had given her enough time to grab a couple of essentials, including a really cute bright blue boy-short bra and panties set. On her lunch break, she had checked out of the Crowne Plaza, bringing her suitcase with her back to Delco, and then had returned her rental car. She had caught a cab to Knight's apartment after work. Claire had given her a spare key.

Now she was waiting for Knight to get home. He knew she was in his apartment, but he didn't know that she had checked out of her hotel. That didn't seem like a phone conversation, letting him know that she needed to stay with him until the weekend when she and Claire were moving into a three-month sublet together.

Better to surprise him in person.

She called her brother Ryan, who was only two years older than her.

" 'Lo?"

"Ry, it's me."

"Hey, Reese-y piece-y, what's up?"

"Not much. I'm in Chicago, I quit my job, I'm investigating a major story of financial fraud, and I'm having really great sex with an FBI agent. How you doing?"

"Well, I can't top you. I'm stuck in New York since the season's over and I haven't had sex in like nine days."

Ryan played minor league baseball and could charm the underwear off a preacher's wife. He was her favorite brother. "Geez, that's like a record for you. Listen, you know how you wanted to share my apartment so you didn't have to have a roommate?"

"And you said no way in hell were you listening to me recreating *Sex and the City* every night? Yeah, I remember."

"Well, I'm not coming back to New York for a while, so I need you to move in and pay half the rent."

"Okay."

That's why she and Ryan got along so well. He was the ultimate go-with-the-flow guy. Usually that flow was in whatever direction women were heading.

"Rick has my keys."

"Why does Rick have your keys and not me?"

"Because Rick won't A—lose them or B—bring strange women into my apartment when I'm out of town."

"Oh, okay, cool. See ya."

"Bye, Ry."

With nothing left to do but wait, Reese hid her suitcase in Knight's bedroom next to all of Claire's boxes and bags, hoping it would blend.

Knight's apartment was small, but less *guy* than she would have expected. In the bedroom was a walnut sleigh bed, covered by a rich wheat colored duvet. There were a few pictures of his parents and Claire on his dresser and one of him with his ex-wife on their wedding day.

What amazed her was not how ugly Dawn's dress was, though it honestly was, but the red-hot stab of jealousy that ripped through her with tornado-force winds. Knight was smiling. He looked happy. He looked at Dawn with love shining in his eyes.

And she was jealous.

She slapped the picture she had been gripping painfully back down on the dresser, disturbing the thin layer of dust that lay there.

Annoyed with herself, she went into the living room, stomping a little in her knee-high boots for good measure. With the carpeted floors, it wasn't all that satisfying, but she'd take what she could get.

It had been an indulgence, deciding to blow off the high heels and get boots to wear to Delco instead. With a knee length black skirt and gray sweater, it was business-y enough to get away with it, and with all the laps she did across that boardroom floor, even with the heels the boots were still more comfortable than pumps.

Now she unzipped the boots in annoyance and tossed them on the floor. And if the boots were off, then why the hell did she need panty hose on? She rolled them down and balled them up, wondering what would happen if she put them in the garbage disposal.

The green-eyed monster had never bitten her this bad before and it was stupid. Plain old what's-up-with-that stupid. Dawn was his ex-wife. She was remarried. She was pregnant. She looked sexually uptight and was in no way a natural blonde.

Knight was not Reese's boyfriend. It didn't matter who he had loved once upon a time. It didn't even matter who he loved now.

It. Was. An. Affair.

Only a certain four-chambered valve in her body was not agreeing with that.

Chapter Fifteen

Derek knew Reese was waiting for him in his apartment. He didn't know she would be bent over looking at his CD's, wearing a tight black skirt that was hiking up snuggly between her bare legs, making him go hard in a nanosecond.

"Hi," she called, still bent over, her hair falling to the left as she tilted her head, her sweater climbing on the opposite side, showing him her creamy flesh.

Derek was still flying high from the tape of Chatterton, and was still edgy and upset about Maddock's hints that Reese might be taking advantage of him.

He knew that wasn't true. He knew it. She wanted him. All the time. The way he wanted her, with hot, wet, grinding desire that pushed out everything else but the need to touch, to feel, to connect together in pleasure.

Like now.

"Hi," he said, coming up behind her rapidly.

He threw his keys on the couch, dropped to one knee and sucked on that ribbon of skin peeping out at him, his hand shoving her skirt up.

"Oh!" She let out a startled cry that quickly converted to a moan as his hand closed over her mound.

With his hand against her, he pulled her back to him until his mouth was touching her thighs, kissing, sucking, running his tongue up and down, along her inner thighs and the underside of her cheeks. She tasted so good, so feminine, like sucking on a peach.

The panties were lacy blue things, almost like short shorts, not tight against her skin at the leg, but loose. There was room to push the fabric aside, to run his tongue over her everywhere until she murmured something he couldn't understand.

Pulling the panties down to her ankles, he stood up and said over her shoulder, "What's that, Peaches? I didn't hear you."

"Nothing, nothing," she said, propping herself up on the bookcase by locking her arms.

He ran his thumb over the front of her, finding her swollen nub, nudging against her backside with his erection, sandwiching her between his front and back strokes. A woman could fake an orgasm, but she could never fake being this wet, this ready for a man.

Derek dug in his pocket with his other hand, found a condom, and unzipped his fly.

When he needed both hands to put the condom in place, Reese cried out in a jagged voice, "What are you doing? Don't stop!"

"Shh. I've got something better for you, Peaches." He eased between her legs, nudging her with his cock, teasing them both by pressing lightly against her, then pulling back.

Reese bowed back, trying to take more of him. "More."

That word ripped through him, shattered all thought of teasing, sent him raging forward in triumphant pleasure, his feeling for her suddenly clear, obvious, unmistakable.

He was falling in love with her.

He wanted her to feel the same.

He sank deep, holding onto her hips, pulling her back against him as he leaned forward, his chest against her back. The layers of clothing between them added to his arousal. He wanted to touch her, feel her, yet the only part of her body he could feel was deep inside, where she wrapped around him with hot, tight, trembling muscles.

Derek found her clitoris with his finger as he pulled back, thrusting into a hard, desperate rhythm. He took her fast, his finger working her as he sent himself careening out of control. He had never been so mindless during sex, so free of thoughts except for Reese, so completely in awe of her.

When she said, "Oh, Knight, I'm going to come," in a soft, breathy, grateful voice, he knew he'd found perfection.

"So, come," he told her, pausing for a quick second before thrusting again, sending her groaning into an orgasm, clawing at the bookcase, arching her back in the most beautiful, graceful way he'd ever seen.

That was all it took for him to join her, pressing his lips together to keep from howling like a dying dog, pumping into her, stroking long past his final shudder.

He didn't want to leave her. Ever.

He wanted to stay together like this, simple, connected, content, for an eternity.

Reese made a mewing sound, her head resting on her arm, her upper half having dropped forward onto the bookcase.

In a lazy voice, she said, "Did you have a good day?"

"Pretty good." He kissed her shoulder, a momentary twinge of guilt overcoming him. He was being very greedy with her, very raw and demanding.

Usually he had more control.

But that wasn't his strong suit when Reese was in the room.

"How about you?"

"Mmm. I went shopping with Claire. And fetched coffee at Delco the rest of the day. Exciting stuff."

Derek brushed across her stomach under her sweater, not wanting to give up his hold on her, wanting to capture this moment of perfect quiet happiness and keep it.

But she patted him on the leg. "Okay, back it up, Knight."

They both sighed when he pulled out of her. Reese turned around and kissed him, a soft gentle kiss that only contributed to his emotional turmoil. Turmoil was probably an understatement. He was a train wreck.

Reese was warring between wanting to kick Knight in the nuts and grab him for another round. Of course, it wasn't his fault she was forgetting everything she had told herself for the last ten years and was falling for him like a dewy-eyed teenager.

Maybe this was fate catching up with her for never acting stupid over a guy in high school. Now she got to act like an idiot over Knight. Except at sixteen it was excusable. At twenty-six it was pathetic.

But all wasn't lost. She hadn't told him her feelings, hadn't admitted anything other than that she enjoyed his company and his penis. He never had to know that she was falling in love with him.

There was no one who could tell him but her, and she wasn't about to say that out loud.

But she needed to stop being so agreeable when it came to sex. He snapped his fingers and she was lifting her skirt and coming. He was that good. And her jealousy over Dawn and the decade-old wedding photo on his dresser had made it all the more satisfying when he had walked into the apartment and wanted her instantly.

But now it was time for her to take the lead.

"Another ugly suit. You've got to stop wearing these." She grabbed the jacket and pushed it off his shoulders. He had the most wonderfully muscular chest under there and she wanted to see it.

"Going to work isn't a fashion statement for me."

"Well, you're home now so take it off." She leaned back against the bookcase and smiled.

He was taking off the jacket, but he stopped and looked at her. "What do you mean?"

"I mean take it off. Take it all off. I've only seen you to-tally naked once, you know. I don't think that's fair, so I want to watch you strip."

"I can show you naked if you want. But I'm not strip-ping."

She laughed at the indignant look on his face. "I don't want you to do a routine to "It's Raining Men." I just want to watch you get undressed."

He wanted to argue, she could tell. But then, those warm rich chocolate eyes trained on her, he started to unbutton his shirt. Her mouth went dry in reaction. Her inner thighs had an equal and opposite reaction.

When he undid the last button, he didn't play around, but just stripped the shirt off, his shoulders muscles rippling as he worked off the sleeves, dropping it to the floor.

Dammit. He had a T-shirt on under there.

Which he pulled over his head and tossed at her. It hit her in the chest and she fisted her hand in it. It was warm, soft cotton, and covered with his scent. She brought it to her nose and took a whiff, loving that deep, rich, guy smell that was so different from her own.

He had peeled off his socks after kicking off his shoes, and he was working open his belt, now. Reese wanted to grab that tuft of caramel hair above his waistband and tug. Haul him right on over to her where she could squeeze his pecs and pull his zipper down with her teeth.

The window behind her was open a foot, letting in a crisp fall breeze, rushing over her arms, raising goose bumps and setting her nipples on end in her sweater.

She shivered. Knight didn't look the least bit cold. He looked hot. Really, really rock solid hot.

All he was missing was oil rubbed over his chest.

He took his pants off. Then his underwear.

Now she was warm. Whew. There was a five-alarm fire burn-ing under her skirt and her sweater was suddenly too thick.

"Anything else you want me to do?" Knight asked, holding his arms up.

There were a lot of things she wanted him to do but it was her turn first.

"Just stand there."

A bus lumbered by outside as Reese reached him. She was dropping to her knees to take him in her mouth when she heard Claire call out, "Hi! I'm home. What are you guys up to?"

The door slammed. Reese froze half bent, before recovering herself to step in front of Knight, attempting to block him from Claire's view.

Knight made a choking, strangled sound.

Claire screamed. "Ohmigod. Oh, shit, Derek!" She closed her eyes tight and clutched her hands in front of them. "Yuck, yuck, I think I'm blind now. Why don't you guys put a note on the door or something?"

Knight's cheeks were a dusky red, in what Reese thought was the closest she was ever going to see him to a blush. He bent over and tugged on his pants without underwear and hastily zipped them up. "A sign on the door that says what?"

He backed up towards his bedroom, swiping the rest of his clothes off the floor. "You can open your eyes now."

"How about a sign that says Do Not Disturb?" Claire popped one eye open and peered through her fingers, like she didn't trust what she might see.

"This isn't a hotel. So I guess if you're going to live here we'll have to make some adjustments."

"Oh, didn't Reese tell you? I guess you were too *preoccupied*. She and I found a sublet together. We move in on Friday and have it for three months. Cool, huh?"

Knight didn't look like he thought it was cool. His jaw dropped, he shot Reese a frown, then stepped the final step back into his bedroom and slammed the door shut.

"Well, that was really embarrassing," Claire said, tossing

her hair back and dumping her purse on the couch. "Don't
you think?"

"Actually, I'm fine." Unlike Knight, she still had her
clothes on. If you didn't count her panties, which were lying
on the floor by the bookcase, but hopefully they weren't noticeable. Now if Claire had walked in a minute later . . . that
might have been embarrassing.

Reese sat down on the ivory couch next to Claire. It was
another piece of furniture she wouldn't have thought was
Knight's style. Curious, she asked Claire, "Did your brother
pick out all this furniture? This isn't really a guy couch, if
you know what I mean."

Claire made a face. "Dawn picked this stuff out. When she
left, she said Derek could have it, because she just wanted to
move forward or something bitchy like that."

She should have known. The couch was kind of ugly. And
lumpy. What was that thing poking her in the butt?

Annoyed, she stood up.

"I'll be right back, Claire." She headed for the bedroom.

"Oh, take your time. I'll just turn up the TV really loud."

Reese laughed and opened Knight's bedroom door.

He was standing by the bed zipping up his jeans. He
looked at her in alarm. "Don't touch me, Reese."

"What? Calm down."

"I'm serious." He held out his hand. "If you touch me, I'm
not responsible for my actions and I really don't want to
make love to you with my sister in the next room."

She rolled her eyes. "I'm not here to rape you. I wanted to
talk to you about me moving in with Claire."

He ran his hand through his hair, making it stick up.
"Yeah, what exactly is that all about?"

"Well, I couldn't afford to stay in the hotel for who knew
how long. And Claire needed a roommate for the sublet for
three months, which will give her time to find an apartment
on her own. So it works out for everyone."

His expression was unreadable. "You could have stayed with me, you know."

Yeah, if she wanted to *completely* fall in love with him. No thanks.

"I didn't think that was a good idea." She wouldn't be able to see him yawning out of sleep each morning, brushing his teeth and smiling at her over coffee and not want to just fling herself in his arms and beg him to let her stay permanently.

That was a humiliation she could do without, when he so kindly explained that she was great in the short-term but as soon as a woman who could do laundry came along, she was gone. It would be hard enough to spend the next three days with him.

"I thought it would be presumptuous."

He still wasn't saying anything. She added, "So is it okay though, if I stay here until Friday?"

"Sure." He shrugged and reached for a pair of gym shoes. "Have you eaten dinner? Want to go for pizza?"

That was it? Sure. Sure, she could stay with him. She hadn't asked him to water her plants for her, she had asked him if she could live with him. For only three days, but still. This was a big deal.

This would push their relationship into a whole different realm. They would be sharing a bathroom, and all he could say was sure?

So much for being in control. She suddenly felt like she'd been dangled over a cliff and shaken hard.

But if Knight could do nonchalance, so could she. "A pizza? Sounds good. Just let me get my underwear."

Derek was sweating his way through a meeting with Nordstrom on Wednesday. There was no one to save him. He was alone, on his own, soaking through his shirt to the jacket of the new black suit Reese had insisted he wear today.

Nordstrom looked ready to pop a vein in his temple and Derek's knee was aching like hell. It was acting up from all the activity lately. Namely, too much sex. Who would have ever thought he would be saying that?

"So let me get this straight. Your girlfriend, who I was subjected to the sight of you PDA-ing in the elevator, now has a job at Delco Pharmaceutical as some kind of gopher for Ashton Chatterton?"

"Yes, sir." He kept his mouth shut about the Public Display of Affection crack.

Nordstrom's jaw worked back and forth. "You know, you're a good agent."

There was a big old fat-ass *but* coming on the end of this, Derek just knew.

"But . . . you have an incredible talent for just sucking trouble right to you. Like dirt to a little kid. I've got Washington on my ass, I've got antitrust chomping at the bit wondering when they can take a look at our case, and what do I have? I have a bunch of papers that indicate possible patent-fixing and one tape of execs acting like maybe they engage in dividing the drug market. I've got one nervous CW who is likely to bolt at any second, and an agent with a personal life that is suddenly spilling over onto the Bureau." He shook his head. "I'm not a happy man."

Derek wasn't sure why making Nordstrom happy seemed to be his job, but he would give it his best shot. "We need to go to New Zealand, sir. We need that entire meeting on tape and camera so we can see and hear everything. We need a surveillance guy to rig a conference room with the equipment. All we need on tape is some kind of verbal agreement from Chatterton and the guys at Stanfield and Ricould and we've got them. Together with all the documents we have, the antitrust prosecutors will be happy."

"Nothing makes those guys happy." Nordstrom snorted. "But okay, we'll go to New Zealand. The three case agents and Schwartz, who can set up the equipment. We'll contact the New Zealand authorities and get permission and you need to try and find out the hotel this is happening in."

Nordstrom leaned back in his chair, making it squeak. He tossed the pen he'd been twirling in his hand onto his desk. "How's Markson holding up? Is he going to be able to handle this?"

Derek sure in the hell hoped so. "He's okay so far."

"And your girlfriend? Can you control her? She can't be running around saying her boyfriend's a Fed."

Derek knew that his ability to control Reese was about as likely as the weatherman ordering sunny skies and seventy degrees. "She's a smart woman. She understands and won't slip up."

His boss's eyebrow rose. "Man, you're completely whipped, aren't you?"

Derek knew he should protest, but he wasn't convinced that he wasn't, in fact, whipped. It certainly seemed like Reese managed to get her way the majority of the time.

"Nice suit, by the way. I'm guessing Girlfriend picked it out for you." Nordstrom gave a crack of laughter.

"She had nothing to do with the suit. I picked it out." With his sister. And was wearing it at Reese's request.

Shit. He was whipped.

Nordstrom shook his head and picked up his coffee mug. "Anyway, I can't believe this case is dragging on like this. New Zealand. Hell, you're going halfway around the damn world. Let's hope they say something worth getting on tape."

Derek had surpassed hoping and had gone to praying. This was it. Make or break time.

Reese was bored to tears. Ashton Chatterton had no meetings scheduled for Wednesday, only phone calls and some afternoon golf. Jennifer didn't seem to know what to do with her.

"Is there anything I could file, or make copies of, or call caterers or something?"

"Well . . ." Jennifer looked around her cubicle at a loss. Jennifer was Marjorie's assistant, who was Chatterton's actual personal assistant. Marjorie's desk was in a real office attached to Chatterton's and Marjorie herself was elusive, squirreled away all day, apparently busy doing things Reese couldn't even fathom.

"I suppose you could book a hotel reservation. Normally our travel department makes flight arrangements and books hotels, but Mr. Chatterton likes one of us to personally oversee scheduling conference rooms when he's out of town. The travel department doesn't always accommodate Mr. Chatterton's specific needs."

Reese tuned the woman out as Jennifer went into a story about Chatterton not being pleased with once having a conference room next to one that was hosting a jump-rope competition.

"Where and when?" she finally interrupted, grateful for the opportunity to do something anything—besides making copies of her face in the Xerox machine to send as postcards to her brothers.

Taking this job had been meant to serve a dual purpose. She had thought to speed the Feds's case along by helping them gather any evidence they needed, or prevent the CW from bolting and leaving them high and dry. Second, she had thought being on the inside of Delco she could conduct her own journalistic investigation into the company and their illegal dealings.

She now realized both were stupidly optimistic.

There was nothing she could do to assist Knight on this case when the only tasks required of her were ordering twelve club sandwiches and buying new batteries for Chatterton's cell phone.

And there was really nothing to investigate. She had access to all the information the FBI had sitting in her suitcase at Knight's apartment. All the paper evidence was there, hidden on her digital camera and laptop. If there was more information to be had, she didn't know where to find it. Even if she did, she probably wouldn't recognize the significance of it.

Her only hope was to hover at these incessant meetings and hope Chatterton or another exec alluded to something criminal, which Knight would be taping anyway.

"Okay, so book a conference room in New Zealand. Got it."

Jennifer handed her the file after a pregnant pause. As Reese took it, Jennifer said sternly, "Now, I'll be at my desk if you have any problems. All Mr. Chatterton's needs are clearly outlined in the file."

"I got it." How hard was it to call and say "book me a room?" A third grader could do this job.

Turning her back on Jennifer, she headed towards the cubicle that had been temporarily assigned to her. No one seemed to know exactly what to do with her, so they had stuck her in the corner by the men's rest room, which had prompted her to decorate her desk with a scented candle.

Flipping open the file, she quickly scanned it. "Okay, meeting room for twelve, including executives from Delco, Stanfield, and Ricould." Those names sounded familiar.

Reese scanned further. "Need lunch, need paper and easel, convenient to airport. No problemo."

It wasn't until she was passing Chatterton in the hall an hour later that she realized why those names were familiar. They were the other companies involved in the antitrust investigation.

When Chatterton nodded and smiled at her, she blurted out, "I made your travel arrangements to Auckland, Mr. Chatterton. Everything's all set."

Though he looked a little startled, he smiled and nodded. "Thank you, Reese."

Reese tipped back on her high heels, wearing a gray skirt and white blouse she had borrowed from Claire. "You know, I've never been to New Zealand. I've never even left the U.S. I bet it's pretty there."

She was babbling, not sure what to say, but she wanted to

keep Chatterton talking. Not that she thought he was going to say anything important, but she needed to at least try.

"It's very nice, I've been there several times."

"You know they filmed *Lord of the Rings* there. Well, not in Auckland but somewhere in New Zealand. It's very green."

There was another small silence while Chatterton looked at her, a slight smile as he seemed to make a decision. "You know, Reese, I always take an assistant with me on these trips. Marjorie can't go, her mother is having bypass surgery. And Jennifer hates to fly. How would you like to go with me? It's only three days, but you'd have plenty of time to sight-see in the evenings."

Reese tried not to grin. She couldn't ask for anything better. "Mr. Chatterton, I'd love to. That's so generous of you considering how new I am."

Then Chatterton gave her that smile, the creepy I've-got-plans-for-you smile that made her want to cross her legs. "I have great hopes for your future here, Reese. You're just the kind of employee I've been looking for."

As he walked down the hall, Reese was left with the impression that she'd just walked straight into grandma's cottage and Chatterton was the waiting wolf.

Derek stared at the ceiling and willed himself to fall asleep. But he'd been doing that for ten minutes and he was still wide awake, painfully aware of Reese lying next to him.

Even though Reese had spent the night in his apartment on Tuesday, they had been so exhausted after another marathon sex session, they had both just tumbled into sleep. When he had gotten up in the morning, Reese was still sleeping.

But tonight was different. Derek had picked Reese up from work, they had gone out to dinner, then come back and had watched a movie together. Then Reese had said she was tired, and so they had come to bed and he was lying there wondering why he felt like a fifteen-year-old on his first date.

Damn, this was uncomfortable. And it was all Reese's fault for flipping out over his calling her his girlfriend. If he knew she was his girlfriend, he would know how to act. But if they were just lovers, they wouldn't be living together, even if it was only temporary. If they were just friends, they wouldn't be having sex.

So he didn't know what they were, or how to act, and it was cutting into his sleep time. Reese had asked to borrow a sweatshirt, saying she was cold, and now she was cuddled up next to him in his shirt and her pajama pants. It shouldn't be sexy, but it was because Derek felt like they had crossed over into something different. He had watched her brush her teeth. Her face crap was intermingling in the drawer with his shaving cream.

He had a boner. Her breath was tickling his neck, and he could smell her minty clean scent. He was flat on his back, legs slightly raised to hide the state of his erection from her, since she didn't appear the least interested in sex.

She was snuggling against him, making little sighs as she settled into sleep. Out of self-preservation he had put on sweat pants and he was grateful for them when her leg brushed against his.

He really, really wanted her. Slow, long, languid, in his own bed, her head resting on his pillow as he filled her, with gentle controlled strokes, pushing her over the edge. But Reese had given him no signals she felt the same and he thought maybe it was time to back off.

They'd had sex every day for the last five days. If he approached her now, she might think he was a pig who was after only one thing.

"Comfortable?" she murmured, dropping a little kiss on his shoulder.

"Yep." If stiff as a corpse was comfortable.

"Good. Me, too."

Derek stared wide-eyed at the shadow from the window

on the ceiling and figured he only had to lie there for eight more hours before he could give up the game and get up. But at least Reese was comfortable.

Reese was so uncomfortable she wanted to sit up in the bed and scream. She could not believe Knight was just going to fall asleep without a touch, a kiss, a hand on the breast, *anything*.

Was he over her? Now that he'd seen her with her face shiny from her cleanser, wearing a big bulky sweatshirt, didn't he find her attractive anymore? Was he *satisfied*? Call her a greedy you-know-what, but she had spent the day looking forward to a little nookie.

She had purposely delayed discussing the New Zealand trip with him, recognizing he might not be entirely overjoyed with the news that she was going with Chatterton. So she figured she would tell him during the afterglow.

Only if they just lay here, there wasn't going to be any afterglow unless she had a really vivid dream.

At first she just thought he was waiting for her to hint, but now she was practically humping his leg and he still showed no signs of making a move.

His arm wasn't even really holding her. It was more like he was tolerating her lying on him. If she turned to the right, she'd probably roll right off him and onto the floor without his noticing. And his left arm was behind his neck.

This was all Knight's fault for calling her his girlfriend. If he hadn't put all that pressure on them, it wouldn't suddenly feel so weird. They could have just gone on having sex, strangers enjoying each other.

Except she knew that no one could keep going on like that, and each moment you spent together pushed you farther away from strangers and more into intimacy.

Which is probably why she'd gone and just about fallen in love with him. Stupid, stupid, stupid. And here she was already, feeling miserable. She might as well slap a sign on her forehead that said Dumb Girl.

Knight's breathing had evened and slowed, his eyes drifting closed. He was really, truly, actually going to fall asleep.

"Are you falling asleep?" she asked incredulously.

His eyes snapped open and he looked at her warily. "I was planning on it."

"Without even a good night kiss or anything?"

He blinked and turned his head to look at her. "You want a good night kiss?"

"No! I want you to want a good night kiss." Duh.

He shrugged. "I always want a kiss from you. But you looked sleepy and I didn't want to bug you."

Reese liked looking at him like this, her eyes just about level with his, that scratchy chin of his inches from her lips, his strong arm now locking around her back. Maybe this wasn't such a disaster after all. Maybe Knight was just being polite.

They were both just kind of feeling their way through this very unexpected and amazing thing between them.

She tossed her leg over his, so that her thigh was firmly against his. "If you're bugging me, trust me, I'll let you know."

There was another pause, and Reese held her breath.

Then Knight said, "So, say, if I wanted to flip you on your back right now and make love to you so slow and good it would take half the night . . . that wouldn't bug you?"

Honey, baby. Reese knew that look in his eye. He hadn't lost interest. At all.

"Why don't you flip me on my back and we'll see?"

Chapter Sixteen

Derek was half asleep and pretty sure he had heard Reese wrong. The coffeepot wasn't done brewing yet, and he was half lying on his kitchen table, yawning. His prediction had been true. He hadn't slept at all the night before, but for a much better reason than staring at the ceiling counting sheep.

"What did you say, Peaches?" He spoke in a low voice, aware of Claire still sleeping on the couch ten feet away, huddled under two blankets. Claire was also the reason he had thrown on a T-shirt and a pair of basketball shorts.

Reese sat on the chair across from him, her legs drawn up and his sweatshirt pulled over them all the way until she tucked her toes under the bottom.

"I said that Chatterton wants me to go on a business trip with him."

Damn, that's what he thought she had said. The last thing he wanted was Reese heading off somewhere with that dirty old man. There was only one reason Chatterton would be taking Reese with him and it wasn't for her people skills.

He was about to point that out when she added, "We're going to New Zealand on October fourth through the eighth."

New Zealand? He sat straight up.

"And I thought you'd want to know that Stanfield and

Ricould are both going to be there, too. Of course, you probably know that already, don't you?"

Yeah, but how did she know? This could only be a bad thing.

"Actually, I did know that. In fact, I'm going to be in Auckland myself." He spoke with caution, waiting to see where this was going.

"Oh, great. We can get a room together, then." Reese picked at a muffin on the table in front of her, crumbling bits between her fingers, then licking them off.

"Because you know, I got the impression that Chatterton might want to pull something, you know, sexual with me, and this way I can just tell him that I've reunited with my fiancé. Also, that way if he sees you and recognizes you, it will be a good cover story."

His ulcer burned. The way she sat there so casually and said she thought her boss wanted her drove him nuts. As did the thought of Chatterton actually succeeding in cornering Reese behind the water cooler or in a conference room. He really, really wanted her to quit that stupid job. "If you thought Chatterton was going to come on to you, then why would you want to go on a trip with him?"

"To help with the investigation. What if Markson flips out? I can take over."

"If Markson flips out, the whole case is in the toilet. I want you to stay home. I don't like you being with Chatterton."

She snorted. "I'll be with you at night. And what's he going to do during a meeting with twelve people present?"

Derek so did not want to go there mentally. "Look, you cannot help the investigation, so I would really prefer it if you stayed home."

That was the wrong thing to say. Reese shot him a mutinous look, her feet dropping to the kitchen floor, her hands landing on the round pine table, rattling it. "I already have helped you. Did you know that the meeting will take place in the Auckland Hilton? Did you know that they're meeting in

Ballroom B, on the fourth floor, and that they requested an easel with paper and that Chatterton plans to stay for three days?"

Wait a minute. She knew what room they were meeting in? "How do you know all that?"

"Because I booked the arrangements, you dill weed."

That sounded like an insult, but he wasn't sure. "What's a dill weed?"

"You. You're a dill weed."

Well, that cleared things right up.

She stood up and got a mug out of his cabinet. She poured some coffee and took a sip.

He looked at the pot longingly.

"I'm not getting you any, so just forget it."

As he pushed back his chair, she made a sound of total exasperation and slammed her mug down. She got out another mug, one that said FBI on the side, and poured coffee in it, sloshing over the sides as she turned.

"Here." She handed it to him, sulking.

"Thank you."

"It's only because your knee looks swollen this morning. Don't get used to it."

It was right then that Derek realized that he cared about Reese way too much.

Reese wanted to stay aloof, she wanted to be tough and in control, distant from him. Yet she cared. Whether she wanted to admit it or not, she cared about him and he wanted her to stay.

Which he knew wasn't going to happen, and he was grateful for that. He needed her to go home to New York, to put distance between them so he didn't get any stupid ideas that maybe this could work out long-term and that maybe Reese wouldn't mind getting married and settling down in the suburbs with an SUV.

He pictured Reese packing leftover chicken wings in school lunches for the kids.

Not a pretty sight.

It was time to think with his brain, and not other body parts.

Later.

After a long sip of coffee, he took her hand and pulled her down onto his lap. She came willingly, but still frowning.

"Thank you." He nestled into her neck, kissing along the warm skin that led down to the tops of her breasts.

Stretching the neck of his sweatshirt, he sucked the curvy swell of her chest. "Thanks for the name of the hotel. That's a big help to me."

She squeezed his shoulders, arching back so her breasts met his mouth more easily. "See? I knew I could help you."

"You were right and I'm big enough to admit it. Markson probably won't know the hotel for a couple of days still."

"Working together isn't so bad, is it? We can both get what we want."

Derek knew what he wanted. He wanted to lay her across his kitchen table and have Reese for breakfast, but a blond head suddenly popped up from the couch.

"Morning," Claire said, then frowned as Derek removed his head from Reese's sweatshirt.

"Oh, geez. You two have a bedroom, you know. Use it and spare me first thing in the morning, please."

Reese reached around him for her coffee mug. Actually, his coffee mug, but then Reese wasn't known for being overly concerned with distinctions like that.

"Sorry, Claire. I'll be more sensitive to your virgin eyes from now on."

"Very funny." Claire yawned and sat up. "But you're about six years too late on that one."

Derek shifted, rocking Reese's behind on his thigh a little as he grew alarmed at the turn in the conversation. He had been joking. Now his stomach began to churn at images of his baby sister being deflowered. He had a whole new appreciation for Reese's brothers and their high-handed methods.

Claire went on before he could find a sock to stuff in her mouth. "Remember Justin, that guy from your training class at Quantico?"

"What about him?" She could not mean that Justin, a friend he trusted, who had spent a weekend with him and Dawn about five years ago, had slept with her.

He was sure Justin valued his balls way too much to risk Derek ripping them off and shoving them down his throat.

"He took my virginity."

Oh, hell. Derek felt his blood pressure go through the ceiling into Mrs. Frajapagne's apartment above him. "Justin? He's ten years older than you! You have fucking got to be kidding me!"

Claire laughed. "I am."

"What?" he asked in confusion, trying to remember when he had last heard from Justin. He'd do a database search at work today, track the guy down, and murder him.

"I'm kidding. I didn't sleep with Justin. He treated me like an annoying little sister the whole weekend he was here."

Reese choked on her coffee, hot liquid spray hitting him across the face as her lips burst open on a laugh. He blinked, coffee dripping down his nose as his heart rate returned to normal and his murderous thoughts shifted from Justin to Claire.

"That is not funny," he told them both sternly.

"I'm sorry," Reese said as she choked back laughter, taking the sleeve of his shirt she was wearing and wiping the coffee mist off his face.

Claire was laughing on the couch, enjoying her joke.

Reese and Claire were both so young, so fresh, so connected to each other in their humor and outlook, that Derek felt a pang that had nothing to do with Claire's sex life.

Given the pains in his chest, and his gut, and his knee, and listening to them lose it over something he found not even remotely funny, Derek felt about as old as dirt.

*   *   *

Reese wondered why she had quit her boring and meaningless job at the *Newark News* to take one even more so at Delco Pharmaceutical.

Nothing of absolutely any interest had happened since her hallway encounter with Chatterton.

Until Markson popped his head into the copy room on Friday and said, "Excuse me, Reese. Can I see you in my office, please? I need some copies made."

What did she look like? Rent-a-secretary? "Alright, give me a second." She had piles of collated reports stacked precariously on every table and surface in the room.

Delco hadn't heard of the concept of a paperless society. Everything was sent via E-mail, then reinforced in hard copy.

Deciding there was nothing she could do with the mess in the next second, she sighed and followed Markson down the hall to his office. He hovered at the door until she was in, then shut the door and locked it.

Not cool. Trying to keep the edge out of her voice, she said, "What did you need, Mr. Markson?"

"I know who you are," he said, taking a step in her direction.

Stan Markson was normally a very average-looking guy, but with that strange gleam in his eye and sweat stains in the armpits of his white dress shirt, he veered into alarming. Scary. Reese took a step back and felt around on his desk for a paperweight to lob at him if necessary.

She said lightly, not wanting him to smell her fear, "Of course you know who I am. I'm Reese, the woman who gets paid to hand you coffee."

"You're Agent Knight's girlfriend. I recognize you from that night in the Holiday Inn parking lot."

"Oh, uh . . ." This was better. Maybe. If Markson didn't plan to murder her and toss her out with the trash, *Knight* would when he found out Markson knew who she was.

"You're really an undercover agent, aren't you?"

Well, that was kind of a cool thought. Special Agent Hampton, going undercover. She was tempted to lie for about a split second, then sanity returned. "No, I'm not. I'm really Knight's . . . girlfriend." She about swallowed her tongue on the word.

Markson looked distracted by that. "I thought he was married."

"He's divorced."

"He looks like the married type. Not your type at all."

Like this goof knew what her type was. It made sense to just explain they had a casual relationship, or even to just let the topic drop. It didn't matter what Stan Markson, Delco informant, thought about her love life.

That's what she should have done. Instead she said, "What do you mean? We're *perfect* for each other. Knight is sooo happy with me. Happy, happy, happy."

Oh, my God. She sounded perky.

"Well, he seems like a nice guy. He's been real honest and fair with me, I always thought. That's why I was worried that maybe the FBI wasn't telling me everything, and you were an agent."

"No, I'm not an agent, I promise." But she was a reporter, and she sniffed exclusive interview. "But I am a journalist, Mr. Markson. This job here at Delco is a cover, just not for the Bureau. I'm doing my own journalistic investigation side by side with the FBI, so that when indictments are handed out, the public will know the whole story."

Markson wiped a bead of sweat off his forehead, glancing around nervously like he expected Chatterton to beam into his office. "I never thought about the story going public. This will all come out, won't it? Everyone is going to know I was the informant."

"I think the FBI will try to keep that quiet initially, but yes, eventually Delco will know it's you. But I think, in order to protect your best interests, you should grant me an exclusive interview with you. We'll hit the public right away with your story, how you wanted to save average Americans hundreds of dollars, how you wanted to stop corporate theft. We've got to spin you as the hero that you are right up front, Stan."

Reese wondered if using his first name was pushing too hard, but she didn't have much time here. Markson already looked ready to throw himself out the window. And she meant every word. Someone needed to look out for this guy and make sure he didn't end up losing his career and his reputation when the whole case blew open.

"I don't know. . . . I really hadn't thought about what would happen afterward." Stan sank into the camel colored leather chair in front of his desk. "Oh, damn. This has gone so much farther than I ever intended."

Reese felt sorry for him. Here he was, trying to do the right thing, and he might very well get squashed in the process. "Think about the interview, Stan. Go home, talk it over with your wife, and let me know. I want to help you."

She reached onto his desk and took one of his business cards from the little gold case. Scribbling her name and cell phone number on the back, she handed it to him. "I'm going to be here at Delco until the investigation is over, and I'm going on the New Zealand trip. Let me know if you ever need to talk about anything. I can do and say whatever I want, unlike the FBI agents, who have rules to follow."

Even if she had rules, she probably wouldn't follow them, but she knew how Knight was skating on thin ice with his boss. She knew he wouldn't be able to go to bat for Markson if need be.

"Okay, I'll think about it." Markson took the card and stared at her, his pale gray eyes searching. "You know, this company is going to be rocked to its very foundation if we get the evidence in New Zealand. There are all kinds of illegal activities going on. The price-fixing is just the beginning."

"So I shouldn't invest in the 401K plan?"

Markson gave a nervous laugh. "Not if you want your money to *stay* your money."

Watching the agony on his face, Reese felt bad for him.

She put her hand on his shoulder and squeezed. "Hey, for what it's worth, you're doing the right thing. That takes guts."

"Or stupidity." He dragged his hand across his face.

"Stupidity is wearing these shoes." She bent her knee and stuck a spiked heel in his face. "You're being courageous."

With another pat on his shoulder, she headed for the door. "Now, I've got to get back or Jennifer will have a cow. Think about the interview and let me know, okay?"

Markson sat motionless in the chair. "Thanks," he said absently, waving at her as she unlocked the door.

When she got back to the copy room, her perfectly collated piles of papers were tossed on a table in a massive jumble and Amber, the twenty-year-old intern, smiled at her.

"I moved your stuff. I hope I didn't mess anything up."

Forget the *New York Times* byline. Reese wanted a freaking Pulitzer Prize after all this hassle.

But first she had to collate.

"Are you really going through with this?" Derek lifted Reese's suitcase, along with an overflowing shopping bag, and headed for the door.

"Yep."

"Why?" He didn't want Reese to move in with his sister. Or more accurately, he didn't want her to move out. Three days, and he was already used to her being around all the time.

"Because it's what Claire and I planned to do." Reese was wearing a pair of his sweat pants, and her ankles looked like the sticks on cotton candy. Two little skinny strips of flesh surrounded by yards of puffy navy cotton.

She might be moving out, but she was taking half his wardrobe with her, including an assortment of sweat pants, T-shirts and jeans.

It amazed him that Reese never seemed to think her permanently borrowing his clothes, a huge girlfriend thing to do, was a big deal, yet she freaked out at any mention of that G word. Nor did he understand why he was allowing her to rob him of practically every item of casual clothing he owned.

"It just seems like a lot of hassle, and you're not going to be in Chicago for that long." He wanted to add, *Are you?* but refrained himself. "Claire can find another roommate."

Reese blew her hair out of her eyes. "Are you jealous or something? Don't you want me to be friends with Claire?"

"Of course I want you to be friends with my sister. But if you're there, and I'm here . . ." He reached out and tugged on the waist of the sweat pants she was wearing. "I can't do this whenever I want."

He kissed her, covering her mouth with his, tasting her tongue as he moved his hands inside the bulky pants to cover the front of her satin panties. His thumb rushed over her as he sucked the tip of her tongue between his lips.

God, she tasted so good, and every time she was near him, he wanted her, a deep quaking quenching need that couldn't be satisfied until he'd touched and tasted everywhere.

"Umm, the silky kind," he whispered as he slid along the heated slope of her panties. "I like these the best."

"I thought you liked the thong." Reese kissed the corners of his mouth, her own hand exploring across the front of his jeans until she found his erection.

Not that it was hard to miss.

Especially after mention of the thong. "Maybe I'm not picky, I like whatever you've got on. Or even better—off."

"Knight, it's time to go. I told Claire I'd pick up the keys from the landlord at three o'clock."

"You're not talking to someone who cares." Squatting down, he took her sweat pants and that scrap of satin down, exposing her dark red curls to him.

"Knight," she warned, her thighs tense, her fingers digging at his shoulder flesh.

Reaching out, he put one thumb on either side of her and

gently parted her until he could see her dewy pink folds surrounded by the halo of hair. He dipped his tongue in and tasted, running from one end to the other until he was throbbing with desire, his thumbs trembling as they held her.

He could feel the moment she gave in, when her fingers slackened on him, her head went back, her breath sighed, and when he tasted her again, she was wet and ready.

"We need to leave," she said, even as the shopping bag she was holding tumbled from her hand onto the floor.

"No."

"You can't hold me here against my will."

He sucked her clitoris, felt her shudder. "Who's holding you against your will? I'm not pointing a gun at you."

"No. And you don't have me handcuffed, either."

Something about her tone made him snap his head up. Her lips were parted, her eyelids heavy, her breasts jutting beneath his T-shirt. He thought about handcuffing Reese to his bed and swallowed hard. Those milky white arms, up over her head, her hair swinging back and forth as she strained to get free, her breasts tumbling over her chest.

His cock about ripped a hole in his jeans.

He didn't know where his cuffs were, since he rarely used them investigating white-collar crimes. But he did know where his gun was. In the drawer of the end table, about a foot from his hand, where he always kept it when he was off-duty.

"Don't move."

"Is that an order?"

"Yes." As he stood up, he stripped her T-shirt up and off, sucking her nipple through the satin of her bra. Above the smooth edge was a red bruise, marring her creamy skin.

It was from his mouth, several days before, sucking hard on her flesh, and the sight of it spurred him on, took his desire to new lengths, pushed him beyond rational. He loved turning her on, making her whimper, caressing her softness and burying himself in her.

Stay. He wanted her to stay.

Reaching around her back, he undid the clasp of her bra, let her breasts spring forward into his hands as she gave a low moan. Then he tossed that bra to the floor, and lifted her right leg. He worked the sweat pants off and then did the same to the left leg.

Leaning back, he took her in, every pale, soft, smooth, awe-inspiring inch of her. Her creamy skin was pinkened, flushed from her excitement, and her nipples were thrust forward. When her hands went up to sink into her hair, to push the thick lustrous strands off her face, he wished he had a camera to capture it. She was perfect. The moment was perfect, including the look in her eye.

She wanted him just as much as he wanted her.

The tip of her tongue came out and wet her plump bottom lip.

Derek, eyes still trained on her, opened the drawer of the end table and felt around until his fingers closed over his gun. When he pulled it out, Reese's eyes widened.

"What the hell is that for?"

She knew precisely what it was for. Her hands pressed against her belly, low, like she'd felt the same jolt of desire that he had.

"It's to make sure you don't leave." Derek removed the cartridge and put it back in the drawer and closed it. "Not until I'm finished with you, anyway."

Her eyes snapped at his tone. "I should kick you in the nuts," she said, making no move to do so.

"Why don't you?" He knew why. He wanted her to say it.

"Because then you wouldn't be able to fuck me."

Her words slammed into his gut, his eyes squeezing shut for a split second as he fought to control himself. He had never been one to like women who swore, but Reese saved it up, then used it when it packed a punch.

Derek ran his gun along her thigh, loving the way she

jumped in surprise. "Nothing's going to stop me from doing that, Peaches."

Even though her breath hitched, Reese managed to ask, "What's with the nickname? You've been calling me Peaches for days."

Reese's fingertips found their way into his hair, tugging hard on the much shorter strands, thanks to Claire and her insistence on a haircut. Taking the gun down past her knee, he kissed her between the thighs, just above her clitoris.

"It's because you taste like peaches. Sweet, ripe, juicy good."

The black steel of the gun against her feminine body made Derek ache for more than his cock deep inside her. It made him aware how lonely, how cold his life was, and how warm and soft and rich with laughter Reese was.

Stay. He wanted her to stay. But if he spoke the words that were hovering on the edge of his mouth, dancing around his heart, she would leave.

So instead he brought the barrel of his handgun between her thighs and teased it across her curls, his mouth dry, his heart pounding, his muscles taut as she jerked in surprise, her fingers tightening on him, her eyes fluttering shut, her mouth rounded into an O.

Reese was stunned speechless, a rarity for her any day of the week. But her shock came more from her own eager reaction than to Knight's behavior. He had a little bit of a dominating streak when it came to sex, and she knew that, wasn't surprised by it.

It surprised her that she liked it, that she craved it, that he made her whimper and claw at him and love every second of it. Reese was used to Knight giving in, indulging her, watching her with amusement when it came to just about everything. Except sex.

Here, he was in control. He made the moves and she gave in, indulged, and watched.

Maybe they weren't as wrong for each other as she had thought.

As wrong as this should feel right now, it felt nothing but exciting, arousing, safe. The cool barrel of Knight's gun brushed back and forth across her as he kissed her inner thighs, sliding his tongue across her hot skin in movement with the gun, until she wanted to push, to pull, to beg, to absorb him inside her.

When he teased her open with his fingertips, when he ran his gun across her wetness, she didn't protest. She bit her lip and sucked air in through her nose, the cold hardness against her warm body titillating in a way she wouldn't have expected. He never pushed it inside her, not even a little, but played with it across her like he would with his finger or his erection, brushing back and forth, teasing her clitoris until she squirmed.

"I want you," she begged, reaching down his chest, trying to pull him up, free him from his jeans before she died of want.

"Are you sure?" he asked, giving her a smirk as he stood up, moving his hands away from her. "Because I thought you had to go."

Reese went for his zipper. "Very funny."

Knight set his gun down on the end table and exchanged it for a condom.

"What else you got in that drawer? First a gun, then condoms . . . are you going to pull out wine and sex toys next?"

He ran one finger over her nipple while he pushed off his jeans with the other hand. "You wish."

Distracted by his touch on her breast, she couldn't come up with a single snappy comeback, and settled for reaching under his shirt and feeling his muscles.

He was so damn big, so guy, so everything different from her, that she loved to run her hands across his chest and twirl her fingers in the soft hair there. His body was becoming familiar to her, and Knight was no longer a stranger, but everything that she had claimed to not want him to be. He was her friend, her lover, her boyfriend.

For once the word didn't send her jerking back in horror, but sent a wave of satisfaction rolling through her, so deep, so intense that she wanted to march her suitcase back into Knight's bedroom and toss her clothes in his drawer.

"I wish you'd quit talking and finish getting that condom on."

"It's on." He nudged her legs apart with his feet while she pulled his shirt off over his head.

Then he picked up her left thigh and wrapped it around his waist, then held her to him with hands locked together on her lower back. Her breasts pressed into his chest, the hair there tickling her already overstimulated nipples.

"Please," she said, her thighs open, her body throbbing, his erection teasing her with gentle nudges.

"You don't have to beg. I'll always give you whatever you want."

Reese wanted to hear more in those words, wanted to ask, *Promise?* but her breath tore out of her in a muffled cry as Knight entered her in one smooth thrust.

And stopped. He stood still, their breath mingling, their eyes locked together, bodies pressed, as he throbbed inside her. Reese swallowed hard, feeling him pulse, holding himself back, too close to an orgasm already. His breath shuddered, and she knew what she wanted.

Rocking her hips back, she thrust onto him, enjoying the way he filled her and the vicious curse that tore from his lips. She moved again, and a third time, squeezing her inner muscles on him until he slid his hands around to her hips and met her with a thrust of his own, sending them both into an orgasm.

Reese clung to him, needing his strength to hold her up as she came in shivers of pleasure, tight and urgent.

And she knew she didn't want to leave. Ever.

Chapter Seventeen

Reese strongly suspected Markson was wearing a wire, and she was having a lot of fun with it. If Knight wouldn't/ couldn't tell her what was going on with the antitrust investigation, even after she had earned his trust and given him two weeks of Richter scale–shattering sex, then she was entitled to have a little fun at his expense.

Besides, the plane trip from Chicago to L.A., then on to Auckland, was half her life long and she was bored. Clip your toenails because there's nothing better to do bored.

Chatterton had insisted she fly on the Delco corporate jet with him, Markson, and four other executives. Chatterton had spent the entire flight so far on the phone, racking up cell phone bills that were probably the equivalent of Reese's New York rent.

He could afford it because he was probably charging some woman named Dottie Slotzsky in Jersey City three times more than her medication should cost. Reese sincerely hoped he got what was coming to him. Even if the case somehow didn't get indicted, she was still going to splash Chatterton's name all over the news, pointing to him as the crook that he was.

But in the meantime, she was talking to Markson, Jenkins, and Goldberg for lack of anything better to do. Russell, a man who would stand five three in heels, was fast asleep, mouth open and emitting a low snore.

Since there was no way to turn the conversation to business without arousing suspicion, Reese was just going for personal entertainment value. "So, are you guys married?"

Jenkins, the youngest of the bunch, and good-looking if you liked big foreheads, laughed. "Why, are you looking?"

"No, but I have an ugly friend who is."

They all laughed, including Markson, who looked more relaxed than . . . ever.

"But she only likes rich guys, so who qualifies?"

"Wait a minute," Goldberg protested with a grin. "If she's ugly, how is she going to hook a rich guy?"

"Good point. You've caught me. I made her up. I just wanted to know how much you guys make." They'd better hope they weren't too attached to their fancy lifestyles, since at least one of them was likely to end up in federal prison.

Reese tried to dredge up sympathy.

"I make enough," Goldberg said, raising his whiskey to his lips.

Jenkins shrugged out of his suit jacket. "Not me. Five hundred thousand doesn't go as far as it used to."

Any sympathy she might have felt shriveled up and died. Reese uncrossed her leg and snorted. The man clearly hadn't tried to live in New York on thirty grand a year.

"What are you spending all that money on?" she asked him. "Hookers and drugs?"

The other two seemed to think it was funny, even if Jenkins was frowning. But he shook it off and winked. "I could spend it on you."

There was a higher probability of Manhattan breaking free and floating off into the Atlantic.

"Thanks, but no thanks. I have a boyfriend." Sort of. For lack of a better word.

Even if she didn't get to see that much of him the last few

days because of this case. Even if they still had never spoken one word about what they actually *were*, and she had moved in with Claire as planned. Her entire life was one big *what-if-maybe-someday,* so why did it matter if she and Knight avoided the L word like meat sold off the back of a truck?

"You do? I bet you take good care of him."

Reese suspected that was a joke, given that she had become notorious at Delco for doing her job begrudgingly.

"Yeah, you know me. I'm Martha Stewart without the illegal activity."

Right now she was Martha with a numb butt, given that she'd been in this seat for three hours. At least the private jet was equipped with large, plush leather chairs and a minibar. She'd sucked down two packs of peanut M&M's, even if the flight was long and the company as stale as the snack foods.

Jenkins laughed at her joke, his voice heavy with amusement and sarcasm. "Yeah, because none of us at Delco would ever do anything illegal."

Derek tried to bend his knee to stretch it and was stopped by his bag in front of him. Kicking his carry-on under the seat, he tried to move his leg again and was stopped by the bump for the wheel under the seat in front of him.

Christ. Coach class sucked.

Maddock was sitting next to him, headphones on, singing in an off-pitch obnoxiously loud voice. Derek leaned against the plastic window screen and sighed.

He should be thrilled. He should be riding high from a tape Markson had brought him two days ago where Chatterton had been blatant in saying they were going to New Zealand to set prices. They were inches away from sending this case to the prosecutors, secure in knowing they had done their job. Nordstrom would be pleased, and maybe would take a week or two breather from riding his back.

Yet he was edgy. Nothing was settled, nothing was firm, this case wasn't closed.

And Reese was driving him nuts.

They spent all their time together joking and having great sex.

Which you wouldn't think would be a problem, and normally wouldn't be, except they were avoiding discussing anything that smacked of commitment or the future, and he was tired of it. He didn't even know if she was going to be in Chicago from one day to the next, or if she was going to head back to New York without warning and nothing but a cheery wave.

He sucked at timing, it seemed. Dawn had wanted nothing but commitment—marriage, a house, big cars, kids, more money, more time with him, and he hadn't been able to give her more than half of those. Now he was ready to settle down and get married again and have kids before he needed Viagra, and he'd fallen for a woman who suffered from that usually male syndrome, Fear Of Commitment.

Maddock hit a high note and Derek winced. Leaning over he pulled one of the earpieces away from Maddock and said, "Shut the hell up. You sound like a dying goat."

Maddock blinked at his unusually surly tone and dropped the headphones around his neck. "You're a little tense. Worried about Chatterton wanting to join the mile high club with Reese?"

Great. Now he had another reason to be pissed off.

"Oh, thank you. I never even thought of that." He fought the urge to groan. "Man."

Maddock turned off his music. "She's got you, hasn't she? You're just a shell of the man I once knew."

Maddock was joking, but Derek could tell he was serious as well, trying to show a little buddy-to-buddy concern. Derek appreciated the gesture. "Pretty pathetic, I know. You think I would have learned, but . . . damn. The minute I saw those legs I think I was gone."

Then she had tried to Mace him and smashed his toe with her high heel. God, he loved her.

"Can't blame you. I've seen her."

"What about you, Wyatt? You ever been in love?" Derek tossed the little cylindrical ice cubes around in his plastic airline cup and pulled his tray back down, playing with the catch on it.

"Nah. Had a serious girlfriend, you know, where you just care about each other and keep going on until something better comes along, but it wasn't really love."

"So what happened?"

"I guess something better came along. She went on a cruise with her girlfriends three years ago, and came back engaged to a guy she met on the day trip to Cozumel."

"No way."

Maddock shrugged with a grin. "Way. It's cool, though. She's happy. I'm happy."

Derek wasn't sure he could be so philosophical if he arrived in Auckland to find Reese had fallen for Ashton Chatterton over the Pacific Ocean.

"You're happy until CJ enters a room, then you turn into a lunatic."

Maddock grunted. "Explain to me why she got out of this trip again? Not that I mind. I'll probably stroll the beach and find me a Kiwi chick to keep me company, but still . . . seems like she should be here. White gets away with murder."

Derek knew exactly why CJ wasn't there and it wasn't his business to tell Maddock if he didn't know. In three years of working together, CJ had just now confided in him and he wasn't going to blab her private business around.

He had known CJ was divorced. He had known she had a kid, and chalked up her lack of conversation about her personal life to her personality. CJ didn't share anything about herself, and plenty of people were like that. But when she had come to him, to let him know she was asking Nordstrom to be excused from going to New Zealand, she had told him her son had special needs and couldn't be left with anyone but her mother. Given the short notice, she couldn't work out the arrangements.

He had been a little floored, but had been pleased she'd told him. She didn't elaborate on what special needs meant, and he didn't ask. He liked CJ, despite her reticence, and respected her. It sounded like she had a tough time of it, and he wanted to accommodate her.

"She had personal circumstances that affected her ability to travel."

Maddock snorted. "What the hell does that mean?"

"It means it's none of your damn business."

Maddock fingered the button of his CD player, his usual smile missing. "See, this is why I'm never falling in love. Women run the show, man, I'm telling you. Love is a circus. They just crack the whip, and all you guys just run around them like fucking trained poodles."

Derek tried to tell himself Maddock was wrong, but he did have a habit of panting whenever Reese entered the room. "Why don't you stick that on a greeting card, Wyatt? Very inspiring."

Reese felt like cat woman. She was hovering in a back stairwell of the Hilton hotel in downtown Auckland, waiting for Knight in a black stretchy top and black cigarette pants.

He had called her on her cell phone a half hour earlier, on his way to the hotel from the airport, and they had arranged to meet. She had no idea what time it was, having lost all sense of time zones somewhere over the Hawaiian Islands, but her stomach was telling her it was dinnertime.

When Knight came around the corner a minute or two later, she was seriously disappointed to find he was wearing khaki pants and a navy blue golf shirt. Not only did he not look covert or FBI-ish, he didn't even look like himself. He looked like an accountant.

He gave her the once over and raised an eyebrow. "Going to a funeral?"

"Where's your disguise? Geez, I thought we agreed to keep it quiet that you're here." Knight had nixed her original idea to have him be there as her fiancé. "I thought you'd be like in one of those skirts and T-shirts that all the Pacific Islander guys wear here. If Chatterton sees you like this, he'll recognize you."

"He won't see me, and nothing could make me put on a skirt."

Oh, please, that whole special agent arrogance got old quick. "Well, he won't see you if you get over here. You're just hovering in plain view."

Reese grabbed his arm and dragged him under the stairwell, where cobwebs were dangling from the steel underbeams of the steps. Dusty, but dark, just what she needed.

Knight's lip twitched. "How was your flight?"

"Fine." She brushed the question off. "Our room is 1212, and here's a key." Handing him the key card, she added, "Make sure you take the stairs. Chatterton will never climb the steps."

He took the key without a word.

"Did you bring your gun?"

"No, I can't be armed. We had enough trouble getting the New Zealand government to cooperate with our recording these meetings. They weren't about to allow me to be armed."

"Well, if you get into any trouble, Maddock should be able to handle it."

"Hey! *I* can handle it."

Reese had forgotten how fragile his ego was, distracted as she was by the excitement of the whole project. Added to that was the dark stairwell, the impending danger of getting caught, the way his hair fell in his eyes, and the fact that she hadn't seen him in over twenty-four hours.

"Knight, you forgot to give me a hello kiss." Reese

fisted her hand over the three buttons on his shirt. She'd never had sex on foreign soil. Maybe it was time to change that.

He gave her a smile, the one she loved, the one that said he saw right through her, and was ready to play the game.

"Missed me, huh? And you've been really demanding lately. Hello kisses, good-bye kisses . . . what's next?"

"How about you make love to me?" Right here, right now. She pressed against him.

"Sorry, Peaches. I've got work to do." He gave her a kiss on the forehead.

On the forehead.

"Oh, come on, just five minutes."

He laughed. "Reese, shame on you. You can wait a couple of hours."

"No, I can't. All this stealth activity is arousing." *Mission Impossible* always got her going. This was like the real-life version.

He bent down a little, easing his legs around her. Sucking her bottom lip, he murmured, "I'll make it up to you later."

Stiffening her body so she wouldn't stick herself to him like a leech, she decided to torture them both. "I've got a better idea. Why don't we go the whole trip without having sex, just to see if we can?"

He pulled back in astonishment. "That's the stupidest idea I've ever heard. I already know we can't go three days without touching each other."

"You're probably right. But wouldn't it be fun? I'm getting horny just thinking about it." Of course, even grocery shopping with Knight could probably get her horny. Him squeezing the melons, all those cucumbers, zucchini, and carrots just staring at her, reminding her of . . .

It was confirmed. She had become a pervert.

"I don't care. I'm not going to share a room with you and not touch you, so forget it." And to prove his point, he went up her shirt and cupped her breast, all while nibbling on the corner of her mouth.

If he insisted. Reese reached for the button on his pants, relaxing her body, shifting back to her original idea of here and now.

But Knight jerked back and shook his finger. "Uh-uh-uh. I see what that was. It was a trick to get me to do it now. I almost fell for it. Forget it, Reese. I've got to go, and this is a stairwell, for God's sake."

It had been worth a shot. But maybe he was right. Later that night they could go out to dinner, stroll down to the harbor, and make out under balmy moonlight. It was spring in Auckland, and the temperature was a gorgeous seventy degrees, perfect for romance.

"Fine." She sighed. This was really the problem with Knight, and exactly why she had known having an affair with him wouldn't work. He refused to be a pig, no matter how many chances she gave him to act like one.

Next he'd be telling her that he respected her.

Derek had tossed his things on the king size bed in Reese's room, then along with Schwartz, their equipment guy, he had gone to the conference room where the meeting was scheduled for the following day.

"How's it look, Schwartz?"

Special Agent Schwartz was a gum chewer, and his jaw moved as he studied the room, walking around, checking outlets, touching here and there.

"It's alright. Not great, but alright. A little too big for good sound quality, so we'll have to go with multiple recorders. One on the CW, then one with the camera, of course, and we'll need another one, maybe in a briefcase or something."

"Where are you going to put the camera?"

"In this ugly flower arrangement." Schwartz picked up the pot from the console table by the sofa and shook his head. "This thing looks like my mother's bathroom wallpaper."

Maddock came into the room, closing the door quickly behind him. He was grinning.

"What? You met some local girl already?"

"No." Maddock pulled a tape out of his pocket. "But you should hear the tape Markson made of the flight over here."

Derek caught his enthusiasm. "What? Did they say something incriminating?"

"No, but Reese asked Jenkins if he was spending all his money on hookers and drugs."

Derek felt a pain behind his eyebrows, and he sighed. "Somehow, I'm not surprised."

"Don't you want to hear it?" Maddock waved the tape in his face as Schwartz let out a laugh.

"No, I'll pass." If he wanted to hear Reese say something outrageous, he could just go upstairs to their room and do it in person.

Maddock looked disappointed. "Don't you even want to hear the part where the guy comes on to her and she tells him she has a boyfriend?"

A boyfriend? She'd said the word boyfriend? That was really damn hard to believe. Not that it mattered.

It didn't mean she thought of *him* as her boyfriend.

He'd look like an ass if he listened to it now.

Like a moony-eyed teenager.

Whipped.

"Maybe just real quick."

Chapter Eighteen

R eese was in the open-air restaurant in the six-story atrium of the hotel, reading *People* magazine and munching on a bag of peanuts, when Markson approached her.

"Uh, Reese, can we talk?" Markson's hand was shaking a little as he tugged at his tie.

Reese shoved her feet back into her sandals and sighed. "What is it, Stan?"

He probably couldn't figure out how to have his shirts dry-cleaned in the hotel. Her eyes wandered back to the article she'd been reading outlining the new rage—orthodontics for dogs. Braces for Fifi so the other poodles don't make fun of her crooked teeth? Reese stifled a laugh.

"Can I sit down?"

Reese looked up at Stan and dropped the magazine. Markson seemed nervous, more so than usual. "Sure. What's going on?"

"I'm ready to do that interview with you." Markson glanced around at the mostly empty restaurant. He winced when the lobby elevators swung open and a crowd of businessmen and -women walked out, talking loudly.

Reese followed his gaze, felt his increasing anxiety. She hoped like hell her voice was soothing. She wanted this interview in the worst way. "That's great, Stan. I promise I'll do the piece your way, with all the facts set straight. We'll show America that you're a hero."

He picked at the cocktail napkin in front of him. "Not a hero. Just trying to do the right thing. I want people to know that I wasn't doing anything illegal, I didn't want to sell out my buddies, but I just couldn't stand by and let Delco cheat its customers."

Where the hell was a tape recorder when you needed one? Reese didn't even have a pen to scribble notes on the napkin with. "That sounds perfect. Let's go up to my room where I can take notes and we can be comfortable, okay?"

Sitting out in the open like this was making her nervous. She could probably explain it with a lie or two if Chatterton or one of the other execs walked by, but Knight was another story. He could see through her BS in about five seconds and would want to know the true story. She could not tell him about the interview with Markson.

At least not until the case had gone to the lawyers and the piece was on its way to the *Chicago Tribune*.

"Sounds good. It's not a good idea to be seen together, is it?"

"No." Grabbing her magazine, Reese felt in her purse for her room key and headed for the elevators, Markson trailing behind.

There was a small alcove by the elevators filled with potted plants and a shoe-shine stand. The stand was empty, but Reese came to a screeching halt in front of it. Markson walked into the back of her, grunting in surprise.

His hands went to her shoulders to steady them both and Reese whirled around, intent on hiding from Jenkins and Goldberg, who were waiting in front of the elevators, look-ing bored. She did not want to explain why she was with Markson, realizing she could probably lie her way through it, but he would more than likely blush and sweat and stam-mer.

"Back up," she whispered to him fiercely.

"What? Why?" His hands still rested on her shoulders.

Given their collision, they were still just about on top of

each other and Reese grabbed the lapels of his suit jacket and shoved, panic setting in. This wouldn't look like a casual *sure, I'll send that fax for you, sir.* Now if they were seen, they would look like they were a little too friendly to be just an exec and a secretary, and the thought of sending that message grossed her out just a little. A lot.

"Jenkins and Goldberg are by the elevators."

Markson swore and backed up, tugging her with him.

"No, you're not supposed to take me with you!" Yikes, now they were holding hands.

Yuck. Reese stumbled forward right as she heard Jenkins say, "What the hell? Is that Markson with Reese?"

That other deep voice had to be none other than Goldberg. "I'll be damned."

Reese ended up catapulting into Markson when his backward progress was stopped by the shoe-shine stand. A fern hit her in the face and she put her hands up to knock it out of her way, considering knocking Markson on the head while her hand was airborne.

Great restraint prevented her from doing so, though she did put her hands back on his chest to shove him out of her way.

"Oh, my God, she's all over him," Jenkins said in wonder.

Idiot. Reese prepared to turn around and hurl her purse at Jenkins. Markson grabbed her hands and squeezed hard, holding her in place. "Just stay still," he whispered fiercely. "This is better than getting caught spilling company secrets to a reporter."

"Yeah, because it makes you look like a stud!" And God only knew what it made her look like. She didn't know what could explain a woman's motivation for having an affair with a married man fifteen years older than her who looked like a bowl of custard with glasses.

The last thing she expected him to do was laugh, but he did, a low chuckle. "I would have loved for something like this to happen in high school, but it never did. Now I couldn't care less about looking like a stud."

She frowned, relaxing a little, though she wished he would drop her hands and back up. Markson was right about keeping his secret her secret. If either of their covers were blown, she wouldn't get the interview, or the Delco story. Let those guys think whatever they wanted, no matter how disgusting it was.

"I'm not kissing you or anything like that." Just in case he got any ideas.

"I don't want to kiss you. I'm a happily married man."

That further relaxed her. Markson was a good guy, trying to do the right thing. It didn't matter if she became known as the Office Slut. It's not like she had a long-term career planned with Delco. She'd give one for the Gipper.

"What does he have that I don't have?" Jenkins complained. "I flirted with her and she blew me off."

"Money," came Goldberg's reply. "He makes more than you and he saves more than you. And a quiet guy like that, she'll have him wrapped around her finger in no time. Hell, he probably got her the job at Delco in the first place. She's the shittiest secretary I've ever seen."

As the voices receded, Reese looked at Stan, whose amusement had disappeared. Tugging her hands out of his, she said, "Do you want to kill them or should I?"

A slur like that couldn't go unchallenged.

She was *not* a shitty secretary.

Wyatt Maddock took a sip of his coffee and scoped the lobby of the hotel. This place was dead. Nothing but businessmen and Asian women who didn't speak English. While there could be some fun in that, he was too jet-lagged to take the challenge.

Now, if White had come along . . . He shook his head. He could what? Listen to her insult him?

It wasn't like she was even attractive. She wore guy clothes and had a bitchy look on her face all the time. He could not understand why she occupied so many of his thoughts lately.

Maybe he was just lonely and bored. The last few women he'd gone out with had been a snore, and watching the sparks fly between Knight and Reese had made him a little jealous. He wanted to feel that kind of connection, that kind of attraction so intense that you got into bed and never wanted to get back out.

White would never do that for him. He wasn't sure she even had a body under those gray suits and white blouses. Maybe she was fat or flat-chested and was trying to hide it. That made sense. What didn't make sense was why he spent so much time trying to figure out what, in fact, she would look like with one of those guyish suits crumpled on the carpet by his bed and her hair falling across her face.

Tossing his cup in the wastebasket, Wyatt walked to the elevator, seeing two Delco executives talking while waiting. This always amused him when he was working a case. Standing feet away from people who had no idea he was working to put them away.

Keeping an eye on them, he followed their gaze when the one nudged the other and pointed.

Wyatt felt his eyes bug out. Damn, that was Reese Hampton, who was supposed to be Knight's girlfriend, doing some kind of weird touchy-feely thing behind a potted plant with Markson, the Cooperative Witness.

They were holding hands, leaning close together and whispering. Wyatt edged closer, hoping to hear what they were saying. Damn, he felt lousy for Knight. Here the guy had all but admitted he was in love, and right under his nose she was cheating on him. With a geek.

This was why he wasn't ever falling in love. To hell with that.

He couldn't hear Reese and Markson, but he heard Goldberg

clear as crystal claiming Reese was in it for the money. Markson was chuckling, Reese was whispering to him, Jenkins was stewing, and Goldberg was nodding like he had predicted the whole thing all along.

Wyatt heard the elevator ding and turned back.

He didn't know whether or not Reese was a gold-digger. He didn't know her, had never even met her.

He didn't even know if he should tell Derek about this or not.

The only thing he did know was what he'd seen didn't look good. Not at all.

Derek was exhausted. Tired from the cramped flight, worried about the case, and whipped from making sure all the equipment was in place and working correctly. He just wanted to curl up with Reese in his arms and order room service.

She met him at the door wearing a dress with a bunch of flowers all over it. The dress distracted him so violently, he barely heard her when she said, "I'm so glad you're back. I'm dying of boredom. I can't wait to go exploring."

Grabbing her purse, she looked him up and down. "If I wasn't in such a hurry, I'd insist you change out of those pretty boy clothes. But I can ignore it. Let's go."

Pretty boy? He glanced down at his khaki pants. He was just trying to look like any other American traveling on business. Casual.

"Reese, babe, I'd rather stay in if you don't mind."

Apparently she did. The way her jaw dropped and her bottom lip went out, he could tell he'd lost some ground with her.

"Knight! I'm wearing a dress. I'm in New Zealand! I want to leave the freaking hotel."

He was about to remind her that neither one of them was there on vacation and that it might be a better idea to just stay in and get some rest.

"Don't be an old fuddy-duddy."

That clamped him up. She knew exactly which buttons to push, namely the one that implied that he was anything less than in the prime of life.

He caved like a sand castle hit by a wave. "At least let me go to the bathroom first."

"Sure." She smiled, with a smugness that made him wince. Wyatt's poodle analogy popped into his head.

Reese was glad Knight had seen her point of view. The sight of the harbor from Prince's Wharf was incredible, the breeze was warm and humid, and Knight was standing beside her, even if he was wearing dorky pants.

This was her idea of perfect.

She reached out and slapped Knight's arm hard, shaking off a mosquito corpse when she pulled her hand back. Who knew what diseases these bugs were carrying.

"Mosquito," she told him.

Knight looked down at her, the corner of his mouth up, something deep and soft and puzzling lighting up his dark chocolate eyes. "What?" she asked.

He shook his head. "Nothing."

But he pulled her in front of him and settled her back against his chest, her butt tucking into his thighs. Big arms wrapped around her and held her snugly, protectively, tenderly. It wasn't a bad way to stand at the edge of the ocean and watch the water lap at the shore.

Reese wasn't normally one to stop and commune with nature, but this was a moment. This was a sunset dropping over the water, the smell of tropical flowers caressing her nose, and a big sexy man watching her back.

"Knight?"

"Hmm?" He sounded as relaxed as she felt.

"How did you hurt your knee?" She had been waiting for the right time to ask him. It didn't matter to her, but she sensed it mattered to him. He resented his injury, and she knew there was some baggage he was dragging around.

The muscles of his chest tightened against her back and he was silent for a long second.

Then he kissed the top of her head and said, "It's a long story, but I conducted a raid without backup, assuming I could handle it. I couldn't. Another agent took a bullet in the arm and I got my knee bashed in. Six months and two surgeries later and I'm still hobbling around like an old man."

It was an answer that made her heart constrict and ache. She loved this man. She really did. It made her want to kiss away that sorrow in his voice, touch him, hold him, show him how much he mattered to her.

Turning in his arms, she rested her head on his chest, her chin digging in a little as she looked up at him, running her hands over the rough calloused tips of his fingers.

"Do you know that I find you the most amazing, kind, honorable, and gorgeous man that I've ever met? Nothing about you hobbles. But even if it did, it wouldn't matter one damn bit."

Not to her, not to anyone. He was one of the Good Guys and she wanted to keep him.

Going back to New York felt just about impossible if that meant leaving Knight in Chicago.

He studied her, lacing his fingers through hers, caressing as his head moved back and forth just a little.

"Reese . . . there are times when you just blow me away."

Hopefully that was a good thing. "Is this one of them?"

The kiss he gave her was so soft, so loving, so worshipful that she felt the urge to burst into tears. That was something she hadn't done since Riley had dropped a loaded fish tank on her foot back in junior high.

Unlike then, this time she squelched it. She didn't want to bawl, for God's sake, she wanted to enjoy the moment. And maybe, just maybe, she could screw up the courage to tell Knight how much she cared about him.

"Yes, this is one of them." He held her, pressed against him, so close not even the breeze could get through. "Reese, I—"

Her stomach growled.

They both stopped, stunned, before Knight gave a rueful laugh. "I guess I need to feed you."

She was hungry, but not just for food. "I'm a slave to my body."

His eyes darkened, the laugh disappeared in an instant. "*I'm* a slave to your body."

The air was too warm and humid, her dress tight across the chest, Knight's sudden and impressive erection resting between her thighs, nudging her a little before he stepped back. Her body went hot, aching, needy.

Screw the view. "You were right. We should have stayed in and ordered room service."

He didn't hesitate, but took her hand as they turned away from the water and strolled down the wharf away from the Viaduct Harbor, where the America's Cup was held.

"I should have taped that. You admitting I was right. You don't say that very often."

"That's because it doesn't happen very often." Giving him a grin, she reached behind him and gave his behind a quick squeeze.

He moved away from her hand, eyes darting around. "Knock it off. There are two dozen people roaming around here."

Reese laughed, feeling something swell inside her like a helium balloon. For the first time in her twenty-six years, she felt completely relaxed, enjoying the now. There was none of the normal restlessness, dissatisfaction that had become so familiar to her.

Now if she could only figure out how to hold on to that feeling.

*   *   *

Derek watched Reese sprawled across the bed, shoes kicked off, her dinner spread out in front of her across the bedspread. After finding out there were no chicken wings on the menu, Reese had ordered crayfish, after determining from the room service employee that crayfish was really lobster.

As he ate his own orange roughy, going over his daily food allowance from the Bureau by about fifty percent, he said, "That cost almost fifty bucks. How the hell can you afford that?"

She licked her fingers. "Well, I really can't. Delco would pay for it if I submitted an expense report, but you know that makes me feel guilty. Like spending someone else's money, you know? Since Delco has basically stolen from people. So I'm just using my credit card."

He was a little worried about her financial circumstances, but there was nothing less romantic than asking a woman what was in her checking account. Well, actually, he could think of a lot less romantic things, but that wasn't the point.

"Yeah, me too." He wasn't worried about his own credit card bill. Since his divorce, he hadn't spent a lot of money and he was doing alright.

"How many times am I going to get to eat lobster in Auckland, New Zealand, you know?"

"I'm guessing this is the one and only for me."

"Me, too. I'm pretty much broke. If I can't get a job from this story, I might be forced to live with my dad or something." She shuddered, showing her feelings on giving up her apartment.

Now was his chance. He should say something about her moving back in with him. Dropping his fork, he wiped his mouth on the napkin and chewed quickly. He went over to the bed, perching next to her awkwardly. Christ, he wasn't any good at blabbering out his feelings.

Reese looked at him suspiciously. "Don't even think about taking a bite of my lobster. You have your own food."

"I don't want your food. I just want to . . . look at you."
Oh, now that was poetic. Derek mentally kicked himself in
the ass Reese liked to grab so much.

Her eyebrow went up. "Should I do something? Make
faces? Sing? Blow bubbles in my wine?"

Knowing he probably looked like a stalker, wild-eyed and
weird, he couldn't stop himself from reaching for her hair
and sliding a hand across it. "Don't be a smart-ass. I just
think you're beautiful."

"Thanks."

Reese was on her stomach, stretched out, arms propped up
with her elbows. She slipped her fingers into her mouth
again, licking off stray butter with long flicks of her wet
tongue. Derek felt his cock harden, and he dropped his fingers down a little, across her graceful neck, to her back
where the zipper of her dress was waiting for him.

"Oh, no. I know that look. But I'm still eating. You'll have
to wait."

Not a chance. He bent forward and kissed the bare spot of
her back, right above the neck of her dress, inhaling her light
scent. "Is that payback for in the stairwell when I put you
off?"

"It's because I'm still hungry, but now that you mention it,
that's a good reason, too."

"Just keep eating." She was fine the way she was. He just
wanted to touch her. Moving lower, he dug into the muscles
of her lower back, massaging with upward strokes.

Reese made a little groaning sound, her mouth wrapped
around a forkful of lobster.

"Lobster and a massage at the same time. I just might have
an orgasm."

"If that's what you want." Still kneading the small of her
back, he ran his hand along the firmness of her curved behind, massaging while his thumb darted closer and closer to
her center.

The fork fell on the bed and Reese's head rolled forward. He moved both hands onto her ass, swallowing hard as he covered her, splaying across her completely with his palms, pressing gently. At the rounded undercurve of each cheek, he slid a finger along, going between her thighs, pulling the shimmery fabric of her dress taut, brushing against her mound from the back through the layers of clothing.

He felt no urgency, no rush to get her clothes off, no immediate need to bury himself in her. He wanted to savor her, the touch, the smell, the taste. Moving down to her thighs, he continued to massage, leaning forward and running his tongue down her back until he reached her zipper. Taking it in his teeth, he pulled, resting his hands on her waist, while Reese sucked in her breath.

The zipper stopped right above the curve of her behind, disappointing him. He wanted to dip his tongue down between her cheeks and make her squirm. Instead, he concentrated on easing her dress off her shoulders, down to her elbows, baring her back to him. He undid her bra, and made long deep strokes across her smooth skin with his hands, wishing they weren't so rough and scratchy.

Then he remembered the scented lotion Reese always carried around with her. Her purse was lying on the desk and he stood up, adjusting his cock inside the khaki pants Reese had made fun of. She might hate the pants, but it hadn't stopped her from wanting him in a stairwell.

Reese whimpered, falling forward onto the bed, her face inches from the tray with her dinner on it. "That was cruel."

"I'm coming back."

"Oh." She shoved the tray back to the other side of the bed. "Good."

Derek turned her purse over on the desk, dumping the contents. Sorting past a toothbrush in a case, a tampon, and a subway swipe card, he finally found the little squeeze tube of lotion with a purple lid. Unscrewing it, he took a whiff.

"Blueberry and vanilla." Sweet and delicious, like her.

When he turned back around, Reese was watching him with a soft smile. "Are you going to rub my feet, too?"

"Sure." Squirting the lotion in his hands, he rubbed them together to warm it up, then picked up her foot. He massaged the arch of her foot, working the lotion into her skin while she sighed in approval.

Her feet were the same creamy fair color as the rest of her, her toes long and thin. When he went between her toes with his slick fingers, she stiffened.

"That tickles!"

Since he didn't want her laughing, he moved away without a word, working up her ankle, around her knee, up her thigh, getting more lotion when his hands dried. The smell of the berries clouded around her, and her head was tucked into her arms as she gave a random soft moan. When he reached her skirt, he dropped down and started with the other foot.

He had meant to tell her he was in love with her, was on the verge of spitting it out when her stomach had growled by the harbor. Derek didn't know if he could make his tongue unstick from the roof of his mouth long enough to tell her now. She was so gorgeous that he didn't know where to start.

This time when he steadily climbed up her thigh, instead of stopping at her skirt, he went past it to her sleeves, which were down by her elbows. Tugging a little to let her know his plan, he said, "Lift your stomach, Reese."

She did, languidly, looking relaxed and in the early stages of arousal. She sank back into the bed when he took the dress past her hips and down her long legs until it was off. Her panties went next.

Reese sucked in her breath, lifting her perfectly rounded ass several inches in the air so he could slide the panties off. His fingers trembled, his mouth went dry, his cock protested at being corralled in his pants.

The view Down Under was fucking fabulous in Derek's mind.

Her bra had fallen half down her arms, but for the most part she was deliciously naked. He filled his hands with more lotion and went for her inner thighs, working over her cheeks, sliding down between her legs, the slick sound of lotion on skin making him grit his teeth.

He was so close to her. All he needed to do was lift her behind a little and he could slide inside her, her face still down on the bed. But he held on to his control, loosening the muscles of her back with deep strokes, before nudging her hip.

"Roll over."

With a sigh, she did, leaving the bra behind and stretching her arms over her head, eyes half closed. "This feels so good."

It looked good, too. He devoured her visually, taking in every inch of her heated flesh, the arch of her neck and the graceful slope of shoulders. Her round breasts rising and following with her slow steady breathing and her rosy nipples reaching towards him.

The dip in at her waist, the lush curve of her hips, the dimple of her belly button, and the triangle of hair that hid her from him.

And he started all over again, from the bottom, moving up inch by erotic inch, giving attention to every muscle, every spot, spreading her legs wider as he went to accommodate himself between her knees. Her moans were coming faster, her breath shakier, her thighs clenching.

Still, he went back to the lotion bottle again and again, running his thumbs along her panty line, nudging her wider and wider apart for him, his mouth close enough to her that he could smell her desire intermixed with the vanilla and blueberry. So close that he could feel the heat pulsing from her, feel the tautness of her thigh muscles, see the moisture that gave away her desire.

His hands slowed, his eyes fixated, his mouth ached to press against her, but he only blew out his hot breath on her, then moved past to her belly. Reese let out a cry of dismay.

He rubbed her arms, her shoulders, her neck, then her

breasts, taking her in his hands, rolling his fingers across her, covering her everywhere but her nipples, which he carefully avoided.

Reese was limp, her gasps of pleasure settling into a steady rhythm, releasing one right after the other each time he moved his hands on her. Goose bumps danced across her flesh as he cupped the side of her breast, coming achingly close to her nipple. She tried to turn, to force contact, but he evaded her and took his hands off her completely.

As she whimpered, he yanked off his shirt, nearly removing the top layer of skin from his face as well, since he hadn't bothered to unbutton the shirt. Undoing his pants, he leaned forward and without touching her anywhere, closed his mouth over the very tip of her nipple and sucked, savoring the sweet taste.

When her hand tried to push his mouth down, and her breasts arched up, he pulled back, enjoying himself with this touch and tease foreplay. Ditching his pants, he swiped a condom from his wallet before letting them drop. Then he bent and repeated the suckle on the other nipple, Reese jerking forward, her head twisting left and right.

Moving out of her reach, he got the condom on and drank in the sight of her. She couldn't be any more spread than she was, and she looked inviting, desperate, drunk from desire, her lower lip swollen from where her teeth had ripped into it.

Her hand lifted up, like she was pleading with him to come back. Her eyes were unfocused. He rubbed his thumb across her clitoris. "Is that what you want?"

"No." Her head went back and forth.

Derek lowered his head between her thighs, resting on his elbows. He could only hold out another minute, she smelled so sweet, looked so hungry, that sixty seconds was probably pushing his limit. But he urged her apart, tugging on her hair, baring her lush pink folds to him.

He buried his mouth in her, eating her with little bites and sucks and licks, wondering if he could come just from loving her like this. Her knees slammed into his head as she jerked and cried out. When he felt she was losing control, Derek stopped, hovering in front of her, licking her taste off his lips.

"Is that what you wanted?"

"Yes. No."

Her hand closed around him as she rose in a half sitting position to reach him. He stifled a moan.

"I want this."

Taking her hand off him before he ended the party early, Derek pushed her back to the bed, holding her hands up over her head.

Then he sank into her, so ready, so tight, that he couldn't prevent himself from calling out, *"Reese."*

If it was possible to die from pleasure, Reese knew her dad should start planning her funeral.

She was lost, limp, taking Knight stroke after stroke, unable to even move against him, so sensitive and swollen and ripped with pleasure. Her mind was empty, her body was engorged, her eyes unable to stay open, her arms over her head, abandoned.

Knight's finger ran over her lip and she kissed him, pulling him into her mouth, sucking lightly.

"Open your eyes, Reese."

The raspy command had her forcing her lids apart, struggling to focus up on him, his body still deep inside hers, moving slower now, languorously. He moved the finger she had gotten wet down to her nipple and brushed across her.

Shuddering, she met his gaze, feeling the buildup reaching its peak, her inner thighs trembling, ready to free-fall into ecstasy.

"Reese," he said, locking those double fudge eyes onto hers, "I'm in love with you."

He thrust hard into her, and the breath rushed out of her from shock and his weight. Before she could think, she ran her hand along his cheek, overwhelmed with emotion. "I love you, too."

His mouth covered hers, tongue plunging into her with an all-consuming kiss and she felt him come inside her, his arms around her head, caging her into his passion. She followed him, crying out into his mouth as her orgasm overtook her in rapturous shudders.

Reese saw the future and it didn't hold double dates in Brooklyn with her brother.

Chapter Nineteen

Reese was on edge. She crossed and recrossed her legs in the conference room the next day, ignoring the chatter of the executives as she thought about last night.

It had been more than good sex. It had been more than mind-blowing sex. It had been a connection, an intimacy she'd never felt with any other man ever.

Yet this morning Knight had said nothing about his stunning pre-orgasm revelation. Instead, he had grumbled about her hogging the sheet, had stumbled off to the shower with barely a backwards glance, and had kissed her on the forehead before leaving to meet the other agents.

The forehead.

The bleeping forehead.

More than likely he was totally regretting his words, remembering that she wouldn't exactly fit the Land's End clogs he had mentally picked out for his perfect suburban wife. White fuzzy slippers were fine for a raucous affair, but you didn't marry the fuzzy slippers.

Which made sense. After all, she didn't see herself in that role, either. Yet it equal parts pissed her off and broke her heart. She should never have told him she loved him back.

Geez. Her stomach rolled and pitched and she felt like she'd come down with a wicked case of PMS. Bloated and weepy, capable of biting off the head of the next man who dared to speak to her.

"Reese, can you get me some coffee?" Chatterton waved his hand towards the coffeepot on the buffet table.

Reese sighed. "Sure." At least Chatterton hadn't come on to her. Whoopee.

Jenkins was standing by the coffeepot and he gave her a sly look. She glared at him.

"That for Stan, Reese?"

Oh, Lord. She'd forgotten about the debacle in the lobby yesterday. Jenkins clearly hadn't. Office Slut jokes were beginning. She was so not in the mood.

"No, Stan already had his coffee this morning. In bed." That ought to shut him up.

It did. Jenkins gaped at her, his hand frozen on his tie where he was adjusting it. Reese dumped coffee in a cup and stomped off towards Chatterton. The executives were chitchatting and she was considering claiming a headache.

She had her interview with Markson on tape. She was of no use here to anyone, as Knight had told her on more than one occasion.

After she passed off the coffee, she sat down again and blinked hard. Her nose was itching and her eyes were watering. It had to be from the ugly flower arrangement sitting next to her on the end table. Why anyone would use gladiolas to fill a vase when there were gobs of gorgeous native flowers right outside, she couldn't even begin to imagine.

Dammit, her eyes were stinging, welling with tears, in what had to be a sudden allergy to ugly flowers, not any reaction to Knight's ambivalent behavior that morning. She picked up the vase and crossed the room, sticking it in the corner behind a big blue chair.

"Reese," Chatterton called to her a minute later. "Your purse is ringing."

*   *   *

"What the hell is she doing?" Maddock stopped pacing in their surveillance room and stared at the screen in disbelief.

Derek knew the feeling. "I have no goddamn idea."

After sniping at Jenkins with a comment that had confused the hell out of Derek, Reese had suddenly picked up the vase with the camera hidden in it. Their only view of the room now was of the back of a chair.

He hadn't told Reese where the camera would be hidden, afraid she would clue in the executives to its presence with her less-than-subtle behavior. But he had never anticipated her moving the camera, for Christ's sake.

Grabbing the room phone, he took deep breaths and prayed her cell phone was on. He could feel Nordstrom's hands on his throat already.

"Hello?" she snarled into the phone.

Before the camera had disappeared, he'd noticed her body language was a little tense. He wondered if the tension in the room among the executives was getting to her.

Or maybe she was tired. He hadn't let her sleep a whole lot the night before. Not that this was a good time to be thinking about that.

"Reese, honey, it's me."

There was a long pause. Then she whispered, "Why the hell are you calling me? We're in the meeting."

"Well." He rubbed his eyes and watched the chair on the screen. "Honey, you moved the camera. It was hidden in the flower arrangement. You've got to put it back."

She made a sound of exasperation. "Well, if you had trusted me enough to tell me in the first place, we wouldn't have this problem."

Then she hung up.

Derek sank back in his chair and said to Maddock, "I think she's going to move it." Not that he could ever be sure with Reese.

Man, he had screwed up last night. Of all times to tell her

that he was in love with her, he had picked in the middle of
sex. No woman in her right mind would believe him. It was
convenient, it was lame, it was totally lacking in even a hint
of romance.

She had probably answered in kind out of politeness and
to get him to hurry up. He'd had her on the edge of an orgasm, she wasn't going to stop and discuss their relationship.

Not that she had that morning. Instead, she'd shot him
wary glances, making him uncomfortable. It was like she was
afraid he was going to lose it and blabber out a marriage pro-
posal or something.

Which he wasn't going to do, because Reese would say no.
He was on the verge of being a washed-up, injured, ex-FBI
agent, he didn't need to add rejected loser to that as well.

"Hey, you know, Derek, I've been debating whether or not
I should tell you this."

Derek snapped his head up. Maddock sounded nervous
and was running his hand through his hair.

"What is it, Wyatt?"

"Yesterday I was in the lobby . . ." Maddock squirmed,
shooting uneasy glances toward the technical agent, who had
earphones on listening to the executives in the meeting.

"Yeah?"

"And . . ." Maddock finally met his eye. "I saw Reese with
Markson."

While he didn't like the sound of that, he wasn't totally
alarmed yet. "So?"

"They were touching each other, um, inappropriately."

Another time he might have laughed at Maddock's awkward explanation but instead he was so floored he just
gaped. "What?"

"Jenkins and Goldberg saw, too. I think that explains that
comment Jenkins made to her about the coffee." Maddock
was grimacing. "It was in an alcove, behind a potted plant,
but I could see . . . well, I could see."

There was no way. There was absolutely no way. He was as sure of that as he was of his own name. Reese would never, ever, in a million years mess around on him. And with Markson? Not in this lifetime. The man wore argyle socks. Not to mention that he wasn't exactly a swinger.

"Maddock, that's nuts. Reese wouldn't do that." But he wasn't disbelieving that she was talking to Markson without his knowledge. Probably for some kind of reason he wasn't going to like.

"If you say so," Maddock said, sounding completely unconvinced.

The picture on the TV screen bounced as Reese walked the vase back across the room. She plunked it down hard, and when it had stopped vibrating, they had a clear shot of everyone in the room except Reese. Perfect.

Derek breathed a sigh of relief.

Maddock swore, giving a little laugh.

No laughter was coming out of Derek until he resolved this. "Hey, Wyatt, can you hold down the fort for ten minutes?" While he went and searched through Reese's possessions.

She wanted to be a serious journalist. If she were talking to Markson, there would be notes.

He couldn't believe it.

There in Reese's briefcase on a yellow legal pad sat notes of a full interview with Markson, where it seemed pretty obvious he had spilled everything. His first contact with the FBI, everything he had given the agents in terms of evidence, and his motivation to see the bad guys at Delco put behind bars.

From the looks of her scratched notes, Reese was already organizing it into a news story, and Derek felt equal parts baffled and furious. How could she do that? Releasing an interview like this, even after a raid on Delco, could tip off the hands of the defense lawyers and jeopardize prosecution.

It was betrayal, plain and simple. He had trusted her, and she had betrayed him.

Derek shoved Reese's notes back into her briefcase and slammed it shut. He had to get back to the surveillance room and see if any progress had been made.

Despite the fact that he felt like someone had sucker punched him, he still had a job to do.

And maybe he shouldn't be so surprised. Derek glanced around the room they had been sharing and shook his head, sticking his key back into the pocket of his navy blue casual pants. Hadn't he always guessed Reese was all about getting ahead in the game, no matter what she had to do to get there?

Yet like an idiot, he'd fallen for her, letting her manipulate him, then in a final humiliation, had told her that he loved her like some goofball kid getting his first lay.

Maddock gave him a look of concern when he entered the room. "Everything alright?"

The look of pity on the agent's face made his stomach turn and his anger rise another notch. "It's fine. Reese is not screwing Markson, so just drop it." She wasn't screwing the CW, but she was screwing Derek *over.*

"Sure, okay, man." Maddock turned back to the screen.

Derek trained his eyes in that direction as well.

Then they both heard it.

"So you agree not to manufacture generic versions of the above analgesics?" Chatterton said to the executive from Ricould.

"Yes, we agree to that, if you agree not to pursue patents for the following." The Ricould exec pointed to the chart where they had listed all the drugs in question.

"Agreed," said Chatterton.

Derek wanted to let out a whoop of joy, but was afraid he'd miss something. These guys were putting the nails in their coffins and he wanted to hear it live, not off the tape later.

The Stanfield executive said, "Does anyone have any concerns over the prices we've set for our share?"

"No, no problems." Chatterton grinned. "You could probably even go higher. Who's going to stop us?"

There was laughter from around the room.

"Hot damn," Maddock breathed. "We've got them. Stupid bastards."

Reese, sitting demurely next to Chatterton, turned and looked directly at the camera, her expression aloof, but her eyes filled with an emotion Derek couldn't pinpoint.

He wanted to reach into the TV, grab her and hold her to him, to have her admit she'd made a mistake with the Markson interview and both pretend they could have a future together.

The triumph for the case soured.

When it was all over, he was still going to have a bum knee, an empty apartment, and no one to laugh with.

Ignoring Maddock's excited chatter and clap on the back, he reached into his jacket pocket and pulled out his antacids. His finger ran over and over across the satiny paper they were rolled in while he watched Reese lock eyes with him.

It felt like she could see right through to him, knew his anger, had her own, eyes staring, wills clashing, always a contest.

Then he broke the contact, the ever present push-pull between them, and flipped the first tablet out and into his hand.

All the antacids in the world couldn't fix his heart and his hurt, but it was all he had.

Reese wanted to be excited for Knight. She'd heard the statements Chatterton and the other executives had made. She knew it was good news, possibly the final piece needed for prosecution. But instead all she wanted was to eat ice cream and buy shoes.

There was a very good reason she'd never been in love before.

It sucked.

Maybe her brother Ryan had the way of it, a merry-go-round of dating and casual sex. Or maybe she had been smarter than she thought in the last couple of years by just avoiding men and a social life altogether.

As she trailed out of the conference room behind the executives, she realized there was another reason to be grateful for the close of this case—she could quit this job. If she wanted to spend this much time serving coffee, she'd prefer to do it at Starbucks where at least she could get a discount and meet people her own age.

Which was where she might be in a couple of weeks since once she quit Delco she had no job. For a minute, she debated groveling to Ralph to get her job back at the *Newark News*. She pictured kissing his very large ass and shuddered.

Markson slowed down and hovered next to her. "Can I talk to you, Reese?"

Did she need this now? She stifled a groan. Markson was a nice enough guy, but he hovered, getting in her way and complicating her life. Like pigeons.

"Later, Stan, okay?"

"This is important. I don't think we should see each other anymore."

That got her attention. She looked over at him, then past him to where Jenkins was listening with no attempt at discretion. The hallway had high ceilings and sound seemed to bounce all around them, sending Markson's voice projecting way louder than she would like.

"Can we discuss this in private?" she asked through gritted teeth, not wanting to give anything away in front of Jenkins and his big fat ears. Besides, when she murdered Markson, she didn't want witnesses.

"No, I don't think that's a good idea." Markson had become a really phenomenal liar during the course of this case. She couldn't imagine why she had ever worried about him, the balding snake. He looked a little nervous, but overall he looked like a wealthy businessman giving his girlfriend the boot in a hotel hallway.

"This was a mistake. I love my wife, and she deserves better than this. It was fun, but now it's over."

Then he walked away. Just walked off down the hall, leaving her staring at Jenkins.

The sting of humiliation and rage left her speechless.

Jenkins wasn't speechless. "Well, now that you're free, maybe you and I could go out."

Sure. Right around the time she could fit into a size two. *Not in this lifetime.* She fisted her hands, gripping the bottom of her blue cable knit sweater, giving herself a calming moment before opening her mouth and shredding him.

He spoke first. "Then again, if you couldn't keep a guy like Markson satisfied, it's probably not worth my time." Jenkins straightened his tie and started off down the hall.

By the time she had ridden the elevator up to the twelfth floor and opened the door to her room with Knight, she was itching for a fight.

So was Knight, given the scowl on his face. "What took you so long? The meeting broke up over an hour ago."

Reese bent over and ripped her black pump off her foot and considered beaning him in the head with it. "They stayed and talked about dinner plans and I was needed to make reservations when they made their final decision. Not that I need to explain myself to you."

"Well, you need to explain this." Knight held up a pad of paper and threw it on the bed.

"What?" Caught off guard, she looked down at the paper and saw her handwriting. Her notes on Markson. He had found them.

Panic rose for a second before she squelched it.

If he wasn't going to feel guilty for digging through her stuff, she wasn't going to feel guilty for interviewing Markson. Besides, she hadn't actually printed the interview yet.

Giving a nonchalant shrug, she said, "What's there to explain? I interviewed Markson, which I guess you can see since you just read it."

He stared at her, mouth open, shoving his hair off his forehead. "Reese! You should have asked me first."

Any effort to remain calm evaporated. "Asked you? Why the hell should I ask you?" Still wearing one shoe, she bobbed up and down to stand in front of him. "It doesn't have anything to do with you."

"It has everything to do with me. This is my career." His mouth was drawn tight and his eyes were flashing. He had changed into a pair of jeans and an untucked T-shirt. He looked disheveled and angry. "I knew this would be a disaster. First moving the damn vase, then everyone thinking you're screwing Markson, and now I find out you went behind my back, knowing I would say no, and compromised my investigation. You should have stayed home like I asked you to."

Reese felt the blood drain from her face. She held her hand out and backed up. "That's really what it's all about, Knight, isn't it? You want a woman who's waiting for you at home wearing an apron, giving you a 'how was your day, honey?' Well, that's not me. You knew that. I knew that."

Something inside her was splintering, aching, leaving her flushed with anger, yet cold with hurt.

"We both knew this was just a fun . . . thing." She swallowed hard. "So I'm guessing now it's over. I can't be what you want and I won't be patronized and bossed around. I spent my whole childhood living with a double standard created by men. I won't do it again."

That was as close to a vow as she was ever going to come.

Derek had no idea how the conversation had gone from her betraying him to their relationship being over, but he didn't like it. If anyone had a fucking bone to pick, it was him.

"Why is it always about you? Just once, I'd like you to take responsibility for what you've done." He grabbed the legal pad off the bed and shook it in her face. "You knew this would piss me off, you knew it was wrong, but you did it anyway."

Mouth open, she ripped it out of his hand and whacked him on the arm with it. "Why are you going through my stuff anyway, Mr. High and Freaking Mighty?"

He grabbed her wrist as she reared back to hit him again. It didn't hurt in the least, but it pissed him off, more than he already was, which was a hell of a lot. "I went through your stuff because Maddock told me that he saw you hanging all over Markson yesterday like a rock groupie. I knew you weren't screwing Markson like everyone seems to think, but I figured that meant you had something up your *Newark News* sleeve."

Reese jangled her arm back and forth trying to shake him off, her auburn hair flying across her face and sticking to her lip. "Look who's talking. You haven't told me anything about this case, forcing me to go out on my own to investigate."

His anger dissolved into frustration, and down into disappoint and resignation. They had been over this so many times. If Reese couldn't respect his professional integrity, she was right. It was over. He could give up his idea of a calm, soothing, maternal wife pretty easily, but he couldn't give up mutual trust and respect.

He let go of her wrist. "I can't tell you about the investigation, you know that. You know that, and you don't give a shit. You push and push even when I promised to give you the story as soon as it's possible."

"We're not going to agree on this, Knight. I'm not apologizing for wanting to move ahead, to have a chance to do a real newsworthy story. Markson deserves to tell his side so that he doesn't get smeared when this hits the stands."

She sounded so driven, so unconcerned about his feelings, that Derek felt like he'd had the wind knocked out of his lungs. Jesus, this was it. It was ending, and it hurt like nothing else. When the tire iron had slammed into his knee, he'd seen the whole world tilt in blurry pain, but this was worse.

There was no surgery to fix this.

"I guess you and I have a different view on relationships. You think they're all about one person being in charge, calling all the shots, and you want it to be you. I want a partnership, compromise."

She scoffed. "The problem is, you're exactly like me. We both want to be in control. I'm just louder about it."

There wasn't any truth in that, he was almost sure of it. Didn't he just about break his back bending over to please her? Hadn't he done that with Dawn? If Reese couldn't see that, then to hell with the whole thing.

He lashed out, said the first thing that popped into his head. "I should have let you go. That night in the parking garage I should have just let you take off with the envelope and saved us both a hell of a lot of trouble."

The color leached from her face, leaving her nothing but white skin and freckles. Tears rose, startling him into swearing out loud. "Shit, Reese, I'm sorry."

Jesus, he hadn't meant to make her cry. Reese and tears didn't go together, and he had brought her to that.

She drew a shaky breath, while he watched her battle to control herself. Not a single tear actually fell down her cheek. She widened her eyes and squeezed her lips shut. "Don't apologize if you meant it. Just get out of my room."

At the last second her voice wavered and Derek felt so lousy he just wanted to scoop her into his arms. Why the hell were they fighting? Did any of it really matter?

"Baby . . ." He reached for her.

She took a step back and held out her hand. "I'm serious. Pack your stuff and get out or I'll take you down like I did in that deli." She glanced down at his crotch, her voice hard, high, and heading towards hysterical. "Only now I know what side you pack your piece on."

That spike-heeled shoe went back onto her foot for emphasis and Derek knew it was time to leave.

Chapter Twenty

Reese was halfway to drunk, debating the merits of another green apple martini and wondering how long it would take Knight to pack, when Markson sat down next to her in the hotel lounge.

She didn't even try to be polite. "Get away from me."

"Reese, I wanted to apologize for that bit in the hall earlier."

She didn't look up from her glass, just swirled the liquid around and around, amazed at how much it looked like green Kool-Aid. "It's fine, Stan. I don't care."

It was the truth. Nothing really seemed to matter at the moment, except for the fact that she was in love with an idiot.

"I know you're probably angry with me, but I thought it was best for both of us if the other executives thought our . . . relationship was over, and it seemed like a good way to make that absolutely clear."

A snort sailed out of her mouth. "Yeah, it was clear."

Reese tilted her head to the right and wondered why the little thatched cabana where you ordered drinks seemed to be undulating like an underwater plant. She was only on her second martini and it wasn't even empty, but she felt a little funny, like she'd ridden a roller coaster three times in a row.

"Well, I'm sorry if I caused you embarrassment. It seems

like I've really botched everything up for the last six months. I just want to go home and have this be over."

Having forgotten that anyone could possibly have a problem except her, she glanced over in sympathy at him sitting in the wicker chair next to her. "You haven't screwed anything up. Without you, the FBI wouldn't even have a case."

He lifted his glasses and rubbed the bridge of his nose. She noticed his jacket was off and his tie was crooked. He looked exhausted.

He said, "Have you ever wondered if you'd done the right thing? That maybe, even though you thought you knew everything there was to know, that just maybe you were wrong?"

Besides right now? Maybe Knight was right, maybe she shouldn't have expected him to tell her classified information. Maybe she could have respected his tenuous position a little more.

"And you can't shake the feeling that you've changed your life forever for the worse."

She sniffed. Yeah, she knew that feeling.

"And that it's not about getting to the top at work, or making more money, it's about the people you love, taking care of each other and sharing the little things every day."

A sob slipped out and Reese dropped her head down onto her arm. Crapola. She didn't know what she wanted anymore, but she was starting to think if she had to choose between Knight and a career, she'd choose him.

She felt a warm awkward pat on her hand. "Hey, are you okay?"

"No. Knight and I broke up." Blowing hair out of her eyes, she stared through the martini glass, face barely off the table. She added, in case he was unclear of her feelings, "I want to die."

Markson sucked in his breath. "Suicide isn't the answer!"

That made her laugh. "No, I wasn't serious. I was being dramatic. I feel like a train wreck."

She should really make an effort to lift her head, but that seemed like too much work.

"Why did you break up?"

"He thinks I'm out to screw up the Delco case, and I think he doesn't take me seriously as a journalist."

"You broke up over *work*?" Markson dug into the peanut bowl sitting on the table and popped one in his mouth. "Trust me, Reese, no job is worth losing the person you love."

If that could explain the sensation of a dull knife scraping away at her heart, maybe he was right.

"You do love him, don't you?"

It took her less than a second to answer. She did love him. He was loving, kind, sexy, everything she could ask for in a man. She wailed, "Yes!"

The martini sloshing through her bloodstream kept her from being embarrassed at the sheer girliness of that forlorn wail. But Markson didn't even blink.

Instead he leaned closer, gaze meeting hers from behind his horn-rims. "Then go fix it. If you love him, it's worth it, Reese."

She wanted to believe he was right. But Reese wished along with his other gems of advice, Markson knew exactly how she was supposed to fix it, because she did not have a clue.

Derek jostled his duffel bag and adjusted his grip on his suitcase with wheels. He knocked on Maddock's door with way more force than was necessary, but he had a ton of frustration to release.

Maddock answered the door in a pair of jeans and no shirt, hair sticking up on end. Derek thought maybe he'd interrupted a nap or something. "Hey, Wyatt, sorry to bother you, but do you think I could share your room?"

He cleared his throat and fought the pain that clamped

around his heart and squeezed. Reese had made her choice and there was nothing to do but move on. "Reese kicked me out."

Maddock darted a quick glance behind him. "Oh, hey, Knight, I'm sorry. And you know normally I'd let you bunk with me, no problem, but right now I sort of have some company." He raised his eyebrows up and down, a slight grin crossing his mouth.

Derek saw a blonde wearing a robe coming towards the door. "Is that the wine, Wyatt?"

She had a local accent and a deep beach tan and Derek was embarrassed, followed quickly by jealous. Reese had looked luscious and beautiful that first night he'd met her, when she had been wearing nothing but a terry cloth robe.

Now Wyatt was getting some action and he had nothing but an empty bed and his job, which wasn't going to keep him warm at night, that's for damn sure.

"Jesus, sorry, Wyatt. Never mind." He started to back up, but the blonde gave him a friendly smile as she draped herself across Wyatt's back.

"Hello, are you a friend of Wyatt's? Are you a computer programmer as well?"

Derek said hello, shooting Maddock a questioning look. What the hell was this woman talking about?

"Sheila, this is Derek Knight and he works with me. He's here for the programming conference too."

Derek tried not to snort as he shook Sheila's hand. It made sense that Maddock couldn't go around the hotel blabbing that he was with the FBI, but leave it to him to make up some BS story, and to find a woman to spend the night with less than twenty-four hours after arriving in Auckland.

Of course, it had been that way with him and Reese. An instant attraction. An instinctive knowledge that they were meant to be together. His heart twisted painfully. Dammit. Everything reminded him of her and how much he was going to miss her.

When they started exchanging lascivious glances and Sheila's fingernails starting marching across Maddock's chest, he knew it was time to get the hell out of there. "Nice to meet you, Sheila. I'll catch you later, Wyatt."

Still hauling his luggage, he went down the hall and to the elevator. It looked like he'd have to book himself a room. Hopefully, they would have some available.

Crossing the lobby, he saw Markson. Ignoring him, since they weren't supposed to know each other, he started to approach the front desk.

A hand touched his arm and he glanced over at Markson, startled. He said in a polite tone, "Can I help you?"

Markson didn't even try to play along. "Derek, I need to talk to you about Reese."

He sighed. "Stan, not here."

"But you need to know that Reese is in the lounge right now, crying into a martini. She loves you and she's hurting." Stan gestured towards the lounge. "You need to get in there and make up with her, Derek, or you're both going to regret it."

"I tried, Stan. She doesn't want to be with me. She's obsessed about making her big break in journalism." And rehashing this in the damn lobby with his suitcase next to him wasn't helping the burn from his ulcer.

"You know, the problem is that Reese is afraid she'll never measure up. She thinks she's not good enough for you."

Stan must have been hitting the martinis himself. Derek dropped his duffel bag to the floor. "That's ridiculous. She's gorgeous, funny, smart, and she doesn't put up with crap from anyone. That doesn't sound like someone with self-esteem issues."

"You're wrong." Stan pushed up his glasses. "She spent her whole childhood trying to be the boy her father wanted and now you come along, she falls in love with you, and what do you want? You want someone quiet and demure with no interest in a career. She feels like you're attracted to her and you want her physically, but she's not good enough for you for the long haul."

Derek stared at his Cooperating Witness. "How long have you been in the lounge talking to her?" It sounded like Stan knew more about Reese than he did. He'd never heard her express those kinds of doubts about their relationship.

"For over an hour. She's in bad shape and you need to go talk to her." It sounded like a reprimand and Derek bristled.

"I told her I loved her."

"But did you ask her to stay in Chicago? To live with you?"

Stan was so right, he was getting on Derek's nerves. "Since when are you a therapist? Jesus, I feel like I fell into a *Touched By an Angel* episode."

Stan laughed, the first real genuine laugh Derek had ever heard come from the man. "No, it's just nice to try and help someone else out with their life, instead of worrying about the mess that mine has become."

Whatever doubts Derek had ever had about Stan's motives disappeared then. Like so many people who walk around quietly, hidden behind unobtrusive clothing and average looks, Stan was a good man, who deserved to be protected when the Delco story hit the news. Reese had been right about that.

"Here, give me your luggage and I'll check it with the front desk. You need to get in there before Reese slides under the table."

Derek handed his stuff to Stan and said, "Thank you, Stan. I appreciate it."

He headed towards the lounge, determined not to leave it until he and Reese had worked this out. He wanted her in his life. He had to have her in his life.

She wasn't under the table, but she was lying across it, licking a peanut off her napkin with her tongue. The napkin stuck to the tip, and she moved her head back, dragging the napkin along with her. When she saw him, she pulled it off.

She was beautiful, and man, did he love her. He'd been an idiot to think he could ever walk away.

"What are you looking at?"

"The woman I love." With all his heart and soul.

Reese looked over her shoulder. "Where? I don't see anyone." Then she laughed, hitting the glass table with the palm of her hand.

He raised his eyebrow and took in the martini glass almost drained.

She followed his gaze. "Don't worry, I'm not drunk. I've only had one and a half martinis in two hours and any effects of the alcohol in my stomach have been absorbed by the three thousand peanuts I've eaten."

Damn Knight for walking in on her misery, looking delicious and telling her that he loved her. Was he trying to kill her along with breaking her heart?

"Can I sit down? We need to talk."

Oh, yippee. "It's a free country. I think."

He sat down, stretching his bad leg out stiffly. She wondered if his knee was bothering him, knowing he would never admit it.

There was a long silence where she rolled a peanut around the tabletop, still lying with her head on her arm.

Then he blurted, "Reese, baby, I never said I wanted you to be some kind of modern June Cleaver."

Pain sliced through her malaise. "No, you never said you wanted *me* to be that. But you said you wanted that."

His finger drummed on the table. "After Dawn, I thought that's what I wanted, though now I honestly don't know why. And that's not who I fell in love with. I fell in love with you, and maybe you can't cook, but you can make me laugh."

Oh, great. She was laughable. "Then why did you act so weird this morning? Last night was . . ." She sighed, unable to find the right words to describe that moment when he had said he loved her, her body singing with pleasure and his eyes locked with hers. "Then this morning you acted like you couldn't get away from me fast enough."

"Because I felt like I'd blown it. I'd been wanting to tell you all week that I love you, and I wanted to ask you to move back in with me, to stay in Chicago, and instead of being romantic about it, I just blurted it out during sex. You deserved better than that."

If he didn't look so sincere, she'd swear he was making that up, it sounded so dumb. "It was romantic! Geez, it was incredible, beautiful."

She sat up, unable to lie still any longer.

His eyes went soft. "Yeah, it was, wasn't it?"

"I wasn't trying to screw up your case, I really wasn't."

He nodded. "I know. And I wasn't trying to cut you out. There are just things that have to stay private."

"I know."

"It was never a competition, it was never about who could win or who was controlling who, and I'm sorry if I made it seem that way. I never meant that you had to make some kind of choice between your career and me. I want you to have a career that you enjoy. I was just trying to protect myself from getting hurt, and you have the power to hurt me, Peaches."

He had the same power. She believed him, felt the first flicker of hope. "I don't want to hurt you and I think when two people are friends, they're equal. No one is in charge."

"I agree. I want to be friends." Though the look on his face was *really* friendly.

Her head started to swim and it wasn't from the martini. She gave a small smile, her hands feeling clammy, her breath hitching. She really wanted this to work out. "So does this mean you'll still give me the exclusive story?"

He leaned closer towards her. "Yeah. And then you have to bake me a pie, remember?"

She'd forgotten that she had agreed to bake him a pie if he

gave her the story. "Oh, yeah." She licked her lips, heart beating faster. "But where should I bake that pie?"

His hand closed over her and started stroking her. "I was hoping in Chicago. In my apartment."

"Like . . . a visit?" If he said yes, she'd shove a peanut up his nose.

"No." He came closer, his chair creaking as he rocked it forward so that his mouth was inches from hers. "As my wife. I love you, Reese. I want to be with you forever."

She wanted to be witty and dazzling, sharp with a snappy reply. Instead she said, "Okay."

Knight blinked. "Is that a yes?"

His lips were almost touching hers, and she was distracted by the musky smell of his aftershave and his knee pressing against hers under the table. It had been twelve long hideous hours since he had touched her and now, they were going to get married.

This was good.

"Yes, I love you. Yes, I'll marry you."

The relief that crossed his face, followed by a tender smile made her break out into a moronic grin. Yeesh, she was one lucky woman.

"Just one thing, Reese." His finger brushed her lip while the other hand went into her hair, stroking, caressing, claiming.

"What's that?" She'd agree to just about anything. She was on the verge of falling into his lap and it was time to head upstairs.

"At our wedding, you have to call me Derek."

Epilogue

Derek enjoyed the view as Reese bent over, her jeans hugging her perfect behind as she pulled a pie out of the oven.

She thunked it down on the counter using the Kiss the Cook oven mitts her brother Ryan had given them for a gag wedding gift. At least, Derek assumed it was a gag gift. Reese looked frazzled, flour all over her tight navy T-shirt, and her hair falling out of a ponytail.

To him, she looked good enough to eat.

He'd been doing paperwork at the kitchen table all afternoon, watching in amusement as she cussed and stormed her way around the kitchen, attempting to fulfill their bargain.

Tossing the mitts down, she said, "Geez, it took me all day to make this stupid thing. Good thing I don't have any deadlines."

It was spring, the wrong time for pumpkin pie, but with the Delco case being handled by the courts, and Reese working steadily as a freelance writer since the interview with Markson had hit the *Chicago Tribune,* now seemed the time for her to make good on her promise.

Reese had gotten the exclusive the minute the raid had gone down at Delco, and had followed the case through the next few months as indictments had been handed out. Several executives, including Jenkins and Goldberg, had plea-bargained, but Chatterton was headed to court and Derek had been re-assigned to a different case, with grudging accolades from Nordstrom.

He had no hopes that Reese's pie would taste any better than mud, but it was a small price to pay for the way she made him feel every day. There had been a few speed bumps getting to the altar, but for the most part they were moving along at a steady pace. Their marriage was a gift, and he had a whole new appreciation for the little things.

Reese was already cutting the pie.

"Aren't you supposed to let it cool?"

She glared at him, blowing hair out of her eyes. "If you know so much about pies, why aren't you making it?"

"Because you look a hell of a lot cuter doing it than I would."

Rolling her eyes, she reached up and got out a plate. He noticed she didn't get two plates. He also noticed, had been noticing all day, that she'd never bothered to put on a bra. Her nipples were showing off in that tight top and he was halfway to hard watching her stretch to pull out a fork.

As she brought the pie towards him, he got up and poured himself a glass of milk. Otherwise he might not be able to swallow if it tasted awful.

She smiled. "Here you go, honey. Eat up."

When she called him honey, she was being sarcastic, he knew from experience. "Thanks, baby. I can't wait."

He sat back down and studied the piece of pie. It looked a little beat up, like she'd hacked it away from the rest of the pie, and the crust had pulled away from the filling. He gave a subtle sniff. It smelled all right.

"Quit smelling it and eat it."

There was no escape. He took the fork, cut off a mice-size bite, and put it in his mouth. He chewed. And raised his eyebrow in surprise. Holy crap, it actually tasted good, like a real pumpkin pie.

"Reese, it's good."

She stared at him. "Very funny."

"No, I'm serious." He took another bite. "It looks like hell, but it tastes really good."

"Really?" She grabbed the fork from him and bit the pie. "No way! I can bake, who'd have thought?"

Not him, that's for sure.

Her fork went back again. "I mean, I followed the directions and it was a huge pain in the ass, but it wasn't really *hard*. Whatta ya know."

Reese was leaning in front of him, her shirt riding up, exposing her smooth belly to him. Since he had lost his fork, Derek stuck his finger into the pie and put it in his mouth, sucking the sweetness off.

"Tastes delicious."

Reese knew that tone of voice, had gotten to love to hear that sound from Knight over the last six months. It meant he wasn't talking about food anymore.

High from her baking triumph, she was ready to be put in the mood. "I'm glad you like it."

"I love it." His finger went back into the pie and came out with a big glob of filling. "Hey, there's something on your shirt."

Before she had time to react, he had lifted her T-shirt and smeared pumpkin pie across her nipple. Then his mouth closed over it and she almost fell to the floor. He sucked, licked, tugging on her with his moist lips and tongue, his fingers digging into her backside as she gripped his shoulders for support, desire stabbing her between the thighs.

"Mmmm," he said, pulling back and blowing on her shiny wet nipple. "Best I ever tasted."

She inched down onto his lap, facing him, giving him a deep, luscious kiss, tasting the pumpkin spice in his mouth. "Plenty more where that came from."

"We've got a whole pie, don't we? I wonder where else I can eat it off?"

An idea or two came to mind, including where she could lick him clean. "I bet I can come up with a better spot than you."

"I bet you you're wrong."

She never was one to turn down a challenge.

Please turn the page for a tantalizing peek at

Good With His Hands

by Lori Foster from

BAD BOYS IN BLACK TIE

Coming from Brava in May 2004

Pete was up with the sun. After hearing that disturbing moan—disturbing on too many levels—he'd tried turning in early. But sleep had been impossible and he'd spent hours tossing and turning, thinking of Cassidy over there with someone else while his muscles cramped and protested. He'd tried to block the awful images from his mind, but they remained, prodding at him like a sore tooth; Cassidy with some suit-wearing jerk; Cassidy getting excited; Cassidy twisting and moaning.

Cassidy climaxing.

He couldn't stand it.

By seven, he was showered, standing at his closet and staring at the lack of professional clothes. Oh, he had a suit, the one he'd worn for his brothers' marriages. Gil had fussed, trying to insist that he buy a new, more expensive one, but Pete refused. He hated the idea of shopping for the thing, trying them on, getting fitted. Then he'd have to pick out a shirt, and a tie, maybe cufflinks . . . He *hated* suits.

But Cassidy loved them.

Stiff and fuming, Pete jerked on khaki shorts and a navy pullover, then paced until it got late enough to go to her place. She generally slept in on Saturday mornings. He knew her schedule as well as he knew his own. Right now she'd be curled in bed, all warm and soft and . . . He couldn't wait a minute more.

He went out his back door and stomped across the rain-wet grass to her patio. He pressed his nose against the glass doors, but it was dark inside, silent. Daunted, Pete looked around, and discovered that her bedroom window was still open.

Shit. What if the guy was still in there? What if he'd spent the night? What if, right this very moment, he was spooned up against her soft backside?

A feral growl rose from Pete's throat, startling him with the viciousness of it. No woman had ever made him growl. He left that type of behavior to his brother, Sam, who was more animal than man.

Now Gil, he was the type of man Cassidy professed to want. A suit, serious, a mover and a shaker. A great guy, his brother Gil. So what would Gil do?

He'd be noble for sure, Pete decided. Gil would wait and see if she did have company, and if so, he'd give them privacy.

That thought was so repugnant, Pete started shaking.

To hell with it. His fist rapped sharply on Cassidy's glass door.

A second later, her bedroom curtain moved and Cassidy peered out. "Pete?" she groused in a sleep-froggy voice. "What are you doing?'

"Open up." Pete tried to emulate Gil, to present himself in a calm, civilized manner. "You alone in there?" he snarled.

Her eyes were huge and round in the early morning light. "No, I have the Dallas Cowboys all tucked into my bed. It's a squeeze, but we're managing."

Pete sucked in a breath. *"Cassidy . . ."*

"Of course I'm alone, you idiot." Her frowning gaze darted around the yard in confusion. "What time is it?"

She was alone. The tension eased out of Pete, making his knees weak. "I dunno, seven or so." The chill morning air frosted his breath and prickled his skin into goose bumps. "Time to get up and keep your neighbor company."

"Seven!"

He took five steps and looked at her through the screen. She had a bad case of bedhead and her eyes were puffy, still vague with sleep. She looked tumbled and tired and his heart softened with a strange, deep thump. "Open up, Cassidy."

Still confused, not that he blamed her, she rubbed her eyes, pushed her hair out of her face. "Yeah, all right. Keep your pants on." She started to turn away.

"What fun will that be?"

Her head snapped back around. Seconds ticked by before she said, "Get away from my window, you perv. I have to get dressed."

The thump turned into a hard steady pulse. "Don't bother on my account."

And we think you'll enjoy an excerpt from

THE ROYAL TREAMENT

by MaryJanice Davidson

Also coming from Brava in May 2004

"Nicky, you little brat, if you don't give that back *right now* . . ."

"That's no way to talk to a prince," His Highness Prince Nicholas, fifth in line to the throne, complained.

"I'm going to smack the crap out of a prince if you don't take my bra off your head this second. It doesn't fit you, and besides," she added coaxingly, "it's my last clean one."

Nicholas, who had been fascinated by the new guest (not to mention the new guest's undergarments), crawled out from under Christina's bed. He had the bra fastened over his head, the snaps tied under his chin, and looked not unlike a mouse with large white ears. He had inherited his grandmother's hair (probably), and looked up at her from a mass of blond curls. "I was only fooling," he said by way of apology.

She snatched the bra away, almost strangling him. "Try it again, and they won't find the body, get it?"

He laughed at her. "You wouldn't."

"Well, probably not," she admitted. "What are you doing here, anyway? Don't you have—I dunno—prince lessons or something?"

"Not on Sunday, dummy."

"Nice way to talk to a guest!"

"Are you going to stay for a long time?"

"I don't know. I mean, there's only so long I can live on your dad's charity."

"It's not charity," the prince said, shocked.

"I *have* to get a job. Maybe I could get one here!" Why hadn't she thought of that? They might be able to use an extra cook in the kitchen. At the least, she could make sure they never ran out of cocktail sauce.

"Um . . . Christina . . . I don't think Daddy wants you to *work* here . . . exactly . . ."

"Well, tough shit. Sorry. Don't repeat that."

"I *am* twelve, you know. I've heard that word before. The King uses it all the time."

"I'll bet," she snickered.

"All the time," David announced from a doorway, "is a minor exaggeration.

Christina jumped. "Don't you guys ever knock?"

"The door is wide open," he pointed out. "Get lost, little prince."

"Awwww, David! It's so *boring* here. An' don't call me that."

"As the king might say, tough shit."

Grumbling, the boy prince took his leave.

"I hope he wasn't bothering you," David said, closing the door as he entered the room.

"He's a cutie, with a disturbing yet healthy interest in women's underwear. Uh . . . what do you want?"

"Have dinner with me."

"I think I'm supposed to have dinner with all of you again tonight." She started peeking under pillows and checking drawers. "Damned schedule's around here somewhere . . ."

"Never mind the schedule. Have dinner with *me*. Whatever you want."

"Scrambled eggs and bacon?" she asked brightly.

He frowned at her. "I'm offering you anything you want, and you want eggs?"

"I love them. I, like, *crave* them. Scrambled, fried, poached, over-easy, over-hard—"

"*Why* won't you marry me?" he blurted, then smacked himself on the forehead.

"Whoa! Easy on the self-flagellation, there, dude."

"I'm supposed to woo you," he explained.

"Well, don't waste the woo on me. Not that it's not a really nice offer. Because it is!"

"So. Why won't you?"

"Because frankly, being queen sounds like a gigantic pain in the ass."

"I offer you a country and you tell me it's a pain in the ass?"

She stared at the ceiling, then nodded and said, "Yeah, um . . . yeah. I'm going to stand by that."

"But you don't have anything!" he exclaimed. "My father said you're all alone in the world and you—uh—" *Don't have anywhere to go, and are entirely dependent on the kindness of strangers.* Never mind. That wouldn't do.

She jabbed a finger in the middle of his chest. "I've got *myself*, pal. And that's more than a lot of people have. Why should I submerge my identity with your family's? *I* can hop a boat or a plane and go anywhere in the world, for as long as I want. You know, if I had any money. Can you?"

". . . theoretically." After the king approved, and the bodyguards were lined up, and the arrangements made, and security triple-checked everything, and—

"Right. Pass. No offense. But thanks for asking. Again."

"Well, you can at least have dinner with me. You know, to let me down gently."

She laughed. "Sure, you're soooo crushed. You don't even know me! Another excellent reason to say no, by the way. But all right. We'll have dinner."

"Scrambled eggs and bacon. And oysters with cocktail sauce."

"You can skip the oysters. And I like ketchup on my eggs."

He managed to conceal the shudder as he bowed, and took his leave of her.

"Hey!" she yelled after him. "I'm not gonna have to curtsey, am I?"

"We don't curtsey in Alaska," he called back. "We only bow."

"Well, good."